SECOND CHANCES

Enriching Life Lessons

By

Michael E. Emrich

Dedication

This novel is dedicated to my Mother, Mary Ann, who has been and remains the most influential person in my life. Her incredible spirit lifted all who knew her that even the pain and suffering of terminal cancer could not defeat or diminish.

It seems unfair, having been blessed with ten grandchildren, that my Mom passed away at age fifty-five before getting to know any of them, and any of them got to know her. It was a cruel twist of fate as she so longed to be a grandmother. With firsthand knowledge of her mothering skills and the person she was, I'm keenly aware of what my five sons, Michael Austin, Brendan James, Grant Addison, Garrett Preston, and Dean Arden, and my nieces and nephews, missed by her physical absence from their lives. Over the years, my siblings and I have tried to pass down our Mom's many teachings and life lessons. This helped our children appreciate, as a result of her, their lineage includes such warmth, beauty, and grace. But I remain bothered they did not get to experience their Grandmother personally.

Second Chances, then, is my attempt to share my Mom with those within and outside my family by placing her in a fictionalized story. In essence, my Mom provides a blueprint of how to live a joyful and rewarding life from which anyone can benefit. Being a parent myself, I'm in awe of how each tender lesson, example, and saying by her resulted in such a coherent and powerful whole, to model how life should best be lived while never being preachy or pedantic. Even though she passed away almost three decades ago as of this writing, she remains with me every day.

I hope you find meaning and beauty in this novel. Thank you for reading it!

Michael E. Emrich

Contents

CHAPTER 1

A Chance Encounter

As she glanced up, she felt his stare – two half eyes fixated on her. His eyes were bright blue, intense, and wild. They stopped her in her tracks, and she instinctively was drawn to him. All she could do was gaze back, momentarily frozen, until she felt too uncomfortable and shifted her eyes away from his. If it were a staring contest, he easily won, his eyes refusing to look elsewhere. Only when he saw her focus back on him did he quickly lift his yellow turtleneck sweater to hide the upper halves of his eyes he had just revealed to her.

Even with his eyes hidden, he believed she still was looking at him. At least, he certainly hoped so, as she was the most beautiful woman he had ever seen, and he desperately needed her attention. He was sure she still was there as he could feel her presence without seeing her. Had he kept his eyes open, he likely could have made out her form through the tiny holes allowed by his sweater's weaving. But he was too frightened to open them, believing if he kept them closed he would turn invisible. After all, he needed to be invisible to withstand her gaze. While he was petrified, he was frightened not of her but of their chance encounter.

She was sophisticated, stunning, and free; he was none of those things. At that instant, he wanted more than anything for her to pay attention to him, talk with him, and care for him. She, to him, represented everything good in life, and he would have been crushed if she thought nothing of his stare and simply kept on her way, ignoring him like everyone else in his lonely world.

With his eyes shut, he tried in his mind's eye to picture her. He did so easily and with precise detail. He remembered her tall frame, thin figure, and white dress with a bright yellow trim rising in the middle all the way up and around the neckline. *It's totally fitting she's wearing such a striking dress, as she's the most remarkable person I've ever seen,* he thought. He could not see her shoes as the window separating them was not full-length, and, thus, he had to do with seeing her only from her waist up. Her ears were pierced with small bright, sparkling earrings, which he imagined to be diamonds. Her hair was light brown, long, and worn up in a tight, neat bun. He'd never seen a bun before, and it made her look very special to him. Her pocketbook was yellow, the same shade of yellow on her dress. *Her shoes likely are the same yellow as her pocketbook and her dress*, he figured. He knew she was not young, but also not old, and he didn't even venture a guess at her age.

He was most excited about her face. Her mouth was full-lipped with a natural pale pink shade of lipstick. In the corners, her mouth turned upward, so it looked like she wore a perpetual smile. He was glad she looked happy, happy to see him, he hoped.

But despite her memorable face, it was her eyes that drew him in and left him spellbound. While he saw them for only seconds before he hid his eyes from hers, he could not forget them. They were bright, shiny, and very blue – a deep blue, not of the sky but of the ocean. He felt her eyes light up the room around her and connect to his soul. Oddly, he thought he knew her well merely by locking his eyes to hers, although, in reality, she was a total mystery. Her eyes were calming, caring, and captivating. He missed not seeing them, which led him to think of lowering his sweater so he could peek over the top and make sure she was there, in full view, and he still held her attention. He craved making another connection with her and those eyes of hers. He hoped her first impression of him was enough to keep her there. He had only one way to find out; he had to do it. He had to pull down his sweater top and show her his eyes, or at least a portion of them, again.

As he lowered his sweater, he first saw her bun. He was so pleased she was there that, without thinking, he fully revealed his eyes, indeed his whole face, making him feel almost naked. She could look at him without the protection of his sweater. He was frightened, but more than that, was so overwhelmed with joy he instantly started to clap his hands. He did not wish to draw attention to himself from the other people on his side of the window but could not control his burst of energy, and it was the only way he knew of expressing what he felt at that moment.

As he started clapping, she smiled broadly and brought her fingers to her mouth as if to hide her smile. Not for an instant did he believe she was laughing at him in a disapproving or mean way as others around him do, but rather, she was smiling, he was sure, because his clapping amused her.

He was right as she had not previously seen someone so easily, naturally, and purely express their joy as he had just done to her. In a way, she felt honored that she could have such an obvious and instant effect on him. That pleased her and made her smile.

As he looked at her again, his mind raced with so many questions. *What brought her to me? Would she like me if I were lucky enough to meet her without anything separating us? Was she really looking at me, or is it just my imagination playing a trick? How did someone so beautiful come to stand right in front of me? Could someone like her actually pay attention to someone like me? Would I faint from shock if she were to join me on my side of the window? If I did, would she just run the other way, never to be seen by me again?*

His clapping was not an ordinary one. It was rather odd in that it started slowly and picked up speed to a crescendo as his excitement built. It was loud and irregularly timed, lacking any consistency or beat. But, yet, it was his clapping, he now was sure, that so amused the fascinating woman who completely enchanted him.

As she lowered her fingers from her mouth, without thinking, she placed her right hand on the glass pane with her fingers fully separated from each other as a sign of recognition and welcome. He then stopped his clapping and placed his right hand on the glass pane as well, overlapping her fingers, which were longer and the width of her hand wider than were his, as much as was possible for him. That simple gesture promptly removed any of his thoughts of wanting to remain invisible to her.

CHAPTER 2

Their First Discussion

As Julia lowered her right hand from the glass pane, Jonathan did likewise. He then motioned to her, inviting her to join him on his side of the window separating them. When she started to move in his direction, he felt a sudden urge to pull his sweater top over his head again out of fear she might not like him after all. But his curiosity of the stranger got the better of him. He watched her intently as she walked up to the front desk and asked if she could visit him.

Jonathan lived at the mentally disabled children's ward of St. Peter's hospital on the outskirts of Boston for as long as he could remember and hadn't had a single visitor during his entire time there whom he could recall. *Well, if she is my first visitor, the wait was well worth it*, he thought.

As he watched her show her identification to the head nurse, Ms. Thornburg, and sign in the visitors' login book, he could barely contain his excitement. *What will I say to her? Will I even be able to speak? Will she ever come to visit me again?* To calm his nerves, he began to rock his body back and forth as he often did when his emotions got the better of him.

He observed her every step as she cleared the admissions desk. *Oh, my God,* he thought, *she's headed right toward me. Me, oh my God!* He smiled as he saw her step elegantly in her yellow shoes that matched the yellow of her dress. She was a sight the likes of which he had not seen in his lifetime, and in a moment they would be face-to-face. Instinctively, his rocking picked up pace as she approached him.

"Hi," Julia said as she gave him a huge smile. As she spoke, Jonathan noticed her eyes glistened and sparkled almost as brightly as her earrings. She held out her hand to shake his. Ignoring her hand, Jonathan did what came naturally to him, and he reached over awkwardly and gave her a quick hug around her waist. As he looked up, he spoke his first words to her.

"Are you afraid of death?" he stammered in a quiet voice.

Julia was startled by his question. She expected small talk and took a step back. "What?" she asked as if to make sure she heard him correctly, although she heard him clearly.

"Are you afraid of death?" he repeated, this time more confidently than the first time he asked that question. The first time, the words just rolled out of this mouth without thinking of them in advance, as often happens with him. The second time, Jonathan felt certain that was the question he wanted to ask her, and he patiently and intently waited for her response, believing her words would greatly affect him and help to address one of his most pressing fears.

"Well, I hadn't thought about it in a while as I used to do when I was younger."

"When you were younger, and you thought about it, what did you think?"

"I thought death was something to be afraid of, something dark, dreadful, and depressing."

"And now?"

"Now, when I think of death, I accept it as a natural part of life. Everyone, and every living thing, must die to make room for the unborn. If everyone lived forever, we'd have lots of problems. It wasn't God's plan for us," she replied.

"So, you believe in God?"

"Yes, certainly. Don't you?"

"I'm not sure. I don't know enough about Him. All I know is He sent his only son here to save us. But I don't understand it at all, and what it means for me. I've never been to church, and I've never said a prayer, at least not to God. If there is a God, though, I think He would love me."

"I'm certain He does," she assured him. "By the way, my name is Julia. What's yours?"

"I'm Jonathan. I don't remember my last name. It's been too long since I've heard it, so I'm sorry for not being able to tell it to you."

"Jonathan is fine. A beautiful name," she said. "Can I call you Jon?"

"Why, no." And then he added for emphasis, "no, no, no. That's only a part of my name. Nobody calls me by that name, and I probably wouldn't answer you if you call me it."

"Okay, then, Jonathan it is."

"I guess there's no short name for Julia, is there?" he asked.

"No, there's not," she replied. "There is Julie, but I don't go by that name just like you wouldn't answer to the name Jon."

"Well, Julie isn't shorter than Julia anyway, so what's the point?"

Julia laughed and found Jonathan to be very direct and engaging.

"Do you always get so dressed up to come to the hospital?"

Julia smiled again. "No, I came here straight from work to visit my Mother. She's at St. Peter's as well."

"Is she dying?"

"As a matter of fact, yes, she is. It weighs heavy on my heart."

"What does that mean?" he asked, confused.

"'To weigh heavy on your heart' is an expression. It means it is something really bothering me, and I am deeply concerned about my Mom."

"I'll pray she gets better, and she doesn't die."

"Thanks, Jonathan. You're a very caring person. And you have very expressive eyes," she said. As Julia spoke her last words, Jonathan instantly looked down at the floor, rather embarrassed.

"Hey, I thought you said you don't pray?" she continued.

"I said I don't pray to God. I'm not quite sure how to do that, or if I did, that He would hear me. And you have beautiful eyes. They sparkle, and I like that," he said.

"Why, thank you, Jonathan. That's so nice of you to say."

"What of?" Jonathan asked.

"What?" Julia asked, unsure of his question.

"What's your Mother dying of?"

"Oh, she has cancer. She's had it for several years, but it's spreading to her liver and other organs, and it's getting worse. The doctors have lost hope she will live much longer. I visit her every day after work and on weekends, and I call her several times a day. I know she looks forward to my visits and calls, and I'm glad I can brighten her day a little."

"Don't you lose hope, Julia. Never lose hope. I'll pray for her." Jonathan felt embarrassed as he realized he repeated his words. He quickly looked away and rocked back and forth.

"Do you bring her anything when you visit her?"

"Well, yes. I bring her food. She's not too fond of hospital cuisine, and I try to bring her meals and drinks I know she likes and are healthy for her."

"Can you bring me food sometimes too?" he stammered, again feeling embarrassed the words did not leave his lips as naturally as he thought of them. That happened too often for Jonathan's liking, but he realized he couldn't control it, so he didn't think of it often.

"I'll have to check with the nurses to see if they'll allow it. But if they do, I will. What do you like?"

"Chocolate cake. I had it for my birthday once, and it was the best thing I've ever eaten."

"Okay, then." After a short pause, Julia continued. "I must be going. But it was a real pleasure to meet you, Jonathan."

"Will I see you again tomorrow?" he asked. "Please say, 'yes.'"

"*Yes!*" she repeated his word emphatically as she started to leave.

Jonathan smiled as he heard her response. He knew his smile was not as natural or striking as Julia's smile. He rose to his feet and hugged her again, a little longer and more self-assured than his first one.

"Bye, Jonathan."

As Julia started to move away from him, Jonathan lifted his right hand as he had when he placed it on the window moments earlier, his fingers spread widely apart from each other, and he invited her to do the same without the window this time to separate them. *It's our own special greeting and goodbye*, he figured, *and I'm happy we share it together.*

Julia met his fingers with hers, smiled at him, and then turned to leave. Jonathan waved to her, a wave she did not see. His eyes focused intently on

Julia, watching her every step as she left him. He saw Julia stop at the front desk to check out and specifically ask Ms. Thornburg several questions. Jonathan was sure chocolate cake was the topic of that discussion. At least, he sure hoped it was, anyway. He watched as she gradually faded from his view and disappeared from his confined space.

What an unexpected meeting, Julia thought as she left Jonathan's room. Julia visited her Mother as she had every day since her Mom was first admitted to St. Peter's on her most recent of numerous stays there. This time, however, workers were reconstructing the front entrance and exit Julia used on all her previous visits. Julia stopped short upon reading the detour sign on her way out of the hospital. Just a couple of hours earlier, she gained entrance through the same doors that now were under reconstruction. The detour led her straight to the narrow hall passing the North wing where Jonathan lived the past thirteen years of his life. The pediatric care unit adjoining the hospital was built approximately fifteen years ago, but Julia had no reason to visit it and forgot it was there until her unexpected detour led her to Jonathan.

Julia was touched by Jonathan's directness, innocence, and caring nature. But as often happens, once she stepped out of the hospital to the darkness of nightfall, her thoughts turned promptly back to her world – text messages with her fiancé, Ben, regarding her visit with her Mom, email messages from co-workers relating to an upcoming assignment, and a quick stop to the grocery store to buy food for her Mother and her own food for the week. As Julia passed the bakery department and saw a vast assortment of fattening-looking cakes and pies, she remembered her promise to Jonathan. She found two slices of chocolate layered cake with rich fudge frosting that looked particularly delicious and asked the baker to write with yellow icing on one of them.

"There, that should please him," she stated, exiting the store.

CHAPTER 3

Mom

Julia arrived at St. Peter's the next evening, exhausted from a busy day at work and appointments to plan for her upcoming wedding. At thirty-five years of age, she long ago wanted to get married and start a family but had not met the right man until later in life. Julia never thought of herself as an "old maid," but with each passing year, she attended countless weddings of her friends and co-workers as a single guest. Now that her big day was finally arriving, she felt relieved others would no longer think of her as an "old maid" but instead as a new bride.

Julia had to admit that wedding planning was not as much fun as she had anticipated. That was due, in large part, to not having her Mother, Mary Ann, available to share that experience, and feeling the weight of her Mom's ill health as Julia knew the spreading cancer refused to give up or slow down.

Yet, despite cancer and hair loss due to chemotherapy treatments, Mary Ann maintains her beauty, both inwardly and outwardly. At 5' 10", she is tall and stunning. Her hair (now wig) and eyes are brown. Although being fifty-five, she has a youthful look and an endearing personality. She is warm, friendly, graceful, and an eternal optimist, and is admired by all who know her. Mary Ann never complains, feels sorry for herself, or lets on that she is ill. Indeed, one could tell that she is not well only by a recent feebleness in her gait, inability to climb stairs, and occasional nausea from the medications. But for those few infirmities, she is doing remarkably well under the circumstances. She puts God and family above all else and credits her faith for her resilience and positive attitude.

Unlike Julia, Mary Ann married young, at nineteen, and had her daughter the following year. The closeness of their ages helped Julia view her as a best friend rather than simply a mother. The two are mostly inseparable and are as close as a mother and daughter could be. They share everything together. For as long as she could remember, Julia considered herself extremely blessed to have Mary Ann as her Mom. That makes the thought of losing her at a young age much more difficult. Not being able to have Mary Ann assist in picking out the wedding dress, choosing the floral arrangements, sampling possible food choices from the caterer, and hearing a preview of songs from the hired band, were heartbreaking for Julia. But she quickly learned to accept that reality and do virtually all the planning herself as Ben's job did not permit him the time to be of much help.

Julia was sure to keep Mary Ann informed of every minute detail of the wedding plans, and to seek her sage advice, most importantly because she knew it gave them something very special to share, and it took the focus away from her Mom's declining health and increased pain, at least temporarily. She was touched as Mary Ann's eyes lit up, and spirit soared with any mention of them. While still three months away, the wedding was thoroughly arranged, and now there was just final fine-tuning to make that day as perfect as possible. Julia prayed every night Mary Ann would have the strength to walk her down the aisle. Mary Ann's health firmly beyond her control, she clung to the hope everything would work out fine.

"You look beautiful," Julia complimented her Mom upon entering her hospital room.

"I think you're going to need to get some new contact lenses! How was your day, sweetheart?"

"Busy and hectic as usual. I'm still researching the weather changes due to the destruction of the ozone layer and global warming, as some continue to insist they are merely a hoax. If all goes well, my article will be published next Tuesday. I still haven't put pen to paper yet. But I'm making a lot of progress."

As an investigative reporter focusing on health and well-being issues for *The Boston Globe*, Julia has few idle moments. But with many of her friends unemployed or under-employed and fearful of losing their jobs, she considered herself truly fortunate to have a busy career with good pay.

"That's my girl. You'll get there. You know you always do."

"I'm sure I will."

After a slight pause, Julia continued, "I don't think I've told you yet about the new man in my life," she teased playfully.

"I'm sure he must be very worldly, charming, and suave for you to be giving up Ben so close to your wedding day," Mary Ann played along.

"Actually, you got one of the three right; he is very charming."

Mary Ann was puzzled because Julia's tone changed in an instant from frolicsome to serious. Catching the confused look on her Mother's face, Julia quickly added, "Oh, but don't you fret, he's only fifteen years old or so, and I'm way too old for him."

"Fifteen. Okay, what's his name, and how'd you meet him?" Mary Ann asked with relief in her voice.

"His name is Jonathan, and he's just a couple of halls away. They were reconstructing the front exit of the hospital, and it was closed yesterday. I needed to leave through the North wing."

"Isn't that where the mentally challenged kids are located?"

"Yes, and according to one of the nurses, he has lived there almost his entire life."

"No parents?"

"I don't know. But I do know no one has visited him, so if his parents aren't gone, they haven't been a presence in his life."

Whenever Julia spoke with Mary Ann since her illness, she intentionally avoided using the words "dead" and "dying," and any related terms, with the word "gone" being a ready substitute, as if by not uttering them around her they would leave Mary Ann alone and move elsewhere.

"Poor guy. How bad off is he?"

"I don't think he's bad off at all. As a matter of fact, as I've said, something is charming about him. He begged me to bring him food from the outside, so I found the best-looking pieces of chocolate cake on this side of the Mississippi. There's one for you and one for him. I hope you both enjoy it."

"If you picked it out for him, how couldn't he?"

Changing topics, Mary Ann continued, "How's my soon-to-be son-in-law doing?"

"Oh, Ben is just as wonderful as ever. He still makes fun of my Southern accent from time to time, but I love him for it. The dear man. I think no matter how long I live up North, I will still retain my accent and have a bit of Southern belle inside of me."

Mary Ann had moved from a suburb of Atlanta to Boston approximately five years ago, upon her acceptance of a job offer to be an account executive at AT&T. She took the position on one condition – that her daughter move with her to Boston to start their new lives together. Julia quickly agreed upon her landing a coveted position at *The Globe*. The timing worked out perfectly, and she was confident she made the right decision. In any event, the thought of living more than 1,000 miles away from her Mother was unthinkable to her, then as now. Not that Mary Ann needed Julia to relocate with her. She was, and remained, a very independent and self-reliant person as she raised her daughter to be. Yet, the two of them were particularly inseparable after Julia's father suddenly abandoned his family when she was only fifteen, and they remained remarkably close ever since.

Before Ben entered Julia's life within the last year, Mary Ann was concerned that her close relationship with her daughter might have helped contribute to Julia's remaining unmarried well into her thirties. But at the same time, everyone who knew them understood their bond was such that neither would have it any other way. Julia could, and did, talk with her Mother about anything and everything, and her Mom always gave her thoughtful advice. Even as she gained her independence at an early age and became a busy professional in a large city, Julia always had her Mother to turn to for words of wisdom, which she often sought.

"Here's your dinner tonight, Mom. A tuna sandwich and a health shake."

"Thanks, sweetheart. But tomorrow, don't buy my dinner. I'm fine with the hospital food. Save your money. I'll eat and enjoy whatever I get."

"I know. I hope you save room for some decadent chocolate cake."

CHAPTER 4

Caren

Jonathan looked at the oversized clock hung on the wall of his ward. As it approached 8:00 p.m., the time when he first saw Julia yesterday, he was fearful she might not reappear this evening. *What if she got busy and doesn't have time for me or, more horribly, what if she forgets?* Jonathan asked himself nervously. Several times during that day, he questioned whether Julia was for real. *Even if she is for real, is she as nice as I think she is? Does she like me, or just feel sorry for my situation?*

Self-doubt and fear were constant companions for Jonathan. Just when he summoned the courage to feel good about life, his constant companions were there to take charge and knock him down again. Yet, despite his twin companions, Jonathan at least was an optimist. He always believed everything would work out in the end. And everyone would live happily ever after. Jonathan was very appreciative of what he did have and long ago learned not to dwell on the negatives in his life – most significantly, his inability to think and act like other kids his age and being an orphan. Jonathan never knew either of his parents or did not remember them, which helped to feed his feelings of being isolated and deprived.

Sure, there were the twenty-four other kids he lived with, but they were a poor substitute for a family. Unlike him, they received visitors from time to time, some more than others. Each of them had family members to whom they were connected and made them feel loved. Jonathan was happy for them. But visits to the other patients were a constant reminder of what he did not have.

The nurses at St. Peter's were pleasant, but it was clear they were just doing a job and did not have time for anything but the business of being a nurse and idle chatter. The staff was reduced from seven to four due to budget cuts. Donna was Jonathan's favorite nurse, but she was one of the three who was required to leave. The others did an adequate job, but they did not care about the patients the way Donna had. She was the most pleasant, always humming a cheery tune, and she spoke with Jonathan often and positively. Jonathan cried for three days straight when she disappeared suddenly from Saint Peter's last fall. He missed her, and he felt an uncomfortable inability to connect with anyone else at St. Peter's, except Caren.

Caren was fourteen years old and had an instant crush on Jonathan when she was admitted to the hospital a couple of years ago. For her, it truly was love at first sight. Jonathan was grateful for Caren's attention, but his feelings toward her were not mutual. Jonathan knew she liked him, and, in his own way, he enjoyed playing hard to get with her. It made Jonathan feel important and gave him something to occupy his time.

Caren was able to keep her feelings for Jonathan a secret for only so long until the other kids would tease her with chants, "Caren loves Jonathan," which she quickly denied. But as the chants continued, she denied them less and less.

Jonathan often played one of Caren's favorite games with her – UNO. He kept the card game at its most basic level. Frequently, he'd let her win on purpose because he knew it brought her much joy and a sense of accomplishment. From time to time, Jonathan tried to play board games with her, but she would be unable to grasp the rules and protest in her confusion. One time, Caren got so upset she flung the board game across the room and started kicking, screaming, and making the most awful fuss, until the nurses gave her an injection, which made her calm and groggy.

Caren often experiences weakness in her knees and legs and spends considerable time in a wheelchair or on crutches or a walker. Using those devices made her look old to Jonathan, and he considered himself lucky he did not need such support.

Jonathan felt sorry for Caren and was embarrassed by her advances and the attention she paid him. He remembered well her fourteenth birthday party. He gave her a card he made, which surprised and delighted her. She put it in her designated draw. Later that day, her uncle brought a birthday cake from the outside. Then everyone gathered around, including the nurses, and sang happy birthday. After the brief celebration and her uncle had left, Caren asked Jonathan in the corner of the room away from the others, "Why didn't you join in singing for me? I watched your face, and your mouth didn't move, except afterward when you ate the cake. Then it went very fast. Your cake was gone in a flash."

"I was embarrassed, and, between you and me, I was not sure I remember the words to that song. I get nervous, and my voice gets shaky when I know others around me are listening."

"Oh, don't be silly. Everyone was singing, and nobody would have stopped to listen to just you, except me, that is. I would have loved to hear you sing. Especially since you would have been singing just for me."

"Well, don't think about it too much. In case you haven't noticed, I don't sing at anyone's birthday, ever. It's just not something I do."

"If you sang quietly, no one could hear you over here. Nobody is watching us, and I would feel my birthday is complete and special if you sang to me now. Please, oh, please. It's the last favor I will ever ask of you. And if you don't, I may just cry all night."

"Well, if it means that much to you. But you must promise you won't tell the others, okay?"

With Caren's nod of her head in agreement and her still pleading eyes staring at him, Jonathan sang as quickly and as softly as he could, occasionally peering over at the other kids to make sure they were not watching.

"See, you did remember the words! That was beautiful."

Then Caren made her move. She was so happy and appreciative she leaned over to kiss Jonathan on his check. But the attention was too much, and he quickly pulled away before her lips had a chance to touch him. The added distance between them caused Caren to extend too far on her crutches, and she fell to the ground. Billy, one of the other kids, witnessed the attempted kiss from across the room, told the others, and they teased Caren for days, which made Jonathan feel even more sorry for her following her fall.

Caren's mom, Tracey, visited Caren quite regularly, and Jonathan got to know her well. She was a heavy-set lady who looked old to Jonathan. Her skin was wrinkled, her clothes were worn, and her hair was always messy. But she was pleasant enough to the point where Jonathan looked forward to her visits. Then, several months ago, Tracey's visits suddenly ended. Jonathan heard a rumor she was locked up in jail, but he had no idea why. Caren's only other adult relative was her uncle, who visited her a few times after Tracey's visits ended. But her uncle also no longer came to visit. Jonathan knew well the heartache of being visitor-less when visits are the only things to which patients have to look forward.

Shortly after her mother's visits stopped, Caren was so lonely she started to sob. She needed to express her feelings and headed straight to Jonathan.

"I just can't stand it anymore. I so looked forward to my mom coming to visit me, and now I don't know if she ever will again. She would tell me about our cat, my cousins, and uncle, and what was happening outside of here. She would bring me things and make me feel happy and loved. Now all I feel is empty. I don't know if I'll ever get over it."

"I know it's hard for you. I miss your mom too. But you'll get used to it," Jonathan said in an effort to brighten her spirit.

"I just don't know if I ever will. And I don't want to get used to her not being around me anymore."

Jonathan saw that Caren's face was red, and her eyes were puffy from her crying. She looked pitiful. But try as he did, he could not stop her tears from flowing.

"I never had visitors. I had no choice, and neither do you. You have to find a way to go on even if your mom can't visit you again just yet. Things will be alright. I made it through, and so can you."

"Thanks for saying what you just said. It means a lot to me."

Jonathan felt sorry enough for Caren, he quickly hugged her. Luckily, no one noticed, so he avoided ridicule and being the butt of jokes by the other kids. *Sometimes, you just need to take chances in life*, Jonathan thought at the time.

CHAPTER 5

Chocolate Cake

Jonathan focused again on the oversized clock with much anticipation as it read 8:03, three minutes after the last time he looked at it. *Will Julia come tonight? If only she knew how important it is to me, she would certainly keep her promise,* he was sure.

Approximately twenty minutes later, he caught a glimpse of Julia through the visitors' window as elegant as she was beautiful. The moment he saw her and the bag in her hand, he started clapping his unusual clap.

"Yeah! She's here," he said out loud.

Julia smiled upon seeing Jonathan so obviously overcome with sheer joy. How wonderful, she thought, that she could brighten one's day simply by her presence (and some cake!). With the desk nurse familiar with Julia from her visit yesterday, she was admitted much more quickly than the previous day. She headed straight toward Jonathan.

Before Julia had time to place the bag she was carrying on the nearby table, Jonathan gave her a huge hug and held out his right hand, fingers spread open as much as possible, and she reciprocated in their shared greeting.

"You remembered! Thanks so much. It's so good to see you again, Julia," Jonathan said quickly.

"Hi, Jonathan. It's so good to see you again too. And I'm absolutely positive you know what's in the paper bag over there," she said, pointing to the table.

"Let's pretend it's my birthday, and the cake is your present for me, okay?"

"Sure," Julia replied, amused at his excitement.

"But you must share it with me so it will be more like a party. You didn't bring any birthday candles, did you?"

Julia laughed as she responded, "Maybe next time."

What music to Jonathan's ears for her to say those two words to him, "next time." *So, now I'm sure she'll come to visit me again*, Jonathan thought as he started to clap.

"You know, I've never had birthday candles to blow out and to make a wish. Maybe that's why my wishes haven't come true until now, that is." Quickly changing the subject, Jonathan asked, "How is she?"

"Who?"

"Your Mom."

"Oh, thanks for asking. She's doing fine. She's definitely as bright and merry as ever."

"May I go to see her someday? She's not too far."

"I don't know if that's allowed, but maybe she could visit you if she gets her strength up."

"Great, something else to look forward to."

Julia was quite sure she knew what Jonathan was referring to by his using the word "else."

To drive his point home more directly, so there could be no doubt about it, Jonathan stated with emphasis, *"I love visitors."*

Then he continued, "Does your Mom look like you?"

"A bit. But she is much more beautiful than I am."

"That's hard to imagine, Julia."

She turned suddenly and asked Jonathan to wait for her.

"I'll be right back."

She walked the short distance to speak with nurse Susan.

What are they talking about? Jonathan wondered as he noticed the nurse hand Julia something.

When she returned to him, Jonathan hurriedly asked, "What did ya get?"

"It's a surprise," Julia said teasingly, as she opened her hand to reveal three birthday candles, one yellow, one red, and one white. "It never hurts to ask, you know. Luckily for us, the hospital keeps some spare candles."

"Yeah, yellow like the sun, and your pretty dress yesterday. Now, this really will be fun. My own little party on a day that isn't even my birthday. What an odd way to get my first birthday candles. Can you sing happy birthday after you light them?"

"I wouldn't have it any other way, young sir."

Upon seeing Jonathan clap, Julia opened the bag to reveal his present, with the words, "To Jonathan," written in yellow icing on top of the deep brown fudge frosting.

"Yum. Now that's a cake. It's the most awesome present ever, and it has my name on it, so it must be mine! I'm so excited."

"But you haven't tasted it yet."

"I know it will be yummy because you bought it for me. How couldn't it be?"

Julia smiled as she lit the three candles and then quietly sang happy birthday to Jonathan.

"Okay, now you get to blow them out. And, most importantly, don't forget to make your wish first."

"I've already made my wish, and it already has come true," Jonathan blurted out while blushing.

"No, wait till you blow out your candles to make your wish and make it a different one, wishing for something you don't have yet. You know," Julia said with a wink to Jonathan, "the smoke from the blown-out candles will reach Heaven so God knows your wish."

"Oh, I think He knows it anyway, but here goes."

Jonathan took the deepest breath he could and blew as hard as possible to make sure it was sufficient to extinguish the three lit candles.

"Wow, that was easier than I thought it would be," Jonathan stated as he was relieved he accomplished his mission with air to spare and thankful he did not make a fool of himself in front of Julia.

"Wish making is not a hard job, Jonathan. It's good to wish for things."

"What would you wish for?" Jonathan asked.

"Well, that's an easy one – the same prayer I ask God to grant every night – that my Mom gets well again, and, in the meantime, she doesn't have to experience pain anymore. What was your wish, if I may ask, young sir?"

"That's funny. My wish was almost the same as yours – that your Mom gets well again right away, and I can meet her soon."

"Why, thank you, Jonathan. How thoughtful to think of my Mom for your one wish when you could have wished for anything in the world. You are a special young man."

Julia was touched that ahead of Jonathan's wishing for improvement in this own health, or he could leave the confinement of St. Peter's, or his parents were alive and he could meet them, he had, so unselfishly, chosen her Mother as the subject of his one wish.

"Now, let's dig in. And, you know, Jonathan, I'm on a diet, and I haven't had a dessert in many months, so this is a special treat for me as well. Just don't tell anyone I'm breaking my diet today."

"I won't," Jonathan promised with a serious tone, as he shared his cake with his new best friend.

"Awesome," Jonathan exclaimed while eating his cake. "The greatest birthday I've ever had, and I get to share it with you."

Jonathan started to clap, but his excitement was tempered by the fact Julia would be leaving him again soon, and he'd have to wait patiently for close to another twenty-four hours before he could see her again. To Jonathan, that seemed like an eternity. But this special visit, of sharing his birthday cake with Julia, gave him renewed confidence he would, indeed, see her again.

After exchanging their special goodbye gesture, Jonathan called after her, "Good night, and thanks again. Be safe." This time she did see his wave as she gave him a wave and a smile before she was gone from his sight.

CHAPTER 6

Ben

Feeling pleased she was able to brighten Jonathan's day, Julia rushed out of the hospital to her parked car. She uncharacteristically was late to meet Ben for a drink. Next week would be the first anniversary of their first date, arranged by Julia's friend, Maggie. Maggie, who had several past successes in matchmaking, was sure Julia and Ben would be infatuated with each other. Both were in their mid-thirties, very attractive, and successful. More importantly, they shared common values, goals, and dreams. Both long desired to get married and start a family as virtually all their friends had done. However, they let the demands of their jobs interfere with the pursuit of that shared goal, and, before their meeting, each had not met the right person to wed.

Maggie met Ben at her friend's party, and she spoke with him for approximately twenty minutes before some of her female friends arrived and monopolized the rest of Ben's time there. Within that short time, her matchmaking skills kicked in, and she was sure to mention Julia and obtain his cell number that, with his permission, would be shared with her.

Maggie called Julia the following morning and informed her about Ben, her excitement building as she spoke.

"He's in his mid-thirties, I'd say, approximately 6' 3", with gorgeous brown eyes and light brown hair. What I remember most is his smile and the way his eyes lit up when he spoke to me. And cute dimples. He's a partner at a major law firm here in Boston, doing corporate law. The best part for you is he's single. I don't know how that could be, but he did say he has a very demanding job and not as much free time as he would like. He volunteers his limited time to coach soccer to kids in junior high school and does pro bono work for the Boston Children's Hospital. In his younger days, he was an associate professor at Boston College teaching prelaw classes and a part-time model for several men's fashion magazines. He loves to go sailing, crewing, hiking and has completed several rigorous boot camp training sessions. Oh, Julia, I just know he's so right for you, and I can't wait for you guys to meet."

Maggie piqued Julia's interest, and upon arriving home from work that evening, she googled Ben's name and found his Facebook and LinkedIn pages. Eagerly perusing them, she was struck by his good looks, how well-traveled he was, and how his personality seemed to leap out of his online pictures. The more Julia saw, the more she became excited he could be her Mr. Right, rolled up into one remarkable specimen of mankind. And when they finally met for the first time, she knew his online profiles did not prepare her enough for that first encounter. He literally took her breath away, and, to this day, every time Julia is in his presence, she feels so privileged to be a part of his life.

Julia had several recent dates before meeting Ben. Oh, the world of online dating and the many horror stories it always seemed to produce for her, that luckily her Mother, and people in her Mother's generation, did not have to experience or tolerate. There were those guys whose online pictures looked like they were taken a decade earlier and conveniently never were updated. Some of the guys posted online images of themselves with a full head of thick hair, only to have thinning hair or bald spots in person with a few strands of hair attempting in vain to hide the bald or balding areas. Others posted pictures they used to represent what they look like to the online universe, which somehow took twenty or more pounds off their stomach or buttock and miraculously transferred that weight to their torso and biceps. Upon her first glance of them up-close and personal, she felt disappointed and deceived before they spoke a single word between them, and she had to resist the temptation to walk, or run, the other way and stand them up.

Not that looks were everything to Julia; she never failed to continue with a date despite her initial shock of meeting a guy for the first time and wondering how his online images could so misrepresent the reality standing in front of her. It was not in her nature to raise the obvious incongruity with them. Instead, she simply ignored it and judged each guy on his personality and spirituality, which she often found to be lacking as well. Even the very few men she had some connection or spark with failed in other ways, either (i) them living too far apart to have a realistic chance at a continuous relationship, (ii) their interests held no attraction to, or repulsed, her, (iii) they were drug users or chain smokers, (iv) the men appeared manly online and effeminate in person, (v) their religious nature and spirituality were nonexistent, or woefully insufficient, for her, or (vi) she discovered the men lived lives that caused red flags regarding their fidelity and trust.

When Julia replayed in her mind the men she had dated before Ben, she was struck by how difficult it was for all the stars to be in alignment and for a man to be marriage material for her. *How could it be such a herculean task to find Mr. Right or even Mr. Somewhat Right?* she often asked herself. As a result of her online dating experiences, Julia concluded Mr. Right and Mr. Online would be mutually exclusive.

Of the thousands of men she would encounter virtually every day, being a somewhat youngish, upwardly mobile, professional in a large American city, how could it be there was no one for her, she would wonder. Yet, she refused to lower her high standards and settle for someone she could not picture being in a "LTR" that would last a lifetime. She had zero intention in dating just to date and merely having a summer fling or a winter cuddle buddy. She'd rather stay single than to be stuck in a wrong relationship, no matter how convenient and artificially appealing it might have been to have a significant other join her when she met with her married friends and their spouses.

Julia's many unfortunate prior dates accentuated how incredible a find Ben was for her. Once she got to know him, looking back, she often wondered how she got to that point in her life without him by her side. While Julia was successful, happy, and optimistic before meeting Ben, his effect on her was immense and immediate. In his arms, she felt nothing could go wrong, and she was so confident of their bright future together. They had many late-night discussions of their yearning to have children shortly after their marriage, with a shared goal of at least four. They discussed every topic with ease, being of similar mind and values. Julia hated for their many intriguing conversations to end so they both could get some sleep before starting their grueling workday the following morning, or in many instances, later that same morning.

As Julia spent more time with Ben, what she came to admire most was his unassuming and humble nature. Here truly was a man who had everything going for him but seemingly was unaware of how he drew people in and caused many a head to turn his way, in admiration by the women and envy by the men.

Ben's and Julia's relationship was now at the point where they knew what each other was thinking and could finish each other's sentences. They shared a similar off-beat sense of humor, laughing spontaneously at the same scene in a movie theater that, apparently, no one else around them thought was funny. That circumstance often made them laugh even harder until tears rolled down their faces, as they tried not to "lose it" and laugh out loud to the annoyance of the moviegoers sitting near them.

Ben and Julia were often surrounded by tens, hundreds, or thousands of people, yet they only saw each other. Their union reminded Julia of the many intricate jigsaw puzzles she pieced together in her youth, with each piece fitting neatly and perfectly to the other and resulting in a thing of beauty, order, and completeness. Sure, the puzzle took many hours, sometimes days, to complete, but upon its completion, she instantly knew all her effort was worthwhile as she admired her masterpiece.

As Julia pulled up to The Watering Hole Bar and Grille, she reflected on her first date with Ben. Maggie's description, and Julia's online search, made her feel as if she knew him well even before they met. Their first date was at Cheers, the pub made famous by the '80s and '90s television show of the same name. As she approached the table where he was sitting, she caught one of her high heels on an uneven spot on the floor and fell forward toward him. He promptly leaped up and managed to catch her before she fell flat on her face. Her embarrassment of the moment was erased by his endearing smile that so put her at ease. Their drinks and dinner went so well that afterward they strolled arm-in-arm in the Public Garden. As they did, Julia was thankful for Maggie's insight and intuition. The evening was perfect, despite the near calamity at its inception.

"Hi, sweetheart," Julia called to Ben, almost out of breath from her rushing into the restaurant as she saw him at a far-off table dressed in a fine suit. "Sorry I'm a little late."

"Hey, gorgeous. No problem, although I was starting to get a little worried because you're never late, and you didn't call."

"Yes, I know. My cell phone battery died, and I got here as soon as I could." While her statement was true, and Julia always was open with Ben, her instinct cautioned her not to mention Jonathan just yet. She would have that conversation at a more appropriate time when they were in a more intimate setting.

"How's Mom today?"

"She's doing well. She got her appetite back and had all three meals without nausea or vomiting. All-in-all, a good day."

"Glad to hear it. Did you get a chance to meet with the band yesterday?"

"Oh, yes. I was so pleased, and I know you will be too. They played 'our song,' and it sent chills down my spine and tears to my eyes. It's so perfect; I couldn't be happier." Julia was referring to the song *You and I* by Michael Bublé, which they chose as their wedding song. They both believe they could "conquer the world" together and were moved by the romantic lyrics that would attest to their incredible love for each other on their big day.

"Great. I hope to hear the band soon when I get back. I've just been so busy at work there's been little time for anything or anyone else, except you!" Upon completing the word "you," Ben flashed his million-dollar smile and gave Julia a wink that erased everyone else in the restaurant as she grasped his right hand in hers and stared lovingly into his big, brown, beautiful eyes.

"Our wedding won't come soon enough, as I can't wait to become Mrs. Julia Anderson. I know it will go by so quickly. After the months and months of planning, the hundreds of hours spent, the attention to every detail, that if we dare to blink, it will be history before we know it. But then, of course, we have a lifetime together to create and live our dream. With Katy, Kathy, Katlin, and Kara running us both ragged," she joked.

"Wait a minute. I think you've made a mistake. It will be with John, Jake, Josh, and Jonah, who will all play football in high school and college, to the delight of the cheerleaders for their teams. After all, we need to pre-serve and perpetuate the 'Anderson' name, especially since neither of my brothers had a son."

"We'll just have to see what God has in store for us, now won't we? Oh, it's all so exciting. I wish I had a dad to walk me down the aisle, and I pray Mom will be strong enough to share our day with us."

All at once, the patrons groaned in unison in defeat, as the New York Yankees got a walk-off home run to win the game against the Boston Red Sox, being aired on multiple television screens scattered throughout the restaurant and bar.

"Oh, not to change the subject, but my travel department got my airline ticket to LAX for my trip. I leave tomorrow at 7 a.m., meet with clients in LA, then head to Silicon Valley for more meetings, then return two weeks from tomorrow. What am I going to do without you for that long? I know, I'll sit in my hotel room and sulk."

"Yeah, I'll be doing much sulking myself. You'll just have to establish a policy from our wedding date forward that all of your clients will meet you here in Boston so that you will never leave me again. Get them to con-vert to be Patriots, Bruins, and Red Sox fans and give them free tickets to the games from your firm so they'll have a built-in incentive to come out East or up North."

"Definitely, darling," Ben laughed. "And if I lose some clients in the process, so be it. If only it were that easy!"

After they finished their drinks and snacks, Ben informed Julia he needed to leave to pack and get a good night's sleep since he had to be at the airport early the following morning. She offered to drive him, but his firm already ordered him a car, and he was all set.

"Get a good night's sleep, sweetheart. And safe travels. Don't forget to call or text as soon as your plane lands."

"Sure, will do. Night, my love," Ben replied as he stood up and gave Julia a big bear hug and a long, tender kiss goodbye, and then he made his way out of the restaurant through the maze of people standing around the bar.

Since Ben entered her life, Julia spent increasingly less time with her many friends, including Maggie, and her co-workers, as Ben and she became inseparable. Although Julia would want it no other way, it did make Ben's business trips and absences more difficult, and she felt an acute emptiness without him in her daily life. But, Julia figured, that longing to be with someone when they're gone from your presence is a true measure of their affection for each other. *Ours is a love that will last a lifetime and only grow,* she thought with a smile.

CHAPTER 7

How to Pray

Working at *The Globe*, Julia became used to the incessant deadlines and time pressures that accompanied her job. As her Mother often reminded her, and as she knew, she always managed to meet her deadlines with success after success. Julia was a rising star at *The Globe*, well-liked and well-respected. But she still felt the pressure of every assignment as if it were her first, and the need to prove herself yet again. That made her new routine of meeting Jonathan after first meeting Mary Ann even more difficult for Julia, and the time she had available to do her chores and spend time with her new puppy, Belle, more constricted. Yet, knowing how much Jonathan looked forward to her visits, she could not disappoint him. And Ben's West Coast trip would give her more time than she otherwise would have had if Ben were in Boston.

"I almost didn't recognize you with your hair down," Jonathan said upon hugging Julia's waist.

"I know. I save my bun for special meetings and when I need to look my best. Today, I'm just plain me," Julia replied.

"Nothing about you is plain, that's for sure! You're the farthest from plain of anyone I have ever known."

"Thanks, Jonathan."

"So, how's she doing?"

Without missing a beat, Julia answered, "She is doing very well today. A great day, actually. A day without being poked or prodded and without much pain. When you're sick, a day without pain is such a blessing."

"I know. I've lived most of my life in pain. Sometimes in my body, and sometimes in my mind."

"In your mind?" Julia asked for clarification.

"Yes, in my mind. I often look out the window, Julia, and see chipmunks, squirrels, and robins, and wish I were one of them. I can't remember feeling sunshine on my face or grass under my toes. For as long as I can remember, I've lived surrounded by these four walls and with kids like Caren, who all have big problems. It's not easy to deal with sometimes. I want to run around, explore, and experience the world outside. But maybe that's not meant to be. Not that I'm complaining. I appreciate having a warm bed at night and three meals a day. That I'm given my medications and have nurses here to help me. Only . . . ." Jonathan trailed off without finishing his sentence.

After a long reflective pause, Jonathan continued, "I don't think most people understand what it's like here – to be woken up in the middle of the night by kids who are in pain or who have temper problems. Kids who throw up their food or pee or poop their beds which can make me hold my nose until the problem is taken care of. I feel sad and scared at times, but I close my eyes and pretend I'm that robin I see flying away. I know I have my own problems, but there are plenty of kids here worse off than I am. And for that, I'm grateful."

As Jonathan spoke, he noticed Julia's face and how intently she was listening to him. After living to that point without anyone paying much attention to him, he so much appreciated he was being heard, essentially for the first time in his life.

Julia looked caringly at Jonathan and responded, "I understand it's not easy on you. But until you just shared your experiences here, I don't think I fully appreciated your life. If I could make things better, Jonathan, I would love to do that for you. I just don't know how."

"I told you what my life is like; what's yours like?"

"Well, as you do, I count my blessings for what I do have. I have the best Mother, a good but demanding job, I can put food on the table and afford my apartment. I do thank God for everything when I pray, especially for the wonderful people in my life and for my new puppy." She was careful not to mention Ben to Jonathan, at least not yet.

"Do you want to get married and have a family someday?"

"Certainly, I want it all, a wonderful husband, kids, and a roomy house with a white picket fence, Greek or Roman columns at the entryway, and a grand piano in my living room. But most importantly, I want a lifetime of love, happiness, and success."

As she completed her wish list, Julia felt a sense of guilt, for she knew these were things Jonathan could only dream of and were not obtainable by him, whereas for her, they were becoming her reality.

"Sorry to rattle on so, but I guess we all have our dreams."

"What's his name?" Jonathan asked.

"Who?" Julia thought that Jonathan might be asking her about Ben.

"Your new puppy."

"It's a her, not a him. Her name is Belle, and she's just the cutest ball of grey fluff you ever did see. She is so gentle and sweet, and she wags her tail a mile a minute. I have to confess I am spoiling her rotten, I love her so."

"You are very lucky. I'm happy for you."

After a slight pause, Jonathan continued. "I have a favor to ask of you."

"What is it?"

"I want you to show me how to pray right."

Smiling and obviously pleased by his request, Julia replied, "Sure."

Pressed for time, Julia knew she did not have much of that increasingly scarce commodity. But Jonathan's request was an important one to her, and she eagerly accepted his invitation to help him learn about God, faith, and hope, all of which could benefit him immensely. As Julia started to drop to her knees to pray, which was made somewhat difficult by her fitted dress, Jonathan promptly stopped her.

"No, not here. There's a small chapel in the East wing. I want to learn to pray there, in God's house."

"What a great idea, Jonathan. I know it well as I often go there to pray for my Mom. But I'll have to ask Ms. Thornburg. Hopefully, it's permissible for us to leave here for a few minutes."

Jonathan watched as Julia approached Ms. Thornburg, and she discussed with her the foreign and novel concept of Jonathan being permitted to leave the confines of his ward with someone other than a nurse. The two women were both smiling, which he took as a good sign. His excitement built as Julia approached him with a grin, shaking her head in a "yes" gesture.

"I can't tell you how much this means to me. You're the best."

"Come, let's go. Here, hold my hand," Julia said as she grasped Jonathan's hand in hers, and they headed in the direction of the East wing.

Holding Julia's hand for the first time, Jonathan believed he floated to the chapel. It indeed was unusual for anyone to touch him. Many times, particularly in public, people intentionally seemed to avoid him. He could go many months in a row without so much as one person touching him, other than his unintentionally touching the hand of a nurse who was giving him medication or accidentally bumping into another kid at St. Peter's.

While Jonathan did not understand the benefits of touch to human physical, mental, and emotional health, starting from birth and the newborn's first touch of a mother nursing him or her, to death and a family member holding the hand of a loved one on the verge of passing on, he did know how the simple act of Julia's taking his hand in hers greatly affected him. That connection of flesh, which was intentional, rather than accidental, was a powerful communication by Julia of caring and support without speaking a single word.

Instead of dwelling on his misfortune of having been touched so rarely in his life, Jonathan's focus now was on holding the hand of this beautiful, vibrant woman who just days earlier unexpectedly entered his isolated world, and with whom he was making a connection unlike anything he previously experienced or could have imagined. All he knew was that he was walking hand-in-hand with Julia to God's house, and he considered himself to be truly blessed and undeserving of her kindnesses.

As they entered the empty chapel, Julia released Jonathan's hand. As soon as she did, he began to spin around several times, with each of his arms stretched out fully by his side. He increased his speed with every turn until he fell to the ground on his knees in a thump.

Looking up at her from his lowly position, Jonathan was embarrassed because he was so dizzy, he could not right himself and attempt to stand up, just yet, on his own.

"I'm sorry, Julia. I didn't mean to scare or embarrass you. I just got carried away by all my excitement. Good that no one else was here to see me look so stupid."

"That was not stupid; it was awesome. I'm sure God has seen how overjoyed you are to be in this chapel, and He is pleased by your excitement. People who believe can feel His love and power in their lives; you just got the chance physically to express it in your own way. Now do me a favor. Never describe your actions or reactions as being stupid. I love how you spun around just now to show your happiness and how you clap when you're excited. Always remember – God loves you."

"Then why did He make me sick and not like everyone else, everyone else outside of where we just left, that is? Why am I so different?"

"Those are great questions, Jonathan, and I can appreciate you would like answers to them. Unfortunately, I don't have the answers for you. But I will tell you what my Mom told me my entire life, and that is: 'Everything happens for a reason.'"

"I don't understand. What does that mean? What does that have to do with me?"

"Well, I'm glad you asked for clarification. I was not as smart as you to ever ask my Mom those questions. But I think I figured them out on my own as I've experienced life."

Julia drew herself closer to Jonathan as she continued.

"They are incredibly powerful words. What they mean to me is God has a grand plan for each of us. We cannot always know what His plan is, but not everything is for us to know. What we don't know, and may never know, we leave to faith. If you believe in God and accept and embrace Him as an important part of your life, you will always have a Father and never be alone. And you'll learn to trust that no matter how bad things are or may get, everything will be fine in the end and according to God's plan for you, in His time. Focus on what's ahead, not what has passed. What's ahead is Heaven and being with Him and all your loved ones for eternity. It doesn't get better than that. Again, I don't pretend to have all the answers to your most pressing questions, but I can tell you those five words are magical. And if you learn to believe them and live your life accordingly, you will have a positive and hopeful life."

"What if God's plan for me is to go to hell? What if I don't make it to Heaven? That would be so awful." As a tear rolled down his face in contemplation of a horrendous fate, Jonathan continued, "And I don't have anyone to meet in Heaven because you're the only person I would want to be there with, and you're not there yet. There is no one else in my life."

"I am not God and cannot be a judge of any man. But I'm certain God loves you, and you'll go to Heaven. And while you may not be aware of your loved ones in Heaven, you can meet your mother and father someday. Isn't that an exciting thought!"

"But how do you know that, that I will go to Heaven?"

"Because in you, I see God's presence. You're an amazing person – kindhearted, sympathetic, caring, and so much more. Those are God-given. I know you would like to be the same as everyone else who don't face the challenges you do. Too often, we all strive our entire life to be like everyone else, or someone else, but we don't see and appreciate God made us our own unique person as He wanted it."

Julia then sat on the floor next to Jonathan and spoke with him at eye level.

"This is important, and please do not forget it. God made Jonathan, and you are so exceptional. There is only one you and, as a child of God, carry yourself high. Focus on your many great qualities and not your challenges. And you'll see, I promise, people love Jonathan for those qualities, and your problems will seem so less troublesome. You face health issues. Everyone has their unique troubles and challenges in life. Everyone. But do not make them define who you are, and to place limits on, and handcuff, you."

As Julia stood up and brushed herself off, she smiled at Jonathan.

"Do you love me, Julia?"

"I do love the strengths God has given you. Those blessings will only grow by having faith, acting in your life with the purpose of being a son of God, and making Him proud of you. Here now, let me help you up."

Julia reached out her right hand to support Jonathan as he started to rise and straighten himself out.

"Nobody has ever said anything like that to me before. I will never forget it."

"That is so good. Now, let's pray."

"Isn't praying like making a wish blowing out candles on a birthday cake?"

"Not quite. A wish just is putting into words what you hope for, while a prayer is your communicating directly with God. Prayer is not limited to something you want to happen, but it can be anything you want to speak with God about. It is much broader and much more important than a wish. Prayers can be very powerful. How great is it that you can speak directly with God wherever you are and whenever you want? It never ceases to amaze me how many people don't partake in the power of prayer, without so much as giving it a try."

"Will He always listen?"

"Why, yes. God is always there for us."

"Will He always give us what we pray for?"

"I can't say all prayers lead to immediate results because often they don't. But what we foresee in the future may not be what's in God's plan for us or others. Again, that's what faith is all about. You may not see changes as a result of prayer, or things may happen that are directly the opposite of what you prayed for, but we do not see what happens later and in Heaven. Only God controls that, and we must trust God."

"Okay, I'm out of questions, and I'm ready to pray now."

"Great. But first, let's kneel like this."

As Julia started to drop to her knees, Jonathan asked, "Do we have to kneel for God to hear us?"

"No, certainly not. Some people cannot kneel, such as an older person or a person strapped into their seat on an airplane. Some people who can kneel choose not to do so. But God will always listen, and He will always be there for us. He is a generous and loving God and doesn't put formalities or requirements in place for us to speak with Him."

After Jonathan joined her on his knees, Julia continued, "Now, we make the sign of the cross, and say 'in the name of the Father, the Son, and the Holy Spirit', the holy trinity. That is how we let God know we intend to speak with Him, and it focuses our attention on our forthcoming prayer. The cross, upon which Jesus died for us, is a powerful symbol in the

Christian religion. It represents God's unconditional and undying love for us. We then put our hands together like this. And, yes, God will listen even if we do not raise our hands in prayer."

Jonathan lifted his clasped hands especially high, well over his head, to be closer to God. "You know what I just thought of?"

"No, what?"

"The way you are showing me how to hold our hands in prayer is very much like what we do with our special greeting and goodbye. We are joining two hands, but instead of being the hands of just one person like in prayer, our greeting and goodbye join your hand and my hand as one. And instead of the fingers together like you just showed me in prayer, in our special greeting and goodbye, our fingers are spread wide apart."

Julia could not believe the words Jonathan just spoke. "How remarkable, Jonathan. What a wonderful connection you just made. I love how you described it, and it makes me feel good you noticed it."

"Didn't you notice it too, Julia?"

"Well, no, not until you just shared it with me. Now, you speak with God, and let Him know what's on your mind."

"But I don't know what to say. I have nothing in my head right now, and I'm a little scared."

"Oh, don't be scared. I usually say prayers without speaking the words out loud, but today, with you by my side and for your benefit, I will."

As Julia began to pray, Jonathan raised his hands even higher to Heaven and waited eagerly to hear what was on her mind that she wanted to share with God, and with him.

"Dear God," Julia began speaking slowly and deliberately. "Thanks so much for this glorious day, and for all the wonderful people You have put in my life. I truly appreciate all You have given me. And thanks for putting Jonathan in my life. I know You know what a special young man he is."

Julia continued, "I pray for all people who are hurting, including those who are sick or have lost a loved one, who struggle to have food or shelter, or who do not believe in You. Your love and blessings make me so extremely grateful and peaceful. Lastly, I pray for Mom, and that she does not suffer and feels well. Thank You, dear Lord." As she lowered her hands from prayer, she said, "Okay, now it's your turn."

"I have to think a while longer. I don't want my first prayer to God to be messy or dumb."

"We have as much time as you want. There is no need to rush. And there are no right or wrong words in prayer, only your words."

Feeling a bit more confident after giving his intended prayer more thought, Jonathan began, "God, this is my very first prayer to You. I'm sorry I haven't done it before, but no one ever took the time to show me how, that is, until now. You did a great job with making Julia because she's so special. I had never met anyone like her before."

Jonathan paused with his face showing signs of his deep concentration.

"There's nothing else I can think of saying, except I hope Julia's Mom has a great day and feels better real soon. I haven't met her yet, but she's an incredible person from what I've been told. I would love to meet her before You take her with You."

Julia remained silent as Jonathan thought some more.

"And one other thing. I hope when people meet me, they don't think I'm stupid, ugly, or strange. I want them to think I'm a good person, and I'm like everyone else, just a little different. I know I have health problems, and my brain doesn't work like most people. I know it's too much to ask I get well because I haven't been well my entire life. And I don't have much in my life. But now I have Julia as my special friend, and I've never been more happy and thankful. You have made my wishes come true without my even praying right before, which makes You my special friend as well. You are an awesome God."

"Jonathan, what a great first prayer. It was so truthful and heartfelt. Thanks for including my Mom in your prayer. I will introduce you to her soon if I can."

As Julia began to open the door to exit the chapel, Jonathan suddenly stopped her.

"Can we stay a bit longer? I never saw anything like the sun shining through those windows with the people and animals on them and with so many colors. See the patterns it makes on the floor? I think God has sent the sunlight through them just for us."

Julia grinned as Jonathan began to clap.

"Can we sit on this bench? I feel so happy right now and don't want to leave just yet. I've heard people talk of this chapel and going to church before, but I never imagined what it would be like. If I did, it wouldn't possibly be as good as this. I love it here, and don't feel so alone."

Julia sat down on the pew next to Jonathan. She remained quiet so not to interfere with his good thoughts and was pleased to witness the sense of peace overcoming him. For the first time Julia knew Jonathan, he looked as if he didn't have a care in the world. She gently placed her hand over his and held it there for several minutes.

Jonathan broke the long silence, "Can I ask you something personal?"

"Why sure, anything. I'll do my best to answer it."

"Do you have a husband or a boyfriend? Please tell me the truth."

"Yes, I do. I have a boyfriend, and his name is Ben. He's away on a business trip now, but someday I'd like to introduce him to you. He has asked me to marry him, and I told him 'yes.'"

"I'm not sure I want to meet him. Oh, I do not mean to be mean, but I don't think we'll have much in common, except you, that is. Do you love him?"

"Yes, I do," she admitted.

"Okay, we can leave now," Jonathan said as he abruptly rose.

"Julia, can you wait outside? I'll only be a minute longer."

"Yes, that's fine."

As the door closed behind her, Julia could hear Jonathan's voice.

"Dear God. I know Julia is happy with Ben, but I hope I never meet him. I'm sure he wouldn't like me, and I don't think I'd like him either. I have to go now."

CHAPTER 8

The Children of St. Peter's

Accompanying Julia from the chapel, Jonathan held her hand, but he was not the spry, happy boy she knew him to be. The news of Ben being Julia's fiancé, and the love they share for each other, was difficult for Jonathan to hear, but it was something she knew he needed to understand and process.

Attempting to lighten Jonathan's spirit, Julia asked Jonathan if he could introduce her to the other children of St. Peter's.

"I'm a bit embarrassed to admit it, but I'm not good with names," Jonathan said with his head and shoulders down.

"That's no problem at all. I'll introduce myself and let the children tell me their names. How's that?"

As Julia entered the children's ward, she met with the patients one by one. Jonathan watched as she connected with each of them in a few minutes that he could not do after years of living there. While most of the introductions and conversations were beyond Jonathan's hearing range, he was close enough to overhear the last few interactions.

"Hi. What's your name?"

"Billy."

"I'm Julia. It's so nice to meet you. I've seen you before, mostly when you were playing board games. Do you have a favorite one?"

"Monopoly."

"Wow, that's a difficult game to play."

"Yeah, I know. My parents taught me the rules. I keep it simple. Whenever I don't remember a rule, I make it up as I go along."

"Do you always play it by yourself?"

"I don't want to, but nobody will play it with me. They say it's too hard to play. And I always win. Maybe because I make up the rules!"

"Well, I'm glad you enjoy it."

"Will you play it with me someday?"

"That would be my pleasure. I used to play it too when I was a girl, but somehow time caught up with me, and I haven't in years. I probably forgot many of the rules myself. You'll have to teach me them."

"You just have to promise to let me win. I can't stand losing. It ruins my whole day."

"Okay, that's a deal."

Next up was Julia's conversation with Agnus, whom Jonathan knew had big problems and seldom talked with anyone.

"What a pretty dress. It looks great on you."

"Thanks," Agnus replied in a monotone voice, speaking very slowly. As she spoke, she turned her head down and away from Julia and avoided making eye contact. She slumped down in her wheelchair in an awkward way, and upon speaking, she slumped even further as if the effort to communicate was painful to her. She looked frail and uncomfortable meeting a stranger for the first time.

"What do you like to do here?"

"Go outside." Agnus's voice was low and barely audible.

"What do you like when you're outside?"

"Feel the sun on my face."

"I love the sun too. Always have. There is something so peaceful and comforting in the sunshine. Its warmth makes me feel refreshed and alive."

"Yup."

"Can you do me a favor? Can you let me see your eyes?"

Slowly, Agnus lifted her head and quickly looked at Julia.

"Beautiful. I knew your eyes would be beautiful. And I was right, they are."

Upon hearing Julia's compliment, Agnus took another quick look at her. "Oh, I don't know about that."

"I enjoyed talking with you. I'd like to do it again soon. Would that be alright with you?"

Agnus attempted to respond, but her voice failed her. Frustrated, she simply shook her head, "yes."

As Julia moved to leave, Agnus lifted her right hand toward Julia. It was shaking uncontrollably. She took Agnus's hand in both of hers and gave it a gentle kiss.

"Goodbye, Agnus."

Agnus managed to smile, which Jonathan knew was a rare occurrence. Last up was Jacob.

"I've seen you here before to visit Jonathan. How do you know him?"

"We met at the visitors' window."

"I see lots of people passing by that window, but nobody comes in here unless they're family or friends. You're not a part of his family or his friend, are you? What made you come inside?"

"Well, Jonathan. He motioned for me to join him on his side of the window, and I did."

"Nobody who doesn't already know us ever comes in here unless they have to. You must be the first one. Jonathan never has any visitors so I'm sure you're special to him."

"Do you have visitors?"

"Lots of 'em. My mom and dad visit at least twice a week. My sister joins them sometimes. I also see my grandma. My grandpa died, though."

"Well, I'm happy you have many people in your life who care greatly about you. I'm sorry to hear about your grandpa."

"Oh, don't be sorry. He was very old anyway. He could barely get around and spent the whole day in bed. He never came to see me, so I didn't know him. My grandma is different, though. I know her quite well. She brings me candy, even when it isn't Halloween!"

"What a treat. Maybe I'll see her here someday."

"I know you'll like her. Everyone does. She never stops talking. And she's good at meeting people. Is your grandma still alive?"

"No. Neither of my grandparents. They were both wonderful and amazing people."

"Then we are both lucky, right?"

"Definitely."

When one of the nurses then came over to them, Jacob explained he needed to take his medication.

"See you soon, Jacob!"

As Julia approached Jonathan again, he shook his head in adoration and admiration of what he believed were her "magical powers" to make people feel good and how she could so quickly bring them joy. Just when Jonathan thought he had Julia to himself again, Caren approached them in her wheelchair.

"It was nice to chat with you. You are beautiful," Caren said, smiling.

"Thanks," Julia replied. "I enjoyed meeting you as well. I love your spirit and energy."

"Oh, many days, I feel I have no energy, especially when I'm stuck in my wheelchair. I get sad at times."

"Why?" Julia asked.

"My mommy used to visit me here, but she stopped coming. I miss her very much." As Caren spoke, she twisted several strands of her hair.

"I'm sure she would be here with you if she could, and she misses you too."

"I've heard about your Mom. Jonnie told me about her."

"Jonnie?"

Jonathan then replied, a bit embarrassed, "Okay, so I let Caren call me by that name because she insisted on it. It's her special name for me. What can I do? I can't have things my way all the time!"

Jonathan and Caren shared a smile as they remembered his initial resistance to being called "Jonnie." But over time, as they drew closer, he reluctantly accepted.

Changing topics, Caren continued, "Have you ever been in love, Julia?"

"Yes, several times. Each time it has gotten better."

"Other than my mommy, I have loved only one person my entire life," Caren declared, as she snuck a glance at Jonathan's reddening face. "It is so special; it gives me goosebumps. And I don't feel lonely when I feel love. I think it's the best thing ever."

"You may think it's love, but how do you know?" Jonathan asked.

"Oh, I know. I can't put it into words; I just know."

After a short silence, Julia asked, "What do you like to do?"

"My favorite thing is riding on the big swing outside. I try to go as high as I can."

"That's very brave of you. I'm sure the nurses have warned you to be careful."

"Yup. I hold on as tightly as I can to make sure I won't fall. I love it when the wind blows fast on my face. I close my eyes and pretend I'm flying. I hate when it stops, and I have to get back in my wheelchair." As Caren looked up, she unexpectedly started to cry.

"What?" Julia asked softly.

Trying to gain her composure, Caren started to answer slowly, "I see everyone outside being able to use their legs all the time and hate it when I can't. I'm upset to need this wheelchair. I don't want to take my medications all the time and depend on nurses to help me. I get frustrated not being able to sit upright. It hurts when I go outside sometimes, and people look at me funny. I don't want to be so different."

Jonathan started to tear up as he witnessed Caren's pain and mental anguish.

"You've got to ignore those people because they don't understand and don't know your strengths," Julia reassured Caren. Julia put her arms around her until she stopped crying.

"One of these days, like every girl, I want to get married. Looking at the magazines by the login desk, I love the pastel floral print on cloud white wedding gowns. They are so beautiful. And I'm getting to know some of the dress designers. But I can't picture myself rolling down the aisle in my wedding dress, instead of walking down it."

"Then don't. Picture yourself walking down the aisle, and maybe you will!"

"I'm starting to feel better. I want you to know I'm not usually this sad. There is a happy part of me, as well. I want to show you my good side the next time I see you. And I'll be smiling instead of crying."

"Oh, I can see your happiness even through your tears. I'm glad you stopped by to finish our discussion."

"I'm sure I'll see you again soon. I look forward to it," Caren remarked as she started to wheel herself away.

As Caren turned to leave, Julia called after her, "It was my pleasure getting to know you. Take care of yourself."

Caren stopped her wheelchair, looked back, and smiled at Julia.

"You know, Jonathan, she's very sweet. I like her very much. Give your relationship a chance to grow."

"Yeah, but I'm not ready for love yet. Don't need it; don't want it. I have enough issues without having 'girl problems!'"

"Well, someday, young sir, you will just need to take a chance. Without risk, there is seldom a reward."

CHAPTER 9

Sharing Wedding Plans

On Saturday morning, Julia was awakened by a phone call. As was her custom, she did not set her alarm on weekend days, but seldom had she slept as late as 9:30 a.m. Thinking it was Ben, she rushed to the phone in a cheerful voice as she greeted the caller.

"Hello!"

"Hi. This is Dr. Ingram."

Julia's heart skipped a few beats as she feared receiving bad news from her Mom's primary oncologist and braced herself for it.

"I just want you to know your Mom had a favorable cat scan, and she seems to be doing well. Don't misunderstand, she is still very sick, but enjoy these times when cancer appears to be held in check."

"Oh, that's great. Thanks for making my day, kind sir."

"I met with her half an hour ago, and I gave her the good news. She's well enough I can clear her to leave the hospital for a few hours. I thought you might like to take this opportunity to spend quality time with your Mom and have her forget about cancer, the hospital, the nurses, and, most especially, the other doctors and me for a while."

"What time is she being cleared through?" Julia asked, her excitement building at the prospect of having a fun day alone with her Mom.

"Have her back by 2 p.m. at the latest. If she gets weak or overwhelmed before then, use your best judgment, or give me a call. Oh, and we have not told her so you can surprise her."

44

"Now, you have really made my day!"

Julia took a quick shower, walked Belle outside and fed her, and then rushed to the hospital. With the entrance to St. Peter's newly renovated and opened, she made sure to avoid the North wing to prevent Jonathan from seeing her. While Julia felt guilty doing so, this day belonged to her Mother, and she knew exactly where she'd take her.

"Hi, Mom."

"Hey, gorgeous. What are you doing here so early? I wasn't expecting you until this evening. I'm sure you have better things to do."

"I had to come early. I have a surprise for you, and I know you're just going to love it!"

Looking at her Mother with a broad grin on her face, Julia could not contain her enthusiasm.

"You're breaking free from this place. I got clearance from Dr. Ingram, and I'm going to show you my wedding dress. How's that for a surprise?"

"Can't wait, let's go," Mary Ann said, tearing up with emotion upon seeing how excited Julia was to have a mother/daughter special day together.

"You're sure you feel up to it, right?" Without waiting for a response, Julia added, "You just have to let me know if you get weak at any point, promise?"

"Sure thing. I just need to get out of this very sexy hospital gown, change my clothes, and off we go." Julia helped her Mom put on a red sweater Mary Ann's mother knitted for her.

"So, this is what sunshine feels like?" Mary Ann remarked as she took her first steps outside of St. Peter's in many days. "It feels so wonderful finally to be free and to spend alone time with you."

"Here, let me help you, Mom. You know how difficult stairs can be, and I wouldn't forgive myself if you got hurt."

"I'm taking my time, don't you worry. I want to leave my cancer behind me in the hospital for today and focus only on you."

As Mary Ann gingerly made her way down the nine steps, with Julia by her side and holding on to her, she took short breaks.

"Funny, I don't remember these stairs being so big when I was admitted," Mary Ann joked.

Julia called Marsh's dress shop while driving to the hospital, so Betsy, who had helped her with her wedding dress, would be ready for their arrival. Both Mary Ann and Julia were jubilant as they entered the empty shop, like two kids in a candy store and plenty of money in their pockets.

"Mom, you wait here while I look for Betsy. She must be in the back. I'll go find her."

As she walked through the rear door, Julia met Betsy, who was holding Julia's wedding dress, just as they planned.

"I better not eat any more desserts for the next three months. It fits perfectly, but any more weight on me and I'll bust a seam," Julia declared, as she slipped on the one wedding dress she absolutely loved and couldn't wait for Ben, and her Mom, to see her wearing. Today, at last, one of them would, thanks to Dr. Ingram.

"Oh, don't you fuss, girl. I can always let it out if need be. I promise it will fit you perfectly on your big day. Then you can eat all the desserts you want, including your wedding cake. Now turn for me, dear."

As she completed putting on her dress, Julia stopped and took a minute to look in the mirror, imagining herself walking down the aisle to join Ben waiting for her at the altar. While it was an image she often thought about in her adult years, her reflection in the mirror was a foreign one. The reality of Julia, the bride, still was so new it had not quite caught up to her. She hoped to make both Ben and her Mom proud.

The dress had more than 5,000 sequins in gatherings that were rose-shaped. The bust showed off Julia's curvy figure but was only modestly revealing. The royal cathedral train was ten feet long and, together with the mid-length veil, repeated the rose shape in a tighter but similar formation. When the light hit each of the carefully placed sequins, the dress truly was radiant, reflecting and bending the light in brilliant rainbow patterns. While the dress was elegant and smart looking, it also had a simplicity that attracted Julia.

The dress would have been overpowering for other women, diminishing rather than accentuating their own personal glow. But it was no match for Julia. Once snuggly in it, she transformed its limpness into sheer elegance, reminiscent of an animated princess of a Disney movie. Silk jeweled strapped-heel shoes completed Julia's new look. On her wedding day, she would wear her hair in a tight bun, and long diamond earrings would dangle from her ears, complementing the sparkle of her dress. She then shut her eyes to complete the image, as she silently uttered the words, "I do!"

Julia could feel her heart pounding as she stepped back into the dress shop where her Mom was patiently waiting on a chair to rest. As Julia turned ever so slowly for her Mother, Mary Ann was rendered speechless. Gaining her composure, she gushed, "My princess, you are so gorgeous. Ben is such a lucky man. Why you should get married at Tara, being the Southern belle you still are. Boston hasn't changed that, you know. Look out, Scarlett, here comes my Julia." She rose to hug her daughter and to touch the sequins. "My, oh, my, you're all grown up and going to become Ms. Anderson. I couldn't be happier."

Julia was thrilled to see her Mother acting young, giddy, and so alive.

"It only took me about ten years longer than I expected, but I finally did find my Rhett Butler."

Julia hated for this moment to end, but she was thankful she shared it with her Mom. The next stop was to finalize plans for the wedding cake. Mary Ann was an incredible baker herself, and Julia was anxious to witness her Mom's reaction to the model of the multi-tier cake adorned with flowers of all shapes and colors. As she rose to say goodbye to Betsy and thank her, Mary Ann suddenly weakened and unexpectedly fell. While Julia and the dress shop owner simultaneously rushed to help her up, Mary Ann quickly informed them she was fine, just a little dizzy and weak from her excitement.

"Mom, I'm taking you back now. I think I overexerted you. I promise to show you pictures tomorrow of what the cake will look like. And, if I can, I'll take a sample back to the hospital for you to try. I just know you'll love it."

"Okay, that sounds like a plan," Mary Ann practically whispered in reply and remained quiet during the ride back to St. Peter's. Once there, they both were so consumed with her fall and feebleness to notice the commotion outside the hospital.

CHAPTER 10

Untimely Deaths

Julia helped her Mom out of the car and called the bakery to inform them she would be a half-hour late for her appointment. While she contemplated rescheduling it, she was eager to move ever closer to being finished with her wedding plans. Ben's current and recent business trips and the daily demands of his job made him unavailable to assist her. He asked Julia only to keep him informed and otherwise was fine with her making all decisions. As each month slipped to the next, what began as pure enjoyment morphed into more of a burden, with the pressure to reach the finish line increasing seemingly exponentially. Adding to her stress, she faced several hard deadlines for her upcoming feature articles.

After checking Mary Ann back into St. Peter's and accompanying her to her room, Julia rushed to say a quick hello to Jonathan before heading to the bakery. But as she neared the North wing, she immediately sensed something was not right and, indeed, terribly wrong. Many unfamiliar people filled the children's ward, including police officers, first responders, and many hospital personnel, each doing their assigned task, and strikingly, no children were present, including Jonathan. At the far end of the pandemonium surrounding her as she entered the ward, Julia caught a glimpse of Ms. Thornburg and fought through the crowd to speak with her.

"What's happened?" Julia shouted in an alarmed voice to Ms. Thornburg above the noise of many people rushing in all directions. Before receiving an answer, she then asked loudly, "Where are the children?"

As Ms. Thornburg turned to respond, Julia noticed with panic Ms. Thornburg's sense of despair. Julia knew it would be a response she did not want to hear.

"It's Caren. She just fell to the ground. There was no warning, nothing we could do. We tried our best to save her, but she didn't make it. The paramedics just removed her body a few minutes ago. I can't believe it. It happened so suddenly. I'm sure I'd be in tears, just like the children, if I weren't in so much shock."

Filled with emotion, Julia hugged Ms. Thornburg and asked, trembling, "Where's Jonathan?" Her voice quivered, and she fought to speak while holding back her tears. But her overriding concern for the children compelled her to focus on them and not her emotions.

"We moved all the children to the chapel. A clergyman arrived and is speaking with them now. They're traumatized and quickly were relocated so first responders, and then the paramedics, had the room they needed. It also was important the children not see more than they already had, and . . . ." Ms. Thornburg's voice trailed off as she shook her head in disbelief and replayed Caren's death over several times in her mind. She couldn't help but contemplate whether there were some missed signals she and the other nurses failed to see just before Caren's death.

Julia released Ms. Thornburg from her hug and told her how sorry she was for everyone who witnessed the tragedy. As she hurried to the chapel, Julia canceled her meeting at the bakery. She knew how upset Jonathan would be and that only she could help him cope and make some sense of Caren's sudden demise.

Looking into one of the two small round windows on the chapel's doors, Julia became concerned when she couldn't locate Jonathan. The children were huddled in the first five pews, many of them crying and visibly upset. Only upon quietly entering the chapel did she catch sight of someone hunched in the very last pew. Jonathan separated himself from everyone else as far as he could. He covered his face in his sweater with his hands on his head so he resembled a ball, furiously rocking forward and backward, intent on drowning out his surroundings and what he had just witnessed in his extreme sorrow.

Like Ms. Thornburg, Jonathan could not help replaying in his mind Caren's death, over and over. He had minutes before spoken with her, not about much, and he couldn't even remember what they said to each other. What shocked him is he had no warning she was a ticking time bomb about to expire. Jonathan wished he could have helped Caren. He was on the far side of the room when she fell, her crutches crashing down in front of her. He clearly saw her face as she began the sudden plunge to the floor. It was full of stress, and her eyes twitched furiously and uncontrollably. It was unlike any face he had ever seen before. For the first time in his life, Jonathan witnessed a person as they were in the process of dying. He stood by helplessly, too far out of her range to do anything but remain frozen and watch, in total shock as to what he was seeing.

By the time the nurses, additional hospital staff, and doctors surrounded Caren a few seconds later, Jonathan lost sight of her. He already was numb and shaking. He wished for the slow-motion replay in his mind of that event to stop, but the more he wanted it to stop, the more it played over, and over, and over, again, in excruciating detail. Jonathan was so tortured by the continuously looping replay that by the time of Julia's arrival in the chapel, he didn't notice her entrance.

Upon seeing Jonathan, Julia quietly sat alongside him. She didn't want to interrupt the pastor, who was trying his best to restore the children's sense of peace and security, of which the tragedy so brutally robbed them. For the next several minutes, Jonathan was so isolated in his secluded world he didn't notice Julia was seated next to him. She finally announced her presence by gently hugging him. Upon feeling her hug, he projected his head from his sweater, like a turtle's head emerging from its shell, his eyes swollen and red. By her simple touch, Julia suddenly entered Jonathan's consciousness, although he still was unaware of his surroundings and the other people in the chapel. But for Jonathan, that's all that mattered. He needed Julia more at that moment than he ever needed anyone in his young life.

Upon Jonathan's acknowledging her, Julia widened her embrace, forming their own cocoon, as she rocked back and forth in unison with him, without missing a beat and without saying a word. Their rocking continued like clockwork, and the two became as one in their unilateral motion. Julia was alarmed when Jonathan's heart-wrenching sobs caused his body to shake violently and uncontrollably, and his shortness of breath caused him to gasp for air. Her instincts resulted in burying her head next to his and humming a soft, soothing lullaby only he could hear.

After the pastor finished speaking, Ms. Thornburg rose to escort the still badly shaken children back to their ward. Julia was relieved when Ms. Thornburg suggested, without Julia even asking, that she and Jonathan remain behind until he was ready to return to them.

Lifting her head from her embrace of Jonathan, Julia noticed the rays of bright white light streaming into the chapel from the small clear windows above the tall stained-glass ones. She took that occasion to speak her first words since she had joined him half an hour ago.

"Jonathan, I am so sorry for your loss. I want you to look up and see the incredible light God is sending your way. Feel its warmth and comfort that words cannot express at this time."

Slowly, Jonathan peeled back his sweater to look at the light.

"I don't understand why God has taken Caren from me but would give light instead."

"The light is not in Caren's place. Nothing and nobody can ever replace her. But I think God is trying to console you and let you know everything will be alright even though Caren is no longer with us. It's never easy losing the people who are central to our life. It's extremely painful, but it is necessary. God designed it that way. We who are left behind focus on our pain, our hurt, and our loss. While that is natural and understandable, there is a bigger picture and a great promise of hope and happiness to come." Julia paused to look at the light as she gathered her thoughts on how best to comfort Jonathan.

After a couple of minutes passed, Julia began in a soothing voice, "I'll tell you something about me very few people know. I experienced death when I was a little older than you are, at seventeen. I had a younger brother, Tommy. We were inseparable growing up; I loved him so. And then, without warning and unexpectedly, he grew ill. Within nine days, he died in the hospital of pneumonia. It crushed me."

In a reflective tone, Julia continued, "Now, almost two decades later, it still hurts. But, and this is the important part, my love of him transcends his death. As I grew older, I realized he never fully did leave me. He's still such an important part of my life that often I don't think of him as not being with me, and I don't focus on my pain but, instead, on all the goodness of his soul and the joy he brought, and continues to bring, me."

"I didn't know you had a brother, Julia."

"I shared my story of Tommy not so you feel sorry for me, but to understand time is a great healer, and realize those we're closest with never truly leave us if we don't let them. We carry them with us, remember them, and celebrate them, and they help us become who we are and influence our values and character."

"Can you tell me more about Tommy? What was he like?"

"I haven't spoken to anyone about him in many, many years. Tommy was a bookworm, meaning he enjoyed reading a lot, and more than that, he loved words. He'd be secluded in his room for many hours at a time with his books and playing all sorts of word games, including crossword puzzles, hangman, and Scrabble. He won more spelling bees at his school than anyone else. One of his favorite things was going to the library and being surrounded by all the periodicals, journals, newspapers, magazines, treatises, and books. He would love to reverse the lettering of any word to learn how it sounded when spelled that way. Doing so, he discovered there is only one state in the United States that, if spelled backward, sounds like another state spelled regularly. He also was wise and seemed beyond his years. He made up a saying I believe is so true – 'everything that is is taken from that that was.'"

"Tommy must have been smart since he read so much. You know, I've never read a book in my life. Please tell me more about him."

"Well, Tommy also enjoyed exploring. He'd always make up some mystery we needed to solve for us to save our planet. He'd ask me to join him on his many adventures and treasure hunts I still vividly remember today. We built this makeshift treehouse in the middle of the woods behind our home. It was so special, our secret place to hang out with each other. We also discovered a small cave in the woods where finches lived that we imagined had never been seen by human eyes before. We'd create stories about how we could use the cave to transcend deep into the Earth to find previously undiscovered minerals that now could be used as a cure for the many diseases plaguing humanity."

"Sounds like you both had a great imagination."

"Tommy was the imaginative one; I joined him for the fun of it all. I was exploring with him when he discovered objects that looked like ancient animal bones with what appeared to be writing on them. To this day, I don't know what they were. We took them to our cave and pretended they gave us magical powers simply by raising them in our hands, high over our heads. We made up our own secret word, 'jumala.' As we'd raise our sacred bones, we'd chant our secret word loudly to scare off any evil spirits so all badness would disappear from the Earth."

"What an odd word, Julia."

"Yes. Getting back to my point, Tommy was so full of energy and fun, life was never the same after he suddenly was gone. I was devastated the day Tommy died. I couldn't comprehend how he could be taken from me without hardly any warning. It seemed all imagination, exploration, and excitement instantly vanished with his passing, and I was lost for words to describe my feelings. I couldn't picture continuing without him. My whole identity, up to that point in my life, was so closely connected with his. I can't fathom how a husband or wife who has been married for many decades feels when the other one is no longer there, and their union abruptly ends, and the two become one."

"It must be so difficult. Kind of like having to start your life all over again."

Julia nodded her head, "yes."

"At first, I was so lonely without Tommy, there were days when I didn't want to get out of bed. My life was stuck on hold, and I was clueless about how I would continue. Since experiencing an unexpected death of someone I loved totally was new to me, I didn't know if I would lose my optimism, joy of life, will to live, or love for God."

"Wow, Julia. I'm sorry you experienced such pain."

"What kept me going, and what got me out of bed on those days when

I didn't want to, was Tommy's tremendous love for me and his continuing to guide me. Without any doubt, I know he wants me to explore on my own, and adjust, adapt, and achieve with a smile on my face and love in my heart. I also came to realize living that way, I would please Tommy."

Julia paused, took a deep breath, and felt the peace of the chapel.

"More than anything, when I think of Tommy now, I feel so blessed he was such an incredible part of my life, I got to be his sister, we shared so many exciting experiences, and we have a bond that stands the test of time and his untimely death."

"I wish I had met Tommy. I'm sure I would have liked him a lot."

"I'm sure of it as well." Julia paused again and tried further to uplift Jonathan.

"Unfortunately, there is nothing I can do or say to bring Caren back. I wish I could. We will all miss her. But as Tommy was to me, Caren is to you, and I am living proof you will get by just fine as I have. I always miss Tommy but draw from our experiences and the love we shared, and they strengthen me and make me a better person. If we leave the big things to God and have faith in Him, then everything will fall into place."

"What bothers me is Caren wanted to kiss me, and I pretended like I didn't want her to. I don't think she knew I did care for her, and most of the time, I acted like I didn't."

"If she didn't know that then, she certainly knows it now. Let her goodness become a part of who you are. And be grateful you had a friend at St. Peter's who cared so much for you."

"What is so difficult is I have no other friend here now, and it will seem less like home without her. I don't look forward to that, and I'm frightened by it."

"Don't worry too much. The goal is to enjoy the time God has given you on Earth despite the thunderclouds overhead. My Mom always says anyone can be happy when things are going well, but the true measure of happiness is whether you can smile and feel good about life when everything is crashing down around you. Do you think you can be happy even after losing Caren?"

"I don't know for sure. But I'll try. I stopped shaking so that's a good sign, I guess. I don't know what I would have done without you here, Julia. You always know the right things to say. One last thing before we leave."

As he finished his sentence, Jonathan knelt toward the altar.

"Can you pray with me, Julia?"

Julia was touched when Jonathan included Tommy in his prayers.

CHAPTER 11

Investigation

Julia was aware that Caren's death instantly gave her new roles to fill for Jonathan's benefit. Now, instead of being just a caring visitor and friend who felt sorry for his plight and tried to brighten his days a bit, she also was his teacher, spiritual leader, and protector. The more Jonathan needed her, the more Julia cared for him and cherished their new relationship. And the more time they spent together, the more she got to know a young man with a great spirit who was so deserving of goodness and joy in his young life.

Julia also knew Caren's death would fundamentally change Jonathan's environment at St. Peter's. While Julia wasn't aware of it before, it became apparent to her now that Caren served as the bridge between Jonathan and the other patients in his ward. Without her, he became further isolated and withdrawn. That strikingly was clear at the chapel and continued in the days that followed. Ms. Thornburg informed her that Jonathan felt lost and was barely functional. He refused to eat or engage in any activity. There were days when he didn't get out of bed or communicate except when Julia visited him. This sudden change deeply concerned Julia, as well as Ms. Thornburg and the other nurses.

Julia spent several sleepless nights worrying about Jonathan and his future. She had nightmares of Caren's fall, the extreme stress on her face at the time she was dying as Jonathan described it, her crutches crashing down in a slow and silent plunge, and the screams of the children while she lay motionless on the ground. Julia also imagined how difficult it would be for Jonathan and the other children to walk on, or near, the area of the floor where Caren died.

Following her last such nightmare, Julia had a dream. In it, she was young again and playing with Tommy in their treehouse. They were having a fun and fabulous time. Suddenly, they heard the noise of someone climbing up the ladder to approach them. That surprised them because nobody ever visited them at the treehouse before and, as far as they both knew, no one else had any knowledge it even existed. She looked down the ladder with some alarm, but more curiosity, to see who was climbing up. Julia saw Jonathan and called a warm greeting, inviting him to come up to join them. In his excitement in doing so, he missed a rung of the ladder and fell to the ground, bruised and hurt. Tommy encouraged Julia to help Jonathan and take care of him. "Help him as you would help me," Tommy called to her. Julia rushed down and assisted Jonathan climb up to the treehouse. She found, and used, a large vine from the woods to tie his leg tightly to help stop its swelling. Julia then called to Tommy to help them, and upon turning her head, noticed for the first time Tommy was no longer there and simply disappeared. She woke up to the image of holding Jonathan in her arms and trying her best to care for him alone.

Especially given her dream, Julia knew she needed to take action. She called her boss at *The Globe* and requested, and was granted, the following two weeks as her vacation time. Julia had always been an ideal employee and built up a reservoir of goodwill. She seldom asked for favors, which made her most recent request hard for her boss to deny. Freed from the obligations of her position, Julia immediately began to use her investigative reporter skills to learn as much as possible about Jonathan's and his family's history.

Working with the assistance of Ms. Thornburg and the hospital's records department, Julia discovered that St. Peter's admitted Jonathan on July 29, 2007, at the tender age of two. Records listed both of his parents as deceased. Oddly, they did not state who admitted him. Since he became an orphan, Julia wondered if he had a relative who temporarily watched him before taking him to the hospital. If the State had done so, the records would have so provided. More than his admission to St. Peter's, Julia was curious to learn who took care of him before such time.

Julia invited Ms. Thornburg to meet with her at a local Starbucks. She thought Ms. Thornburg was easily in her early fifties, a matronly looking lady, on the heavy side, with brown straight, wispy hair. Her black wire rim-glasses gave the impression she could be a librarian. Her face was beautiful, with high cheekbones and dimples, which just was starting to hint at Ms. Thornburg's age. Julia was sure she had been quite attractive in her younger days. While friendly and approachable, she appeared to have little time or temperament for anything other than fulfilling her duties at St. Peter's.

Julia thought it best they meet outside of the hospital and away from Ms. Thornburg's job so their conversation could be deliberate and focused. She quickly learned that Ms. Thornburg was never married and had no children of her own. Yet, she professed her love of children and her burning desire to be a mother in her younger days. However, the right man to wed and start a family with always eluded her. Julia sympathized and considered herself blessed that Ben was her answer to not becoming a Ms. Thornburg.

"When did you arrive at St. Peter's?" Julia asked.

Taking a sip of her piping hot latte, Ms. Thornburg responded, "On October 30, 2007. I remember it like it was yesterday. We only had five patients back then, so I started pretty much at the ward's beginning. At age two, Jonathan was already there, and couldn't speak, and made few sounds. He was very much a loner from the start, unable, and then unwilling, to communicate."

"Please tell me about those early years. You and Jonathan have a long history together."

"As I know you are aware, Jonathan is an exceptional young man. He's very much a worrier and always seems to have the weight of the world on his shoulders. I wish he were more social but being social never appeared to be one of his priorities. I remember all the children during playtime. Jonathan refused to have any part of it and would be off in the corner all by himself. I'd often encouraged him to enjoy other children's company in the earlier years, but he had no interest, and I found some things I could not change no matter how much I wanted them to be different. Often, he was, and is, very much alone. It worries me. How long can he be his own island?"

"I know," Julia chimed in. "Especially with Caren's death, I had hoped he could share his grief and be open with the other children. But that certainly does not appear to be happening."

"No, it's not. But that's why you've been like a fresh cool breeze on a hot, muggy day in August. He so has taken to you. When you arrive, he seems to wake up for the first time that day, and is so alive. But once you leave, he immediately reverts into isolation. I feel so sorry for the poor guy. I wish there were something I could do to help him."

Changing the topic, Julia asked, "Do you have any information regarding his parents? I understand from hospital records they are both deceased, and Jonathan was an orphan before he arrived at St. Peter's."

"Yes, that's my understanding as well. I heard his parents died in the same car crash, and Jonathan, luckily, was not in the car with them at the time. But that's about all I know."

Julia continued without missing a beat, "Do you recall if he's ever had any visitors at St. Peter's other than myself?"

"No, none." Then slightly changing her answer, Ms. Thornburg added, "Certainly not in many, many years."

"So, he did have visitors in his early years at St. Peter's?" Julia pressed.

"Let me think. Many people come and go. Wait, now that I'm thinking of it, he did have an elderly lady visit him a couple of times, but only in the first two months after my joining St. Peter's. But I can't recall her name or how she knew him. She was in and out of Jonathan's life so quickly. There seemed to be little connection between them. But he did appear to recognize her."

"Do you recall what she looked like?"

"No, my memory's not that good. Possibly, if I saw her picture, it would jog my memory. I'm sorry I can't be more helpful."

Julia thought for a few seconds, then proceeded. "Visitors at St. Peter's need to sign a login book upon entry. Did they have to do so back then as well?"

"Why, yes. I'm quite certain that's been the policy since the start."

"Where would the login book from 2007 be kept?" Julia asked, leaning forward toward Ms. Thornburg.

"We don't keep that sort of information on-site. Most of the hospital records and documents are sent off-site to a warehouse in Springfield."

"Do you think the 2007 login book is in the warehouse?"

"I can't say with certainty, but, yes, I expect it is."

"And you're quite certain all visitors were required to sign in and state who they were there to see so if I could locate and view the relevant login book, I could determine the identity of Jonathan's mystery visitor?" Julia asked, more excited than before.

"Yes, I believe so."

"Do you know if it exists and can be found, would I be permitted to view it?"

"That's my understanding. It's treated as public information and is not confidential. If you have any problem in viewing the login book once found, please let me know. I have been at the hospital for so long, I know everyone, and they know me. It never hurts to have friends in high places," Ms. Thornburg said with a smile.

"How about records regarding Jonathan's medical condition?"

"That information is kept on-site and is readily available; however, unless you're Jonathan's family or his guardian, I am not at liberty to share it with you, and you cannot see it. Let's say, though, he has significant medical issues and is not a healthy boy, and that's separate from his mental challenges."

"I understand. You've been so helpful, and I appreciate your time and insights. One last question – who can tell me whether the login books are at the warehouse?"

"That's an easy one, Roger Banin of Administration. He coordinates all shipments to and from the warehouse. I'll let him know you're planning on speaking with him. Let me look." Ms. Thornburg then fiddled through the items in her pocketbook from which emerged her cell phone. "Here it is," Ms. Thornburg said after a slight pause as she glanced up from her iPhone contact page. "I'll text you his cell number."

"Thanks again, so much! You're a dear soul."

Julia wasted no time in speaking with Mr. Banin. He assured her the login books were at the warehouse, and he provided her with the work address and contact information of Thomas Wills, the head administrator of the warehouse, who further would assist her.

Arriving at the warehouse later that afternoon, Julia was struck by Mr. Wills' businesslike manner, and believed him to be the male counterpart to Ms. Thornburg in demeanor, although not in appearance. He was seated at a desk at the warehouse's entryway, which was walled-off from the rest of the space. Upon seeing Julia, he slowly rose to greet her. Mr. Wills was tall and lanky, with a frailness that made him look like he would have trouble maintaining a vertical position against a strong headwind. His hair was jet black and cut short and straight at the sides so as to make his face appear especially elongated. Black bi-focal glasses sat on the very edge of his nose so low that when he moved his head, Julia instinctively jerked her hand out in a gesture to catch them. His complexion was pale, with only a hint of color, and he moved with the stiffness of a man twice his age. Mr. Wills wore black suit pants with a crisp, starched, white dress shirt with only the upper-most button unbuttoned and a white tee shirt visible underneath. It looked like he was more suited for attending a funeral than working at a warehouse. As she approached him, he extended his hand in greeting and shook hers with a profound limpness.

"You must be Julia. I know why you're here. Follow me, and I'll do my best to assist you," he said, unlocking the door and holding it open for her to enter the cavernous space overflowing with folders, files, and corrugated boxes of every size.

While attempting to help, Mr. Wills spent the first couple of hours in one futile search after another. Unfortunately, he moved extremely slowly such that Julia wondered whether he could make it out alive in the event of a warehouse fire. He reminded Julia of the "oldest man" character played by Tim Conway on *The Carol Burnett Show*. On several occasions, when the timing of his pace seemed like the flowing of thick molasses, Julia thought of giving him a gentle nudge to confirm that he was still awake. He was sure as to where the 2007 login book should have been located; the only problem was, it was not there. Finally, Mr. Wills had a hunch that proved to be correct. In addition to St. Peter's records, the warehouse stored books and documents from several other hospitals. Sure enough, upon reviewing the section where the login books of St. Patrick's hospital were located, he discovered the St. Peter's 2007 login book mistakenly was filed there. Problem solved.

Being handed the relevant book, Julia eagerly searched the months of November and December, the first full two months after Ms. Thornburg's arrival at the hospital. Under the column of the patient's name who was being visited, Jonathan's name appeared exactly twice, just as Ms. Thornburg remembered. On both occasions, the name of the visitor was Samantha Wharton, having an address of 39 Barfield Drive, Marlborough, Massachusetts.

Julia hurried her thank you and goodbye to Mr. Wills so as to reach Marlborough, which was slightly less than an hour and a half drive from Springfield, before nightfall. She attempted to find Samantha Wharton's phone number online but had no fortune doing so. Having no telephone information for Ms. Wharton, Julia hoped an unannounced visit nevertheless would be welcomed.

As she approached the neighborhood, Julia admired the large Victorian homes, the well-groomed spacious lawns, and the spotless public roads in a well-to-do part of town. Rather than feel nervous, she summoned her investigative professionalism to guide her to the front door. *I just pray someone is home*, she thought, as she rang the bell of the large bright white Victorian house that stood before her. Within twenty seconds, a skinny elderly lady answered the door. It remained chain locked, and Julia spoke through the three-inch width of space allowed to her.

"Hello, ma'am. My name is Julia Richards. I'm so sorry to come to you today unannounced, but I ask a favor of you, please. I am looking for Samantha Wharton and urgently need to speak with her. I hope you can help me."

"I'm sorry, she doesn't live here," responded the elderly lady as she moved to close her front door.

"Oh, please. I've come a long way to get here. Do you know the name and where I might find her?"

"Yes, I do recognize the name. I bought this house from her over a decade ago. However, I don't have contact with her anymore. I'm once again sorry, Ms. Richards. Good day." The lady again moved to close her door.

"No, please wait," Julia begged firmly and forcefully. "Did she leave you her forwarding address in the event you received any of her mail here?"

"Yes, I believe she did."

"Did you ever receive mail for her you then forwarded on?", Julia persisted.

"Certainly, in the first year I lived here, but it's been years since, and I'm not sure I kept her address."

"Say you were to receive mail for her today, however unlikely that would be. How would you find where to send it to her?"

"I might be able to locate her address. I have a few ideas as to where I kept it. Can I ask what you need her contact information for?"

"It's a long story, but I'll try to be brief. It revolves around the most adorable boy who is at St. Peter's hospital in Boston. He's mentally challenged. I visit him often, and we have become close. He's quite remarkable. It appears the only visitor he ever had at St. Peter's was Ms. Wharton many years ago. I very much need to speak with her to learn more about the boy's past. The poor soul, I understand he lost both of his parents in a car crash, and he has been at St. Peter's essentially his entire life. I am looking to make his life better because, well, because he deserves it."

Julia spoke with such sincerity the lady readily capitulated.

"I'm sorry I can't let you in. But if you wait here, I'll look for it." And with those words, the lady closed her door and was gone for approximately ten minutes.

As she waited, Julia admired the large wraparound wooden white porch, the hung swing bench, and the sweet-smelling deep blue and purple hydrangea bushes dotting the landscape. The house had a kind of Southern charm that made her feel at home.

As abruptly as the elderly lady disappeared, she suddenly reopened her door and reappeared. "Guess it's your lucky day. I wrote her address for you, dear. Here it is. Her address is, or at least was, on Martha's Vineyard. I couldn't find her phone number, even though I believe I had it at one point in time. Good luck, dear."

"One last question, please. Do you know if Ms. Wharton had ever adopted a child?"

"No, I'm sorry, I don't know. I do hope you find what you're looking for."

"Thanks again so much, ma'am. Again, I apologize for intruding."

With night approaching, Julia would leave Martha's Vineyard for another day – tomorrow.

Arriving at her apartment, Julia quickly arranged for her trip and Belle's care. After a full day, she finally sunk into her oversized accent chair in her living room, exhausted. Julia was confident of learning much more of Jonathan's life story tomorrow, as she was satisfied of being on the right track to solving her latest puzzle.

CHAPTER 12

The Truth Revealed

Julia was on a mission to learn as much as she could to help Jonathan. Her most recent visit was discouraging. Jonathan appeared unable to cope and remained emotionally drained, stuck, and traumatized. Having a grief counselor visit with the children was of little help to him, unlike the others.

Julia arrived at South Station to catch the first Dattco motorcoach to the New Bedford terminal. From there, she boarded the Seastreak ferry to Oak Bluffs in Martha's Vineyard. Julia heard much of Martha's Vineyard's charm, and it had been on her "to do" list for a long time. Now, she actually had a purpose for making the trip. Julia sat on the ferry's uppermost deck, loving the fresh air and the early morning sun. The cool breeze off of Buzzards Bay put her to sleep almost immediately, and the calmness of Vineyard Sound helped to keep Julia in her slumber until the ferry docked, and the noise of the passengers awakened her as they gathered their children and personal items to disembark.

Upon her arrival, Julia quickly hailed a cab for the twenty-minute ride to her destination. She asked the cab driver to wait a few minutes until she could confirm Samantha Wharton still lived there and was at home. Given Julia's persuasive charm, Southern politeness, and a generous tip, he readily complied.

While smaller than Ms. Wharton's former house in Marlborough with much less acreage, the Edgartown house was no less impressive. A clean white picket fence surrounded the property. The house was a stunning, immaculate, bright white with tan shutters and the same tan in stucco siding that perfectly framed it. The attached three-car garage had a pair of bay windows and a balcony on top. The lawn was a deep green and was neatly manicured, and the birch trees, shrubs, and flowers appeared as if they were newly planted. The garage entrance had a two-tone grey stone that sparkled in the sunlight. Red claystone formed the short walkway to the front door. Behind the house was a small beach leading to the deep blue water. *How quaint,* Julia thought, as she turned to ring the bell. She was met by a pleasant white-haired lady who exuded confidence and sophistication. The lady wore her hair in a bun and had expressive, bright blue eyes. As with the house, Julia liked her instantly.

"You must be Julia," the lady said in a welcoming voice, to Julia's surprise.

Before Julia could respond, the lady, witnessing her shock, explained. "Rachel, whom I understand you met with last night, called me to let me know to expect you. She found my number after you left. I hadn't spoken with Rachel in many years. She apologized for giving out my address without having spoken with me first, but she didn't have my phone number available at the time. I assured her I am fine she did. We had a lot of catching up to do. Speaking with Rachel, I understand why you are here. It's a long story, so I have a suggestion to make. Have you been to Edgartown before, Julia?"

"No, this is my first time in Martha's Vineyard. It's simply breathtaking."

"Great. My suggestion is this. Let's ride bikes to Lighthouse Beach. I have a spare one, and it's a lovely area I think you will enjoy. We can chat there."

"I'm with you, Ms. Wharton. Thanks."

"Please call me Sam. All my friends do."

Julia motioned to her cab driver that he could go on his way without her. She had come to the right place, was standing in front of the right person, Jonathan's mystery visitor, and she knew Sam was holding many, if not all, of the remaining pieces necessary to complete her puzzle. Sam grabbed an oversized straw hat with printed colorful flowers on it, tied it on her head to protect her face from the strong sun, and off they went.

Julia was surprised by Sam's stamina. The older woman rode at a quick and constant pace, so Julia found it challenging to keep up, despite being three decades younger and in excellent shape herself. They stopped at a short, stocky white lighthouse.

"These lighthouses are such an important part of our history. I just love them. Too bad many are no longer used and are falling into disrepair," Sam said without so much as missing a breath from the long bike ride.

Without giving Julia an opportunity to respond, which she appreciated being a bit out of breath herself, Sam continued, "I understand you know Jonathan and would like to learn more about his early years and how he got to St. Peter's. Is that correct?"

"Yes, Sam, it is."

Sam moved to sit down on the beach, and Julia followed her there. Staring out into the peaceful blue water, Sam began again to speak.

"I have to start by confessing I have much regret regarding that poor child. I hope you don't think badly of me."

Julia shook her head, "no," to encourage Sam to continue.

"Let's start from the beginning, then, shall we?"

So there Julia found herself in an idyllic setting, overlooked by the lighthouse, with a breathtaking view of the water and the salty-smelling cool breeze. It was a perfect place for a chat, peaceful and quiet, with only periodic interruptions by the sounds of the seagulls frolicking overhead. Finally, she'd get the answers to the questions she longed to hear.

"I grew up outside of Nashville. For a Southern girl, I kept a swift pace. I met Jack, my husband, in my junior year at Vanderbilt. It was love at first sight for both of us. Sure enough, he proposed to me shortly after we graduated. We married, but soon after that, discovered Jack could not father a child. I was devastated. Having children was a lifelong dream of mine and Jack's. But my Jack was my everything. He was strong, charming, intelligent, determined, and hardworking, but he also had an endearing sensitive and empathetic side to his personality. Ours is a true romance story."

Sam paused with a slight smile, her eyes glistening in the sun as she adjusted her hat.

"Within a couple of years of our wedding, one of our former classmates at Vanderbilt had an idea to start a semiconductor company and locate it up North outside of Boston. He knew Jack was entrepreneurial, and they had big dreams. I was hesitant to leave behind my family, friends, and everything I knew up to that point in my life, but I let Jack decide what was best for him, and I followed him to Boston. You could say, dear, ours was a traditional marriage," Sam said with a wink to Julia.

"Their business in Boston thrived, Jack was his own boss, and we bought the Marlborough Victorian you were at yesterday. I loved that house, and we had no intention of leaving it. We planned to sell Jack's business for a hefty sum, and we would be golden in our golden years," she said with a curious laugh.

"One of Jack's employees, Jill Singler, gave birth to a child out of wedlock. Jill had her problems. She had little money, was an alcoholic, and abused drugs. She should have been fired many times, but Jack had a huge heart and felt sorry for her. He tried his best to protect her. While she had her strengths, motherhood was not one of them. The child was unplanned, and there was no husband or relatives to help to raise him. It was clear soon after his birth, the child had mental problems. Jill was helpless. She didn't begin to know how to work and care for her newborn."

"What a dilemma to be in," Julia remarked.

Sam nodded in agreement, and then she continued.

"Upon returning to her job, Jill suffered greatly. She had a horrible case of postpartum depression. Things quickly went from bad to worse, and she attempted to commit suicide in the lot behind Jack's business. Jack was galvanized by that event to help her. He proposed a plan for us to raise Jonathan for six months to a year tops until Jill could find her footing and become the mother Jonathan needed. We proposed our plan to Jill, and she was very thankful and relieved. And I finally had a baby I always wanted. But we all understood at the outset the plan was a short term one, a year at the most. So, I intentionally did not get too emotionally attached to Jonathan because I knew my role only was to serve as a bridge until Jill got better, and she could then raise him herself."

Sam stopped speaking for a few minutes as a couple of ships passed by, increasing the lapping of the waves on the beach, and waited for the seagulls overhead to quiet down after they found their lunch on the nearby sand.

Sam then continued, "While Jack's plan for Jonathan was well-intentioned and generous, it didn't work out as we originally envisioned it. Jill had a nervous breakdown and was in no position to resume her role as his mother. Our one-year plan turned into a two-year plan. Shortly after Jonathan's second birthday, Jack died in a car crash. The rug was pulled out from under me, and I felt lost without my beloved Jack by my side."

Julia gasped upon learning of Jack's sudden death and put her arms around Sam to help comfort her decade-old wound. Sam appreciated Julia's gesture of support and continued with her story.

"Without Jack, my life was transformed yet again. I quickly sold our house to Rachel. I also came to the sad conclusion I was not the right person to be Jonathan's mother. I was in my mid-fifties at the time and never intended to be a single mom at that age. I truly believed despite my love for Jonathan, he would be better off with children who shared similar difficulties as he did and should be where he had around-the-clock care and access to medical treatment, as needed. I remember the day I brought Jonathan to St. Peter's. I cried uncontrollably and felt tremendous guilt, and I still do to this day. I had so longed for a child, and there I was giving away a beautiful baby boy." Sam shook her head at remembering how torn she was on that day. "I think of Jonathan often. I visited him at first, but once I moved to Edgartown, the visits became more difficult, and I'm sorry to say they ended entirely." After a brief pause, Sam asked, "Tell me, Julia, how is Jonathan?"

"First, Sam, thanks so much for your heartfelt honesty and sharing the pains you went through by Jack's death and Jonathan's hospitalization. To say those events were devastating to you, I know is a great understatement. I could feel your pain with every word of your story."

The two women sat and embraced each other again.

"You're a special lady, Sam. I'm fortunate to have met you and for your sharing your life story with me, a total stranger. I'm so sorry for your losses."

Julia then proceeded to address Sam's question.

"Jonathan has such a great spirit. I have connected with him so quickly and at such a deep level. I want to help him; I need to help him. He just experienced a painful loss himself. One of his fellow patients at St. Peter's, who he was closest to, unexpectedly passed away a few days ago. Jonathan is trying hard to cope with his loss, but, sorry to say, he isn't doing well. I think he'll be fine in time and the right environment."

"What do you mean by the 'right environment?'"

"I'm thinking of having Jonathan come live with me and, if that goes well, ultimately adopting him. I have come to love Jonathan and care greatly about him. I need to help him and what better way than for him to live with me."

"Wouldn't that be wonderful, Julia! You would become the mother to him Jill and I were not able to be. Are you married, dear?"

"Not yet. I'm engaged. His name is Ben, and I know he'll make a great father."

"And he's ready to adopt Jonathan?"

"One slight problem, Sam. I haven't told Ben about Jonathan yet, or my plan for him. It all happened so suddenly while he's been away on a lengthy business trip. I need to discuss it with him in person. If all goes well, that's in the very near future!"

"Oh, good luck, dear. I trust that God has a plan for you and Jonathan, and you will make the right decision for you and Ben. I'm quite sure of it. Now, follow me."

Sam showed Julia the lighthouse up-close and personal. She pointed out a heart with the initials "S" and "J" etched inconspicuously into the lighthouse's exterior.

"My Jack was so romantic. During our last summer together, we vacationed here. We came to this very lighthouse, and he made this heart for me using it as his canvas. I love looking at it and remembering how excited he was for me to see it. It was his way physically to express his love for me that has withstood the test of time. I hope it never is painted over or disappears. So, when I was looking to relocate after Jack's death, I do believe this heart was like a beacon to direct and welcome me here." Sam then ran her fingers over the heart, held them there for a brief moment, and smiled.

"How special. Thanks for sharing that with me. Seeing Jack's heart, I feel a connection with him even though we never had the chance to meet," Julia said as they headed back to their bicycles.

When Sam entered her house, she offered Julia a bite to eat. Julia politely declined. Sam then insisted on driving her back to the ferry. As the two women sat outside waiting for the ferry's arrival, Julia asked Sam one last question. "So, when did Jill die?"

"Oh, my dear," Sam responded. "Jill's not dead. She moved to Texas years ago to begin anew. I believe she's still there. I have her address, but I lost her cell number years ago. We exchange Christmas cards and keep up with each other year-by-year. I can text it to you if you wish. I'm sure she would be fine with that since you have befriended her son."

Still in shock, Julia replied, "Yes, please do."

As the ferry arrived to start the boarding process, Julia hugged Sam. It delighted them that they so quickly and naturally formed a strong bond with each other, with Jonathan at its core.

Julia was heading back to the mainland and city life that contrasted so starkly to the way of life offered by Edgartown. On the ferry ride back, she wondered how Jack's car crash became mistakenly associated with Jonathan's parents. That was one question it appeared would go unanswered.

CHAPTER 13

Mom's Words of Wisdom

Julia arrived back in Boston and looked forward to her visits later that day with her Mom and Jonathan. Neither was doing particularly well. Since Mary Ann had fallen, she was in increased pain and could not get an adequate amount of sleep. Julia worried her Mom might not be strong enough to fight her illness.

While Mary Ann was struggling with her physical health issues, Jonathan still was reeling in mental anguish and pain. He told Julia several times he much rather be in physical pain than mental pain. His mental pain mercilessly would not leave him alone and let him forget he should have been more appreciative of Caren when she was alive.

Julia knew she needed to discuss her plan for Jonathan with Ben and have him agree to that plan as soon as possible. Ben would be returning in a few days, and she wanted her Mom's advice on how best to approach him. She knew he very much wanted to be a father someday. Her plan would require he become the father of someone else's child, who already was in his teenage years, with mental disabilities and health issues, and that some-day would need to be very soon. While she was confident in Ben's love for her, she knew her request would be extreme and life-altering, and she was uncertain whether he was ready to become a father as quickly as that would require.

Despite her Mother's ordeal, Julia was aware Mary Ann had her mental facilities very much intact, and she would receive sage advice. She informed her Mom about her meeting with Ms. Thornburg, her discussions with hospital administration, her several hours together with Mr. Wills at the Springfield warehouse, her visit with Rachel in Marlborough, and her meeting and talk with Sam in Edgartown the previous day. She also told Mary Ann about Jill and her plan for Jonathan.

"Wow, my sweetheart. You have been through a lot. I know you have given it much thought, and I trust you will make the right decision. I have two questions for you. First, will you be able to provide Jonathan with the around-the-clock care he needs? Second, what if your plan does not become Ben's plan?" Rephrasing it, she asked, "What happens if Ben is not ready, willing, and able, before your wedding, or shortly after that, to care for, or adopt, Jonathan? Instead of joining a man and a woman, you are asking him to join a man, a woman, and a teenager. That may be asking a lot of him."

"I'm aware of those obstacles and have thought them through. I will ask for a leave of absence to get Jonathan settled and interview a personal 24-hour nurse for him, if needed. Once I return to work, I'll try to do some of my assignments remotely to have more time with him. He's not associating with the kids at St. Peter's now, and he has no friends, so there's not much of a loss if he's moved. And he will continue to see his same doctors at St. Peter's."

"How long of a leave of absence will you be asking for?"

"Somewhere between six months to a year, depending on the circumstances."

"You might have to factor in that request being denied outright or the possibility they find someone to replace you, and there's no job to return to when you're ready to start working again."

"I know. That is a bit scary. But I'm remaining focused on Jonathan now and his welfare. I trust that everything else will fall into place."

Julia continued, "Concerning Ben, I truthfully have not had time to give it much thought. Maybe I'm intentionally avoiding it. But my view is if he truly loves me, he will trust me to do what's right, and once he appreciates how important it is to me, and after he meets and gets to know Jonathan, it will become important to him as well. It will not be the same family we have been planning, but it will be a family nevertheless, with an incredible young man who needs us."

"And if he doesn't feel the same as you?" Mary Ann repeated.

"I will have to think about it some more and cross that bridge if, and when, I come to it. I don't believe that's likely to happen, but if it did, what would you do?"

"It's a delicate decision, and I don't want to sway you one way or the other. I do want you fully to consider the implications."

"Mom, I need you to tell me in no uncertain terms. What would you suggest I do if Ben were to reject my plan?"

Mary Ann took some time before responding, acutely aware this could be a turning point for Julia, and a radical departure from the life she had been planning since Ben proposed to her.

"Well, as I see it, there are three possibilities:

1. leave Jonathan at St. Peter's, the status quo, so to speak – do nothing;
2. move Jonathan to your apartment with Ben's prior consent; or
3. move Jonathan to your apartment despite Ben's opposition."

Julia cut in, "Mom, because of my love and concern for Jonathan, the first scenario is not an option."

"I figured as much. I know you too well, my sweetheart. The second scenario clearly is optimal. If it comes to the third scenario, knowing my daughter, as I do, you will go forward and let the chips fall where they may. Ultimately, you need to ask yourself, which is more important – becoming Jonathan's mother or Ben's wife? I know giving up either one of those would be devastating for you. But you need to be true to yourself and follow your heart. And do not have regrets either way. Always remember, everything happens for a reason. If you're meant to be Jonathan's mother, you will be. If you're meant to be Mrs. Anderson, I do not doubt you will become her. Hopefully, you'll become both. With faith, anything is possible."

"What bothers me is if my wedding were canceled, you would not be able to walk me down the aisle. I know how long you have waited for that day to come and how much you want it to happen, so you know I'm cared for and loved."

"Don't think that way, my Julia. I appreciate you thinking of me and how your decision could affect me. But this is not about me; it's about you, Ben and Jonathan. I don't, and shouldn't, come into that picture. Say, for example, you chose to become Ms. Anderson, but that choice precludes your chance to be Jonathan's mother. You might ultimately regret it, which then could negatively affect your marriage and your happiness. In that circumstance, even though I got to see my daughter get married and walk you down the aisle, most important to me is your long-term happiness. I want you to follow your heart, do what you think is right, and accept whatever the consequences are without regret."

"You always know what to say." Julia thanked her Mom and kissed her on her forehead. "I can't imagine my life without Ben in it. I love him so, and we have a bright future together. At this point, I don't know what I would do if he refuses to adopt Jonathan with me. I am uncertain and torn, and you know how I dislike uncertainty. I'll have to give it more thought, in light of your advice."

After a slight pause, Julia continued.

"Ben gets back by week's end. I need to do one more thing before I decide how to proceed."

"Let me guess. Go to Texas to pay a visit with Jonathan's mom, right?"

"You know me too well!"

"What's a mother for, sweetheart?" Mary Ann asked smiling and winked at Julia.

Julia left her Mom's room and walked the short distance to Jonathan to give him her daily dose of comfort. As she arrived at Jonathan's world of the North wing, she stopped to look through the visitors' window where they first met. Unlike the boy she saw through the window then, Jonathan was curled up on his bed in a ball, shutting out his surroundings entirely, so he did not see her.

Julia entered the children's ward, signed in, and gave Ms. Thornburg a brief hug. When Jonathan heard the sound of her high heels on the hard floor, he uncurled himself and peered out from under his covers. He immediately hugged her but with such desperation this time that it hurt Julia's back. She instinctively stroked his hair and gave him a gentle kiss on the nape of his neck. He was soaked with perspiration and trembling. They spoke few words. Jonathan, most importantly, just needed to be held. Before Julia left, she explained, as vaguely as possible, that she needed to take a short trip and would not be able to see him tomorrow. She then gave him her cell number and told him to borrow a nurse's phone and call her if he needed anything.

As Julia headed home, she arranged for Belle to spend the night and the following day with a neighbor. After quickly packing for her trip to Texas, she sunk into her comfy, easy chair. Her world, which until recently was unmessy and uncomplicated, suddenly became uncertain and unpredictable. "I leave it to you, God," she said out loud, looking up. "My life, and the lives of the people I most love, hang in the balance. I pray I make the right decisions in completing the most important puzzle of my life, and for that fairytale ending that's so elusive."

CHAPTER 14

Jill

Julia obtained a direct flight from Logan Airport to Dallas/Fort Worth International Airport and was off on her latest adventure the following morning. She was prepared to pay a premium markup for a last-minute air-fare purchase, and that she did. But time was of the essence as she needed to finish the trip before Ben came home.

She arrived in Dallas by 10 a.m. local time, with plenty of time to rent a car and drive approximately 100 miles to Mexia, located between Dallas and Houston. Stopping only for a cup of coffee, she arrived at Jill's house by 1 p.m. In sharp contrast to Sam's former and current dwellings, Jill lived in a run-down trailer park. The smell was that of a backed-up sewer emanating from the garbage and scraps of food that littered the landscape. They provided a scent quite unlike the hydrangea bushes she had the pleasure of smelling in Marlborough. Dogs and mice were ever-present, and several naked toddlers were chasing the dogs unattended.

Jill's trailer was small and looked to be cramped. There were centrally located communal bathrooms and showers, one for men and one for women. The place was scarce of charm or smiling people.

Julia's knock on Jill's rusting and deteriorating door went unanswered. She decided to grab a bite to eat and return later when, hopefully, her knock would produce a different result.

Julia proceeded to a nearby restaurant, the name and address of which popped up on her GPS. Whenever she traveled, Julia was sure to take her trusty GPS from her car and toss it in her travel bag. *What did we do before the invention of the GPS and smartphone mapping apps?* she wondered. She conveniently tried to forget her several misadventures before owning a GPS, getting lost while on vacations that ate away at her time for fun and enjoyment.

As Julia entered Jim's Krispy Fried Chicken, she was greeted by the pungent smells of cooked chicken and freshly homemade desserts blended together. It was a simple, basic place, presenting large white hung boards with black plastic lettering setting forth the day's menu, the pricing appearing in red plastic numbers to each choice's right side. The walls were covered with old signs, including the names of companies no longer in existence and ones that long ago changed their names, including a large "Esso" sign. It had the look and feel of a 1950's diner, but instead of being nostalgic, this restaurant was authentic in a way that time seemed to leave behind.

Julia noticed the restaurant's customers were also without smiles, going about their day as if they could not wait for it to end. Their faces were tanned from overexposure to the sun, apparently not because of fun outdoor activities by choice, but rather the result of the necessity to make a hard-earned living that dictated the need for long hours of tedious outdoor labor.

Mexia was a small town where everyone seemed to know each other. Julia, in her smart, well-fitted white and light blue dress, with matching heels and pocketbook, appeared more ready for a runway shoot than dining at a local watering hole. She was very aware of how out-of-place she appeared to the locals, which made her a bit uncomfortable.

"What brings you to Mexia, hon?" a buxom, middle-aged lady who approached Julia's table to take her order asked in a strong Texan accent.

"I'm from out of town and meeting a friend of a friend. It's my first time here."

"Could have guessed. What I can't guess, honey, is what you want for lunch today. We have a bunch of specials listed on the boards over there," the waitress said, pointing to the wall.

"I'll take the chef salad with balsamic vinegar and olive oil on the side. A glass of iced water would be great, thanks."

"Sure thing, hon."

Julia was seated in a booth, and upon finishing her order, she noticed a young man who sat in the next booth directly facing her. She couldn't help but be aware of his staring at her as he made it painfully obvious. He clearly was a local, and Julia found him ruggedly handsome, in his late twenties, she surmised. He looked as if he could be a cowboy but had no cowboy hat or lasso, at least not that accompanied him at his table. His face was tanned and had more wrinkles than it should for his age, she thought, but for her the wrinkles added to his allure. Julia glanced back at him and flashed him a welcoming smile, although she obviously was the visitor. Her smile caught him off guard as he rose to introduce himself, which, in turn, surprised her.

"Hi, ma'am. Couldn't help but notice ya. You truly are a sight to be seen, especially 'round these parts. Name's Ron. Mind if I join ya?"

His Texas accent was unmistakable, and he sat down at Julia's table even before she could reply. His cool confidence impressed her. He wasted virtually no time getting her attention and making his move to join her.

"Where you from? Somewhere Southern, I imagine."

"I'm originally from Georgia, but I now live in Massachusetts. My name's Julia."

As she extended her hand to shake his, he politely took it and gently kissed it. His boldness in doing so amused and flattered her.

"Pleased to make your acquaintance, ma'am. Can I be of any help to ya in these parts?"

"It's a long, complicated story, but I'm here to meet someone who lives in town I haven't met before."

"Don't need no explainin'. But it is a small town. Lived here my entire life. Know everyone here. If you don't mind my askin', who you here to see?"

"Jill Singler." Julia could tell immediately from his reaction that Ron knew Jill, and she'd hear his opinion of her whether she asked for it or not.

"Oh, Jill works at Bealls. It's a department store directly diagonal to the Walmart Superstore. If ya could believe it, there's only one Walmart anywhere 'round here. It's right down the road a ways."

"Do you know what time she works until?"

"Let's see. Today is Wednesday, so she'll be finished by 5:30."

"Thanks. I went by her home, but when Jill didn't answer her door, I figured she must be at work."

"Yeah, that Jill's a simple girl. Doesn't go out much but for her job. Never been married, never had any kids. As I recall now, she moved here more than a decade ago from Massachusetts. Never been there myself and never been out of Texas. Have everything I need right here, but for romance," he said with a wink.

Ron stopped speaking for a short minute as their food arrived. Julia could tell he was enjoying her company, as she was enjoying his. She was amused by how different he was from the men she had dated up North, who were much more guarded and polished. His roughness and brashness gave him a sensuality that was undeniable to her. Julia smiled, thinking if she were only ten years younger, willing to give up the big city for Mexia, ready to compromise significantly on her long-held dreams and aspirations, and if there were no Ben in her life, then maybe she'd give Ron a chance. Julia let her imagination run wild, imagining what her life would be like if Ron were her significant other and what she'd look like in a cowgirl hat. Ron's voice interrupted those thoughts.

"Jill's nice and all but has a hard life. Barely makes enough to pay for her trailer home. She works six or seven days a week and has some health issues. She needed to declare Chapter 7 bankruptcy to move on and get rid of her most pressing debts. A trustee was appointed and sold what little she had that couldn't be claimed as exempt. Didn't start with much and doesn't have much now."

"Yes, I understand she has had a difficult life. I feel sorry for her."

"I'll tell ya, though, I give her credit. Jill's cheerful enough, smiling despite her troubles. I've often suspected it's a front. Don't believe she's happy but wears that smile on her so as to fool ya. I think she always wanted a husband and a family, but it just didn't happen for her, and likely won't as long as she stays here. This town knows she's a troubled soul, and all the guys steer clear of her. Most everyone here has their own issues and problems and don't need no more. Mexia ain't overrun with rich folk in case you haven't noticed."

Ron finished his words with an endearing smile. As he took a break to eat his food, which by now was starting to get cold, Julia asked him out of curiosity, "Did you order?"

"No, I didn't. Very perceptive of you. Don't need to here, ma'am. They know me, and they know what I eat and drink. I'm a simple kind of guy. She knows what her tip's gonna be too. Not much mystery here in these parts, now is there?"

After they finished their meals, Ron asked Julia if he could buy her a beer at "good 'ole Jim's." At first, she politely declined his offer, but having plenty of time to spare and enjoying Ron's company, she changed her mind.

As they started to drink their beers, Ron turned their conversation back to Jill.

"How do you know her if you don't mind me askin'?"

"I don't, but I know of her. We have a mutual friend back in Massachusetts who gave me her contact information. I want to meet her in person. She has no idea of my visit, so it will be a surprise," Julia replied. She didn't want to provide Ron with any information concerning Jonathan, as he made it clear that Jill led the town's people to believe she didn't have a child. *Who am I to blow Jill's cover?* she thought.

Halfway through their beers, Julia and Ron noticed two women who entered the restaurant, speaking loudly and laughing. Ron pointed out the taller one and informed Julia he dated her years ago and got her pregnant when he was only 18, and she was 17, without being married. She wanted to get an abortion, which he opposed. She proceeded to carry the baby to term, but the boy died at childbirth.

"If he lived, he'd be in his first year of elementary school by now. I often wonder why my son was taken from me before I even had a chance to hold him. But some things just ain't meant to be, I guess."

"I'm so sorry to hear that, Ron. Do you still want to become a dad?"

"Yup. I've matured a lot. Although I thought I was ready for parenthood then, looking back, I was so ill-prepared. But that wouldn't have stopped me. I would have done anything to support my kid. I didn't have the chance, but I know I would have been a good father."

"What kind of work do you do, if you don't mind my asking?"

"My dad and uncle own a ranch not too far from here. I'm a ranch hand working for them. Gets me by. But I do have bigger dreams, though."

"What are your dreams, Ron?"

"Well, I like good clothes. In case you haven't noticed, we wear a different type of clothing down here, and I'd like to take the best of it and open a chain of stores to sell them to the rest of the States and internationally. It makes us unique here in Texas. I envision my chain to be to clothing what Texas Roadhouse is to food. It's nice to dream. As long as I'm dreaming, I'm gonna dream big."

Ron took another large gulp of his beer to finish it off and continued, "Don't know if you're aware there was a girl who used to live in Mexia. Poor as could be but was awfully perrty and had a lot of potential. She couldn't leave here fast enough for her likin' and followed her big dreams to Houston. Knew her before she changed her name to Anna Nicole Smith. In Houston, she changed her life and some body parts," Ron said, smiling broadly at Julia. "Realize that, like her, I stand a better chance of attainin' my goals if I leave this place."

Ron then promptly changed his tone to a more serious one. "Well, ma'am, you still have time to kill before Jill gets home. There's not a whole lot to do in town, but I'd be mighty glad to show you around or take you to the ranch if you'd like. You could milk a cow, feed the pigs, or ride a horse. Be my pleasure."

"Thanks. That's mighty kind of you, dear sir. But I must decline your generous offer."

Julia did not provide him an excuse and did not see a purpose to mention Ben, and her engagement to him. Most importantly, she didn't want to lead Ron on and thought it best to say their goodbyes at the restaurant as soon as they finished their beers. She then mentioned to him her plane out of Dallas left early the next morning and her remaining time in Mexia was quite limited.

Ron waited like a gentleman until Julia finished her beer. He then got up, wiped his mouth with his shirt sleeve, and said to her, "Hope that I wasn't too direct for ya, ma'am. That's the way I've been and will always be, I guess. Not making any apologies, just explainin'."

"Hey, I don't know anything about you. How could I possibly give you my blessing?"

Julia was taken aback by Jill's hostility. She attempted to convince Jill of the benefits of her plan.

"Unfortunately, Jonathan doesn't have much at St. Peter's. He just unexpectedly and tragically lost his only friend there, and he has no one else. He deserves better – a better place to live, healthier meals, and more love and attention than St. Peter's possibly could give him. I can provide those for him, trust me. I love your son, and I will take great care of him. Please believe that."

"Why should I trust you? I'm sorry to hear of his loss, but that doesn't mean he's better off with you."

As she turned to Jill, Julia saw her become emotional and start to cry.

"Giving up my only child was the hardest decision I've ever made. But I was, and still am, in no position to care for him. My mom was a drug addict, and my dad was a dealer. They never had time for me even when they were off the drugs. I wasn't given the skills to be a good mother, as I had no one to model that for me. I wanted what was best for my son, and I determined that being absent from his life, with all my problems, was in his best interest. Nor was Sam able to care for him once Jack died. I approved of him being taken to St. Peter's."

"But since you love your son, don't you want what's best for him now?"

Taking a deep breath and trying to check her emotions, Jill responded, "I can give you an assurance and nothing more. I can assure you here and now, if you do adopt Jonathan, I will not contest your adoption or seek him back. You have my word. That's what you really want anyway, isn't it?"

"Truthfully, no. I prayed about this meeting, and I was hoping you would . . ."

"Well, I can't give you anything more."

"Do you think St. Peter's remains his best option?"

"Why wouldn't it be? Jonathan has everything he needs right there."

"Unfortunately, that's not so. Jonathan feels trapped, and he's not living his life how it is meant to be lived. He's barely surviving. He yearns to

Borrowing a pen from a waitress, Ron wrote something on his napkin and handed it to Julia. "If you change your mind, here's my number."

Julia took the napkin and placed it in her purse.

"It was my utmost pleasure to meet a lady, such as yourself. Enjoy the rest of your stay in Mexia."

Julia wished Ron well and expressed her hope that he follows his dreams and open those clothing stores he described to her. When Julia rose to say her goodbye to Ron and thank him for her beer, he again took her hand, gave it a gentle kiss, and with that gesture, he was gone in a flash.

Driving aimlessly around town and not seeing any reason to stop, Julia decided to head southwest on Route 14 until she came upon Fort Parker State Park. She locked her rental car door and admired the white pelicans romping on the nearby lake. The pelicans flew away when the young children of a group of families having a picnic intentionally tried to scare them. It didn't take long for the hot Texas sun, the flight to Dallas, her drive to Mexia, and the beer with Ron, to take their toll. Julia quickly surrendered to her exhaustion and fell into a deep sleep by the lake.

When Julia woke an hour later, it took her a few seconds to realize where she was and how she had gotten there. Her gaze on the pelicans, which returned after the picnicking families left the park, quickly reminded her. Julia was glad that, without setting her iPhone alarm, she was up with plenty of time to arrive at Jill's home before Jill did.

Julia then took a stroll along the entire perimeter of the lake. Enjoying her surroundings, she imagined her upcoming discussion with Ben. She smiled, picturing him being so thrilled with her plan for Jonathan and the happiness the three of them would share, along with the strong sense of fulfillment of doing something good, positive, and pleasing to God. Although they didn't agree on everything, with Ben having a more liberal bent than her, they relished their shared views and humbly respected their differences. That they could speak about anything and everything together, still have their differences, but always respect each other's opinions without arguing, gave her great comfort.

Julia arrived at the trailer park shortly before Jill. She waited patiently, reviewing in her mind what she planned on saying to Jonathan's mother, someone who, until yesterday, was believed to be deceased. Julia recalled Sam's sad story of Jill's life before she left for Texas, and by the looks of her surroundings, things haven't gotten markedly better for her here than they had been up North. Ron's description of Jill just a little while earlier and how the men of Mexia viewed and avoided her made Julia feel a sudden rush of sympathy for Jill.

Hearing a loud noise that sounded like a cannonball being fired, Julia turned to see a big yellow car emitting smoke and fumes approaching her. It jerked forward with one final deafening sputter as it came to a stop in front of Jill's home. A middle-aged woman with shoulder-length, red, wildly tossed hair that was graying stepped slowly out of the car. She was around 5' 9", skinny, and her complexion was light, with a face that had numerous freckles. Her eyes were a dull, pale gray and bore little expression. The woman was pretty, despite wearing no makeup. She wore a cheap, flowing sundress with printed flowers of blue, violet, and purple and green leaves against a white background and had on no jewelry of any kind. As the woman stepped further away from the car, Julia noticed her tattoos consisting of a small red rose partly covered by snow on her right ankle and a larger tattoo depicting a red heart on her upper right arm with the words "Always in my heart!" directly underneath. Unlike the image of her dress, which looked carefree and loose, the woman gave an appearance that more closely resembled her car, beaten down and barely functional. Julia watched as she walked slowly along the worn grass path leading to Jill's trailer.

"Hi, Ms. Singler?" Julia stopped Jill's short walk to the door of her trailer.

"Do I know you?"

"No, you don't. Excuse me for interrupting."

"If you're from the IRS or any other tax agency, or a bill collector, I don't want to see you."

"No, it's nothing like that."

"Look, I'm sorry. I've had a long day, a hard day, and I'm looking to relax. I wasn't expecting company at this hour, just as I'm getting back home." Jill proceeded toward her door.

"It's about Jonathan." Those three words did more to stop Jill c her tracks than anything Julia physically could have done to halt the for her door.

"What about Jonathan? Who are you?"

"I'm an acquaintance of his. He's a terrific young boy. I'm try make his life better."

"What have you told Jonathan about me?"

"Nothing, absolutely nothing, rest assured. Jonathan, and the h believe you and your husband died in a car crash many years ago."

"There was no husband. I don't even know who his father is. Loc done some things I truly regret, and giving up my son tops my list. I you'll excuse me, I don't need you to cast judgment on me. I just be left alone and go inside my trailer." Jill started again toward he but Julia persisted.

"Look, Jill. I'm in no position to judge you or your actions fro ago. Nor would I ever do that, even if I were qualified. I understa were young and without the means or the ability to care for him. I that. I can't even begin to understand your life, your needs, and wl best for you and Jonathan at the time. From what little I know, I thi made the best decision you could, for what it's worth to you." Jul explained of her meeting with Sam and that she obtained the pres dress through her.

"Well, what do you want from me? What can I possibly do for I'm looking to adopt Jonathan with my husband-to-be. I kn don't need your approval. As I've said, Jonathan and the hospital you're dead. And I can promise you unless you intend to tell them alive and well, and ready to care for your son, then my lips are se you did choose that, I would help you anyway I can."

"Unfortunately, I can't, as is rather obvious from my surrou Take a good look at this place. So, if you don't need my approva again, what do you want from me?"

"I would very much appreciate your blessing. Regardless of wh pened long ago, Jonathan is, and always will be, your son. It would g great peace of mind if you approved of it."

know what it's like to live outside of the hospital. I know I can change that for him, and I'm determined to make things better."

After hearing Julia's emotionally charged plea, Jill responded curtly, "Okay, then, you win. Do what you need to do. But I'm not giving you my blessing. Now go and just leave me alone." And with those words, and a slam of her door, Jill ended their tense conversation.

On her drive to Dallas and her flight back to Boston, Julia couldn't get the image of Jill, who was so consumed with regret and guilt, out of her mind. But Julia's disappointment with Jill's remarks and her hostile attitude continually gave way to a stronger feeling – an extreme sorrow for a mother who abandoned her only child because she couldn't afford to take care of him, and, more importantly, her perceived inability to do so. *How awful it must be for a mother not to be able to provide her child with one of the most universal expressions of love, that of being a parent,* Julia thought. As Julia's plane landed at Logan, her visit with Jill seemed so long ago, and Mexia seemed so far away.

CHAPTER 15

A Most Important Discussion

Another visit with Jonathan convinced Julia she needed to do what was best for him with or without Jill's blessing. With Ben's return tomorrow, she didn't want to think about what she would do without his support. But her Ben was compassionate, understanding, and supportive, and she was confident in his love for her and the strong relationship they built together.

Upon Julia's entering the ward, Ms. Thornburg informed her that Jonathan hardly got out of bed for two days. "The poor dear, he has a heavy heart and grieves in his own way. Who am I to tell him what to do or how best to express his sorrow?" she commented.

Jonathan was so thrilled to see Julia that he leaped out of his bed, jumped up and down, and gave her his waist-high hug and their special greeting.

"My Julia. I've missed you so. When I didn't see you last night, I thought something terrible happened to you, which scared me. Then I remembered you told me you'd be away, and I felt so much better."

"I missed you too. I met with someone last night and did not have the opportunity to come."

"Did you meet with Ben?"

"No, he's not back from his trip yet. But he will be soon."

"Did you meet with your Mother?"

"Nope."

"Then who did you meet?"

"Nobody whom you know." Julia hated to lie, but she figured her statement was, in fact, true.

"Will you see them again?"

"Probably not, but I don't know for sure."

"Did you get what you wanted out of the meeting?"

"No, I didn't. But I know we can't always get what we want on our time, but we might get it in God's time, which can be two very different things."

The next day, Jonathan had a special request for Julia. He asked she take him to the hospital playground. "I remember each time we'd go there, Caren would ask one of the nurses to push her on the large swing. She would laugh and have such a great time. I don't like the swings much, but I thought I'd give it a try today for Caren's sake. Can you help me?"

Obliging Jonathan's request, Julia took his hand as she led him to the playground. She then assisted him onto the large swing and gently gave him a push to his delight.

"Hold on tightly," she told him as she released the swing from her grasp. "You can pump your feet to keep the momentum, but don't go too high."

In less than a minute, Jonathan fell off the swing, his head hitting the ground hard, which resulted in his right cheek being cut and some blood and tears.

"Now I know I hate the swings. Not everyone is made to do everything, and I'm surely not made for that swing," Jonathan remarked.

The cut was only a superficial wound, but Julia felt awful Jonathan got hurt under her watch. As they started walking back into the ward, he muttered, trying to hold back his tears and appear to be mature, "Definitely not the way Caren would have wanted it."

Once inside, Jonathan was laid flat on a cot to be attended to by nurse Susan, who determined he did not need stitches. As the nurse went to apply an antiseptic to the cut, she informed Jonathan that it could sting and burn him. Upon hearing that, Julia put her head over his forehead and held his body with both of her hands and arms to help keep him still. She then assisted in his cleanup and bandaging, and gently kissed his swollen cheek. By the time of her visit later that same day to see how he was doing, the bandaging has been removed and Jonathan's wounds were already starting to heal.

"I have another request," Jonathan called to Julia as she approached him.

"No more swings," she joked.

"No, not that again. Instead of going on a swing for Caren, I want to pray for her in the chapel. I know you told me God could hear me anywhere, but I think the chapel is the best place because I feel closer to God there."

"At least neither of us will get a bruise this time," Julia again said kiddingly to Jonathan. "Let's go."

"Thanks, Julia. By the way, you look amazing today. I know you can't say the same about me with my cuts and scrapes," Jonathan remarked, in his own attempt to be humorous. They both burst out laughing.

"I never saw windows so awesome. Is it mainly for prayers and to go when people die?"

"Yes, chapels, churches, and other places of worship are where people pray. And for funerals, but also weddings, holy communions, and baptisms. All special events."

"So, are you and Ben going to be married here?"

"Well, we're planning on getting married, not here, but in a larger church. We'd be so cramped trying to fit two hundred guests in this tiny chapel."

"Yeah, they'd need to sit on each other's laps, right?" Without waiting for a reply, Jonathan asked her to lead him in prayer.

"I have an idea. How about you say your prayer out loud, and I'll listen? I'm sure telling God how you feel will be good, and I'd love to hear it. Can you pray for us, Jonathan?"

Jonathan dropped to his knees. He held his hands up very high in the air in prayer and thought for several minutes before he began.

"Dear God. I've been thinking about Caren's death for days now. I still don't understand why You would not save her. I feel sad I was not as nice to her as I could have been. There were many times when she would try to talk with me, and I pretended I didn't hear her. I acted like I didn't want her there with me; now that she'd gone, I wish I had the chance to be with her again. The thing is, I never thought she'd be taken from me for good. I'm not sure if I can ask You for a favor – but if I can, here goes. Caren was a good person, so I'm sure she's there in Heaven with You. Can You please tell her how much I miss her and how sorry I am I was not nicer to her? And can You please take care of her for me? I'm still confused, and I know I have no choice but to accept I'll never see her again. That's sad. I hope I don't feel sad forever. Thanks."

As Jonathan looked up at Julia, he asked her, "How was that for a prayer?"

"That, why that, that was an awesome prayer. You told God how you feel, asked Him to care for Caren, and expressed you want to feel better. Jonathan, sometimes expressing how we feel is an important first step to healing. I want you to know that healing doesn't happen in one day or several days. It takes time, however much time you need. One thing always to remember in life is we never know how long anyone has to live, anyone, so we should be understanding and kind toward everyone."

"Do you want to know when you are going to die, Julia?"

"If I knew that specific date and time, I would care less about the trivial things and everyday annoyances and pressures to focus more on the big picture. But I've learned, with the help of my Mom, we should live every day as if it were our last. There is a song I'll play for you someday. It's called *Live Like You Were Dying* by Tim McGraw. If you do that, then you will always have your priorities straight."

After leaving Jonathan at his ward, Julia rushed to pick up Ben at the airport. Unexpected traffic caused by an accident resulted in her being twenty minutes late. Ben was already outside, surrounded by his travel bags waiting for her as she pulled into the terminal's arrival section. Since Ben's phone battery died on the plane, he did not receive her text message she would be late.

As her car approached Ben, Julia rolled down her passenger side window when he was within hearing distance, whistled at him and yelled, "Hey, handsome. Need a ride?"

"Sure do, gorgeous. Boy, did I miss you. I'm so glad to be home. Give me a hug."

Julia quickly jumped out of her car into Ben's waiting arms. His big embrace engulfed her as he passionately kissed her.

"Now, that was good, really good. Just what I needed," Ben said upon releasing her from his strong grip.

After placing Ben's suitcases in the trunk and starting to drive away from the airport, Julia asked, "How did your meetings go? Productive, I trust."

"Long, boring, and tiring, but I do believe we accomplished what we set out to do. It seemed like forever I was away from you. How is Mom doing?"

"She's still weakened after her fall. The doctors had to cancel her next scheduled chemo treatment until she regains some of her strength and stamina."

"Hopefully, that will be soon. I'll stop by to see her during the week. Did you meet with the bakery?"

"No. I didn't."

"I thought you had an appointment with them."

"I did. But I couldn't make it. Something came up. I'll explain a little later."

"Okay," Ben said hesitantly, aware for the first time Julia was acting strangely, and he was concerned about what was bothering her.

As they entered Ben's apartment and settled in, Julia wasted no time addressing Jonathan with him.

"Ben, there is something I need to talk with you about."

"Sure, what's up, babe?" Ben replied in a concerned voice.

"Is now a good time? You look tired."

"Yes, it is; I'm fine. What is it?"

At first, Julia thought about jokingly saying there was another man in her life as she did with Mary Ann but decided against it.

"I recently met this nice kid, Jonathan, who's fifteen years old and is mentally challenged. It was when St. Peter's was repairing their front exit, and I was routed past the North wing of the hospital. I've gotten to know him, and my heart breaks at his plight. His best friend, Caren, who lived with him there, suddenly died, which he witnessed as it was happening. He is devastated, and he hasn't begun to heal yet. Jonathan has no family and has not had any visitors, so I've visited almost daily to give him the support he needs. He's a wonderful boy, and I can't wait for you to meet him."

"They repaired that exit more than two weeks ago, didn't they? I know because I visited with Mom before I left on my trip."

"Yes, that's right."

"So, why are you telling me about this only now?"

"Caren's death changed everything. Jonathan is torn apart because she had a huge crush on him, and he is haunted by guilt that he ignored her advances and played hard to get. It's his first brush with death, and he is ill-prepared to deal with it. I've been trying to help him through it."

"So, what's that got to do with me? With us? I don't understand. You want my permission you can devote some of your time to go to see him, you got it."

Julia noticed Ben's sudden change in his tone, which went from curious to annoyance to anger in a few seconds, and it concerned her. She marched on with her attempt to awaken Ben's empathetic qualities.

"No, it's more than that. Jonathan's not doing well, and I'm genuinely concerned for him."

"So, how can I help?"

Julia was relieved at Ben's latest question. However, his next one caught her off guard again.

"Where is this going?"

There was no choice now, but to be as direct as possible.

"I want him to move in with me for a period so I can more effectively take care of him. If that works well, then I want us to adopt him."

"What?" Ben shouted. "Are you kidding me? You met this retarded kid, know him for a few weeks, and now on the eve of our wedding, you want to adopt him?"

Julia witnessed the rising anger expressed in Ben's face and eyes, which was an unfamiliar face to her on a face she knew all too well.

"Have you thought about me? Whether I'm ready for that, ready to be a father before I'm even a husband? And to some retarded kid whom I've never even met?" Ben looked at her with half bewilderment and half annoyance.

"Please stop using that inappropriate word."

"Why, it's not politically correct? Sorry."

Julia knew Ben was sarcastic rather than apologetic.

Ben continued, as his approach changed to being more rational than re-active, and his voice softened. "Julia, we're about to become husband and wife, two people beginning their new lives together. Frankly, it's not fair of you to ask me to start as three. We need time for us first, and to grow closer in our relationship as newlyweds. Adopting a child now makes no sense for us, whatever the situation with Jonathan. Have you thought through what that would mean for your job?, how much alone time that it would leave for us?, and whether you're even capable of caring for a very needy kid by yourself?"

"I have been praying I wouldn't have to do it alone," Julia replied, as she looked directly and pleadingly into Ben's eyes, her eyes getting misty with emotion as she spoke. After a slight pause, she continued, "I'm think-ing of taking a leave of absence. Maybe it wouldn't need to be long. If things work out, then we could hire help for him, as needed."

"Wow," Ben exclaimed, as he returned to his reactive approach. "I go away for a couple of weeks, and I return to a different woman. What do you expect, I would embrace your rather – I'm searching for the right word – *weird*, plan? First, I'm not happy you've been visiting him without so much as mentioning it to me. Second, before I have the chance to meet him, you concoct a plan for us to adopt him. We've never been parents before, and I don't think we're ready, or at least, I'm ready, for it."

"Ben, listen. I understand what you're saying. I had not thought of adopting Jonathan until Caren's death, which happened suddenly when you were away. It's something I obviously didn't want to discuss with you over the phone, but I needed to do it upon your return, face-to-face. Before Caren's death, my visits with Jonathan were to help brighten his day a little. Now, he needs me much more. I understand the strains this could put on you and us if you agree to it. But think of the good we'd be doing. If you love me, you will trust my instincts that this move is the right one and necessary. I'm not asking you to agree to it now. I just want to let you know what I'm thinking of doing. Of course, you should meet with Jonathan and get to know him first. But we couldn't let too much time go by."

Fully aware he'd annoy Julia and unable to hold back, Ben replied, "Look, I wouldn't prematurely agree to adopt a normal child; why would I agree to do that with a retarded one? I have zero interest in meeting with him. You want to play fairy godmother, hero, and savior, fine, but that's not my plan, and you're being shortsighted and extremely unfair to me. How could you just assume all this would be okay with me? We're so close to our wedding day, *don't blow it!*"

"I don't like your tone or attitude. You're treating me with disrespect, and you have never done that before. I won't stand for it." Despite her words, Julia delivered them not in an angry voice but rather almost as a teacher to her pupil.

"How do you expect me to respect you with what you just sprang on me? You're doing things behind my back and hatching a plan with life-changing consequences for me and our future together. I'm surprised at you."

"I'm sorry if I went about it the wrong way for you. I know this, though. If the tables were turned, I have enough love and respect for you that I would trust your judgment to do what was right. Sure, it's not the way we planned it. It is kind of 'weird,' but my heart tells me I must help Jonathan."

"Whether or not I agree with it, right?"

"I certainly hoped and prayed you would."

After attempting to calm herself down, Julia picked up again and began, "I discovered Jonathan's mother, Jill, is alive. Both the hospital and Jonathan think she died long ago, along with his father, in a car crash. I found out her employer's wife took care of Jonathan because Jill couldn't. She left him here and moved to Texas as an escape from her problems back East."

"So, let me guess, you flew down to Texas to meet with Jonathan's mother, right?"

"Yes, I did."

"And again, without telling me first. Jonathan has a mother. It's her obligation to take care of him, not yours, and certainly not ours."

"That would be a good response if Jill were able to care for him. But she can't. That's why she gave him up in the first place and moved away, leaving her only child behind."

"I'm sorry to hear how messed up his mother is. But because his mother is incapable of taking care of him doesn't mean you should, or we should, period."

Ben paused a minute to give Julia time to come around and see things his way. He looked at her and did not see the woman in front of him he had asked to wed.

"Look, I wish I could be your hero, but I'm afraid that I can't be. It's not what I bargained for when I proposed to you. I want us, I believe in us, you and me and, at least for now, only you and me."

"I believe in us, too. I want us, too. But doing the right thing shouldn't weaken us; it will strengthen us. I'm not asking you to take care of Jonathan. That would be my role. I'm only asking you to tolerate and support my role, nothing more."

"Are you listening to what you're saying? Jonathan is not an ordinary boy. That role you envision for yourself would have to affect me and our relationship, not to mention your career and Mom. They're not mutually exclusive. I just don't see the future as brightly as you do. I just don't see it working out." Ben, rubbing his eyes, continued, "Look, I'm exhausted. I've got to get to bed. Let's call it a night."

"Sure. I understand. And I know all this is coming at you suddenly and out of left field. I apologize for that. I'd like to continue our discussion again tomorrow if that's alright with you?"

Ben shook his head, "yes."

Julia believed she made her best arguments, but they made no headway in convincing Ben. Continuing to press forward tonight, with Ben not receptive to her and tired from his travels, would do little good and might further alienate him. This is a conversation she knew would need to be continued, hopefully with a better result next time.

Julia gave Ben a gentle kiss on his cheek, which was not reciprocated.

She stumbled back into her car in a daze as if she were a prizefighter who had just been struck straight on the head. When she sat down in her car, she collapsed her head in her hands and placed them on the steering wheel, crying hysterically. *How could it have gone so badly? How could I have not known Ben as well as I thought I had? How could he use the word 'retarded' not once, but three times, and even after I pleaded with him to not use that disrespectful word?* Julia was in total despair. She replayed her discussion with Ben over in her mind as she tried to think about how she could have been more persuasive. She quickly decided to focus on her next meeting with Ben instead of the one that just ended so miserably. *I must do a better job to convince him. Thank God I have another chance.* Trying to remain positive, she exclaimed, "After all, tomorrow is another day!"

CHAPTER 16

The Surprise of a Lifetime

Immediately upon waking up the next morning, Julia knew what she needed to do. She headed to St. Peter's and purchased a dozen red roses at the hospital florist. As soon as she entered her Mom's room and gave Mary Ann the flowers, Julia lost her composure and started sobbing.

"Ah, my sweetheart," Mary Ann said, hugging her daughter.

"I picked up Ben from the airport last night," Julia explained through her tears. "I told him about Jonathan and my plan to adopt him. It didn't go well. He essentially said he wasn't ready to be a father to a 'retarded' kid. He was rather annoyed, and for the first time in our relationship, he was disrespectful and insensitive."

"A combination of factors might explain his negative response," Mary Ann replied. "I imagine he was exhausted from his trip and it being the end of his grueling workweek. And I bet he was disappointed you did not tell him about Jonathan sooner than you did. It must have come as a total shock to him, and he was not ready to deal with it. He likely sees Jonathan as an intrusion to the dynamic you would have as a married couple. Maybe after he has time to absorb the news and reflect on it, and after he has met Jonathan, he would be more receptive to your plan."

"The problem is that he already closed the door to that idea. He refuses to meet with Jonathan and wants no part in helping me. He might be in a better frame of mind today than yesterday, particularly after his sleep, but I doubt he will change his mind."

"Maybe. Maybe not. I think you owe Ben another chance to respond to your plan after the initial shock of it has worn off. Sometimes when we feel threatened, we become defensive, and we say things we don't mean and act foolishly. Julia, I don't think you can blame him for his initial reaction. It's what came naturally to him under the circumstances. Today's another day, and maybe, just maybe, he'll react differently. Hopefully, he'll change his mind to meet with Jonathan."

"And if he doesn't?"

"I think we already discussed that. Follow your heart and do what you believe is the right thing to do. Good things happen when we're true to ourselves. They may not be apparent immediately, and you might have to wait patiently for them to materialize, but I believe, with time, they will occur."

Julia buried her head in her hands and cried, "We've come so far. I love him so. I don't want to lose him. But if he loves me, then I think he'll see things the way I do."

"Julia, don't give up on Ben just yet. See how things go and don't lose hope."

After Julia went to the sink in her Mother's hospital room and washed her tears away, she sat down next to her Mother's bed and continued.

"You know, Mom, I've never felt so torn in my life. I love Ben with all my heart and soul, and I have come to love Jonathan in the short time I know him. They are so amazing in very different ways, and the incredible bond I share with each of them is undeniable. What is so clear is how much Jonathan needs me now. So much so I had a dream about Jonathan involving Tommy."

"Tommy?" Mary Ann asked, surprised.

"Yes. It was so real. In the dream, Jonathan visits Tommy and me at our treehouse back when we were kids. As Jonathan's climbing the ladder, he accidentally falls to the ground and gets hurt. Tommy yells to me to go help him. I do, and I manage to bring Jonathan to the top of our treehouse, and when I get there, Tommy just disappeared. I was left caring for Jonathan alone."

"Come here, sweetheart."

Mary Ann stroked Julia's hand the way she used to do when Julia was young. Just her Mom's touch was better than any meditation, or medication she could have taken, to relax.

"I understand what a critical decision this is for you, as it affects the lives of two people who you so love. I feel for you. But I have total faith in your ability to make the best decision, the right decision, and you will do that. And God will help you along the way. I do not doubt that, and neither should you."

Smelling the roses, Mary Ann remarked, "They are so lovely. I don't want you to spend your money on me, but I do so appreciate them."

After thanking her Mom for her support, Julia checked in with Jonathan. The nurses notified her he had an altercation with Jacob resulting in a short fistfight until the nurses blocked Jonathan's intended punches. When Julia asked him what happened, he told her Jacob said Caren was strange and never fit in with the other kids anyway, and that's why God took her away from them. Jacob's statement so angered Jonathan he "had" to lash out at the boy.

"I know I shouldn't have hit him, but I got so upset with Jacob."

"It was your way of protecting Caren. Your intention was good, but you should have acted differently. When someone upsets us, it's often best not to react immediately. That way, we can control our temper before it controls us and our words or actions. After the argument or fight is over, if you overreacted, or should have responded differently, apologizing often helps the other person to be forgiving and put the argument behind him or her."

Julia left St. Peter's that day so unsure of where her life was heading. Knowing the significance of her next meeting with Ben, she could feel her heart pounding and palpitating irregularly during her drive to his apartment. *Our whole future could be determined in the next half hour*, she thought with a sense of dread.

Julia's anxiety heightened when, upon opening his front door, Ben kissed her on the forehead instead of on her lips, and he did not give her his customary bear hug. His face seemed solemn and uninviting. She figured it best for Ben to start the discussion, as the tension and anticipation began to build. Julia remembered Mary Ann's advice, and she wanted to listen and understand how Ben was processing her news now that he had additional time to reflect on it.

"All I could do after you left last night was to dwell on our discussion. Despite being exhausted, I couldn't sleep a wink."

Ben paused, then he continued calmly, "I know you have a big heart and are well-intentioned. I respect you're trying to improve Jonathan's life, and feel an obligation to do that, and want to heed God's calling. Look . . ."

"Oh God, please don't start a sentence with 'look.' It's always bad news."

Ben continued, "It's not what I want and what I envisioned for us. Things come up in relationships, and either you find common ground, or don't. I guess what I'm trying to say, in an inartful way, is I can't be a part of your plan or a part of your life that includes Jonathan. I ask you to reconsider, to think of our future, and to do what is best for us."

Julia took a nervous sigh before she could reply. She was grateful for Ben's tone and attitude but disappointed with his conclusion. She spoke with a quiver in her voice.

"I have given it a tremendous amount of thought, Ben. Obviously, this is not a decision I possibly could take lightly. I've searched my heart and my soul. I've prayed that God gives me the wisdom to make the right choice for all of us. I've also spoken with Mom about it. I've seen what Caren's death has done to Jonathan and it's alarming. He's barely surviving."

Julia paused and then looked directly into Ben's eyes.

"I don't know if I could live with myself if I shut him out, like everyone else. I think God led me down the narrow corridor to him for a reason. Certainly, as we are finalizing our wedding plans, the timing couldn't be worse for us. But God put me in Jonathan's life just shortly before he was to experience his greatest pain. In one way, I know it's the most selfish thing I could do to focus on him at this time, just before our wedding. But in another way, it's totally unselfish for me to follow what I believe is God's plan regardless of its effect on me and us. I'm truly sorry for that."

Ben raised his hand. "No need to apologize."

"I have no doubt you, with all of your good looks, intelligence, and success, have all the tools at your disposal to lead a wonderful and fulfilling life, with or without me. Contrast that with Jonathan. He is frightened, confused, unsure of his future, and his role in life. I see the change in him the instant he sees me enter his room. He goes from darkness to sunshine. It's like turning on, and turning off, a switch. That's why I visited with his mother. I had to see for myself if she could be that light for him. Believe me, I was hoping I would reunite them. I prayed that in her, I found a person who wanted to be a part of his life, and she was ready and able to do that. But, sadly, that is not what I found in Texas. I can't imagine losing you, Ben. But I also can't imagine my life not doing what I believe is right."

"Well," Ben said very emotionally. "It sounds like you've made your decision. I do hope for your sake, and his, it goes well. I do love you, and I always will. But there is no other choice, then, but to call off the wedding."

Julia paused as she looked lovingly into Ben's eyes. Then, choking on her words, she continued.

"I didn't see this coming, Ben. It's numbing and surreal to me. I do love you so much, as well, more than you know, and I'm so grateful we shared so many incredible experiences. I will always treasure them and your decision to choose me to be your wife. I wish I would have been, and I hope your life is a fabulous journey." Julia then removed her engagement ring and returned it to Ben.

After tearful goodbyes and hugs, Julia headed back to her car. The only words she could hear in her mind on her drive home were "call off the wedding." The "Save the Date" email blast was circulated months ago. She wondered how she would let all the intended guests now know there was no longer a need for them to save that date.

Upon reaching her apartment, she raced to her bathroom and promptly threw up in the toilet, hovering over it for a long time as she sat on the cold floor, too weak to move. The sense of nausea was overwhelming, and she felt drained and depleted. Somehow, she commanded enough strength to hobble to, and collapse on, her oversized chair, where she found herself the next morning. She needed time to adjust to her new reality and the quick shattering of her dreams. She reflected on how fragile relationships can be, even the strongest ones.

The next couple of weeks were troubling and unfamiliar to Julia. She missed Ben terribly. She felt like a spinning top that was beginning to wobble. She knew the direction she was going, but it nevertheless caught her off balance and "out of whack."

Julia had much to do to prepare for Jonathan's arrival, including her giving notice at work and finishing up her outstanding projects for *The Globe*, setting up Jonathan's bedroom, and making arrangements with St. Peter's. But keeping busy only temporarily masked her extreme pain and coming to terms with her crushing loss. The sight of Ben's pictures and her many thoughts of him throughout the day reminded her of what could have been, and what she had given up. While she was able to take down his pictures in her apartment and her office at work, removing his image from her mind was much more difficult. She felt a sense of despair she hadn't experienced since her father's abandonment decades ago, with the difference being she intentionally caused her current circumstances rather than being the recipient of someone else's hurtful action.

Several days after her last meeting with Ben, Julia informed Ms. Thornburg of her plan for Jonathan, upon Ms. Thornburg's promise of utmost secrecy. Ms. Thornburg was thrilled for them. She then assisted Julia in dealing with the "Hospital Oversight Management Committee," culminating in the Committee's interviewing Julia. Approximately a week later, the Committee informed Julia of their decision that she was authorized to remove Jonathan from St. Peter's for one month. Afterward, she and Jonathan would be obligated to attend further meetings with the Committee. If all went well following those meetings, she would be permitted to adopt Jonathan. In short, her plan was cleared for takeoff, and she was thrilled about the new trajectory for Jonathan's life. Now, for the first time, she could share her plan with everyone else, and most importantly, with Jonathan.

As Julia drove to St. Peter's to pick up Jonathan, thoughts of her recent confrontation with Ben began to fade as she focused on lightening the load and brightening the life of a young man she was privileged to call her friend, and hopefully soon, her son. She would return to her heartache later. Now, as she turned into the hospital parking lot, she sensed something beautiful was about to happen.

She couldn't wait to see Jonathan's face upon informing him of her surprise and seemingly flew by the doctors, nurses, hospital staff, and visitors to get to him.

Julia entered the children's ward and gave Ms. Thornburg a thumbs-up gesture and a hug. They then approached Jonathan, lying on his bed, face down, with the blankets completely covering him.

"Jonathan," Ms. Thornburg called in a high, joyous voice, rising as she reached the "than." "You have a beautiful visitor here to see you."

And with that cue, Jonathan slowly peered over the blanket with the two upper halves of his eyes focused on Julia. Upon seeing her, he ripped off the covers and greeted her with their special greeting.

"Hey, buddy. Today is an amazing day," she called to him in a teasing tone.

"Is it your birthday?"

"No," she replied coyly.

"Is it your Mom's birthday?"

"No," Julia repeated in the same tone.

"Is it my birthday?"

She shook her head, "no."

"Well, I know it's not Jesus's birthday – there's no snow yet, and it's not cold enough."

"Let's take a walk outside, and I'll tell you."

Julia helped Jonathan into his light jacket and, holding his hand, led him to the small garden beside the North wing of the hospital.

"What is it? What are you going to tell me? What's special about this day?"

"Well," Julia began slowly. "I want you to know, I see you. I see the young man who you are – your courage, your spirit, your goodness. God brought me to you for a reason, and now I know what that reason is."

"I have to admit; I don't understand what you're saying. Did God tell you what to do?"

"He certainly did, and I know you'll really love it," Julia replied, clearly enjoying the anticipation building in Jonathan. She moved to sit on the low-lying stone wall separating the outside patio from the hospital lawn.

"Are you buying ice cream for me?"

"Absolutely not."

"Are you bringing me more chocolate cake?"

"Nope, that's not it."

"Are we going to visit your Mom?"

"No, not just yet, anyway."

"Are you taking me to the chapel?"

"No, no, no."

"I think I'm out of guesses. What is it, Julia? What? Please tell me!"

"God made me realize what a blessing it would be for you to come live with me for a while."

Julia's surprise so moved Jonathan he could not verbally respond. Rather, he rushed over to give her a huge hug, only for the force of his forward momentum to spiral them both onto the freshly cut, dark green grass surrounding the garden. With the mixed smell of the freshly cut grass and the nearby flowers filling their nostrils, and the feel of the afternoon sun on their faces, they both laughed from their unexpected fall and the overwhelming joy they shared.

"You know," Jonathan started, "each time we went to the chapel, I prayed something good would happen for us. I wasn't sure what that could be or even if God heard me. Now, I know He has. And He's given me a miracle."

Jonathan could barely finish his words as tears of joy started to gush, first by him, and then by Julia as well.

"This is the most special thing to ever happen to me, other than, that is, the first time I saw you at the visitors' window."

As Julia embraced Jonathan, she felt the heaving of his chest as his tears continued to flow. She gently rocked him in her arms and held him tightly. Without a further word being spoken, Julia gave Jonathan comfort his life was about to change profoundly for the better. Rocking on the sweet-smelling grass with Jonathan in her arms and witnessing his reaction to her surprising news, Julia felt confident she made the right decision, just as her Mother told her she would.

CHAPTER 17

Meeting Grandma

"**Y**ou know, one of your many guesses as to what my surprise for you was will now come true," Julia told Jonathan as she walked with him, holding his hand, back into the hospital. "I'm going to take you to visit an amazing lady."

"I don't need any guesses with that one – yeah, your Mom!" Upon saying the word "Mom," Jonathan excitedly clapped his hands. "I can't wait to meet her. My wait finally is over."

"Ever since I can remember, she has been my best friend."

"What happened to your father, Julia?"

"He left my family when I was young. I was sorry that my Mom had to raise me on her own."

"Why did your father leave you and your Mom? Didn't he know how special you both are?"

"That's an interesting question. My dad suddenly disappeared one day, and I never got the chance to ask him why and say goodbye. He didn't inform my Mom of his plan to desert his family either, so she was as devastated as I was. And we never heard from him again. I learned very quickly, though, how to live my life without him. Sure, there was, and remains, great hurt and a big void in our lives. But time is a great healer, and it helped me deal with unexpected loss and become independent. After a while, you try to bury the pain and move on."

Julia added, "It reminds me of the song *Piece By Piece* by Kelly

Clarkson, about her father abandoning her family when she was a little girl. I have to admit that song is so personal, I tear up each time I hear it. But the important thing is that God gave both my Mom and me a wonderful life despite my dad leaving us. And I learned invaluable lessons from him, like how to forgive someone who hurts you, especially when that person is your father."

"Well, at least you know who your father was. I don't know anything about mine. Nothing. Other than he died with my mom in a car crash. I must not have been in that car 'cause I'm still here."

"So, Jonathan, we both have another thing in common. We both grew up without a dad."

"Yeah, but at least you have a mother who loves you. I don't remember mine. I often wonder what she looked like and what she thought of me."

"I'm sure she loved you very much."

"I hope so, but in case you haven't noticed yet, I'm not like the other kids. I have big problems. My mind doesn't work right. And if it weren't for you, nobody would care about me."

"Well, I'm glad you are who you are. And as long as you're living with me, I won't have any of this negative talk – only positive. Agreed?"

"Yup. Did you and your Mom ever have a fight or an argument?"

"Hum, not that I can recall. To be able to say that at thirty-five years old says something about my Mom."

"And you, too," added Jonathan.

As Julia reached her Mother's hospital room, she knocked on the door to announce their presence.

"Knock, knock."

"Come in." Mary Ann greeted them with a twinkle in her eyes and a welcoming smile. "You must be Jonathan. I knew I would meet you some-day, and I'm so glad that day is today. I've heard so much about you."

Then Mary Ann turned to look directly at Jonathan's eyes and gave Jonathan the most amazing wink he had ever seen. It touched him so deeply, and from a person whom he met only seconds ago. He experienced an instant connection with her.

"Wow, you are beautiful," Jonathan exclaimed as he ran over to give

Mary Ann a Jonathan hug, and she held him for several seconds lovingly in her arms.

"Looks can be deceiving, Jonathan. I'll let you in on a little secret. I lost my hair, and this is a wig."

"Where did your hair go?"

Mary Ann and Julia chuckled in unison.

"My cancer has stolen it from me. I must get treatments, and one of the side effects is you often lose your hair and sometimes throw up. But you do what you need to do."

"If you feel like you're going to throw up, can you give me some warning so I can run the other way?"

"Promise."

"Is it painful, your cancer?"

"It can be, at times. But at those times, I think of great things to keep my mind off my pain."

"What great things do you think about?"

"Oh, about being at some wonderful tropical paradise on vacation, about the beauty of God's creation, and, of course, most importantly, about my incredible daughter. And when I need to have my chemo treatments, I designate each of them for a loved one, and imagine that I am taking the pain for them. That helps me get through it, as naturally I would do anything for someone I love."

"Did you want more children?" Jonathan asked, without thinking about Tommy first. As soon as the question left his lips, he was sorry he asked it. It was not his intention of raising something that could be painful to discuss.

"My husband and I didn't set a number. I knew I always wanted to be a mom. I was very blessed by the time my husband left, I had Julia. How much more fortunate could I be?"

Jonathan was glad that Mary Ann answered his question in a way that did not need to address Tommy.

"Did you miss your husband after he left?"

"Well, honestly, yes and no. At first, I did very much. But I quickly learned how to join the workforce, handle the bills, and take care of my daughter the best I could on my own. I can certainly say that if Richard had not left, I would be quite a different person today. From hardship, good things can grow."

"Oh, I knew that already!" Jonathan turned to Julia and smiled at her, clearly enjoying they shared a great surprise they soon would be revealing to her Mother.

Jonathan continued by asking what remained his most pressing question.

"Are you afraid of dying?"

"Absolutely, not! It's a part of life. And I can tell you I know when I will die. That will be whenever God is ready for me. I love my life and the beauty God has put in it, but I know Heaven is much better still, and I'm ready to go there when it's my time."

Mary Ann then took a minute to rest.

"I'm fortunate I've lived a full life. I feel for those who don't, like your friend Caren. Julia told me about her. I am sorry for your loss. We're seldom ready to lose those we love. And we shouldn't blame ourselves when that happens. Sometimes a person who lost a loved one feels miserable they didn't tell that person they loved them one last time or didn't get a final chance to hold them, or maybe their last words were an argument. But you know what? None of that matters in the end. What is important is your love for each other, not what happened immediately before they died. God wouldn't want anyone to feel guilty about those things, only blessed for having that person in your life. I am certain, Jonathan, Caren knows exactly how you feel about her."

"I certainly hope so."

"I know so. You can count on it," Mary Ann assured him.

"Did you hear the exciting news?" Jonathan asked her.

"No, not yet. But I think I know what it is."

Julia shook her head, "yes." "I told Jonathan just before coming to meet you."

"I don't know what's more exciting, going to live with Julia or meeting you for the first time. It's been the greatest day of my life."

"What a sweet thing to say."

"I told you what a charmer Jonathan is, right, Mom?"

"Jonathan, you're an incredible person. Never forget that," Mary Ann said with another wink meant only for him.

"If Julia's going to be my mom, can I call you Grandma?"

"Well, I've never been a grandmother before, but I would be very honored if you call me 'grandma.' You know, I've had many titles in my life. 'Grandma' is a new one. It does make me feel a bit old, but if not now, when?"

"You're the youngest looking, and most beautiful, grandma I know," added Julia.

"Thanks, sweetheart. You know, Jonathan, I have wanted to be a grandmother for a long time now. And, while under my current circumstances, I will not be able to meet all my future grandchildren while on Earth, I know this with certainty – they each truly will be remarkable and so special, and they will make me so very proud of them. I often close my eyes and try to picture their smiling faces and the sound of their laughter."

"I can't wait to live with Julia. I'm so excited. Did I say thank you yet? If not, thanks so much, Julia. I can never repay you."

"Some things never need to be repaid. I'd like for you to think of things you've always wanted to do or see. We'll add them to our own 'to do' list."

"I know of one thing already. Want to know what it is?"

"Tell us," Mary Ann chimed in.

"Go to a parade. I once saw one on TV, and it looked like so much fun. I'd love to see one in real life someday. Have you ever been to one, Grandma?"

Mary Ann smiled lovingly at Jonathan as he uttered his last word to her.

"Many in my lifetime. But, then again, I have lived a few more years than you have. I remember when I was a little girl, around seven, I believe, my parents took me to New York City to see the Macy's Thanksgiving Day Parade. For a couple of minutes, I somehow got separated from them, and, with the huge crowd, I'd thought I lost them and started to cry. But my mom soon found me, and she held my hand until the parade started. Then my dad put me on his broad shoulders. I had the best view from up there and felt so privileged and tall. The floats were so large, creative, and incredible to a little girl. And, of course, my favorite one was the Santa float at the end of the parade. Some things you just never forget."

After a nurse came into the room and introduced herself to Jonathan, she checked the monitors alongside the hospital bed and the bags of fluid attached to Mary Ann by long tubes.

With the nurse still present, Jonathan asked if they hurt her.

"Only when I try to run my laps around this hospital floor, I forget I have these tubes in my arm, and I drag all this stuff with me up and down the hall, and the people around me try to avoid me in fright," she laughed.

Mary Ann was glad to see Julia looking so radiant and joyful. It was the first time since she parted ways with Ben that Julia looked happy. Mary Ann took comfort in knowing she now would have Jonathan to occupy her time and attention, so the loss she just suffered from not becoming Ms. Anderson could be drowned out, at least in part, by her new role as Jonathan's mom.

"We must be going. Jonathan and I still have much to do today."

Julia rose and gave her Mom a goodbye kiss. Jonathan followed her lead and awkwardly kissed his Grandmother goodbye, waving as he left and, looking back, he called to her, "Bye, Grandma. See you soon."

CHAPTER 18

Great Great-Grandparents

As Julia was rushing to her car from the hospital and holding Jonathan's hand, she purposely avoided passing Ms. Thornburg and the children because her focus was on moving Jonathan to her apartment.

As they were just about to exit the hospital, Jonathan suddenly stopped short and looked pleadingly at Julia.

"What is it, Jonathan, what's the matter?"

"Can we go back to see Grandma?"

"Now?" Julia asked.

"Yes, now."

"Well, we just left Grandma. Did you forget something in her room?" Julia asked, trying to think of what that possibly could be.

"No, not at all. But I desperately want to ask Grandma something else, and I just thought, now would be a good time."

Julia looked again at Jonathan's big, beautiful, blue, and still pleading eyes, and could not refuse his request to see his Grandmother, despite the rush of the day, and that they just left her. With not even taking the time to ask Jonathan what his "pressing" question was going to be, and trusting if it were important to him, then it would be important to herself as well, she simply said, "Sure, my Jonathan. Let's go." They then instantly retraced the steps they just had taken a few seconds ago.

As they reentered the door they just left, Mary Ann looked surprised to see them.

"Back so soon?" she asked. "Jonathan, when you said, 'see you soon' when you left me, I didn't think it would be this soon."

"I know," replied Jonathan. "But Grandma, I forget to ask you something."

"Okay, shoot," she replied.

Julia and Jonathan pulled up two chairs next to each other to take their place and sit at Mary Ann's side.

"Grandma," Jonathan started. "Remember when you just told me about the parade your parents took you to when you were a little girl?"

"Sure, do," Mary Ann replied sweetly, waiting to hear what Jonathan returned to ask her.

"Well, Grandma, what were they like?"

"You mean my parents? What an excellent question, Jonathan. Why I'd love to tell you more about them." Jonathan could see how excited his Grandmother was to share the story of her parents. He wished he brought some popcorn to munch on as Julia and Jonathan made themselves comfortable in their chairs.

"Grandma," Jonathan stopped Mary Ann before she had a chance to start her story.

"What, sweetheart?" she replied to Jonathan.

I've heard the word "sweet" before and the word "heart" before, Jonathan thought, *but I've never heard them put together like that.* Then he remembered his Grandma called Julia "sweetheart," and, realizing that, he knew whatever it meant, it had to be something very good. Jonathan was thankful that being in Julia's life exposed him to new words he never heard before, even though he had yet to understand their meanings.

"Since the people you are going to tell me about are your parents, and you're my Grandma, wouldn't I be related to them in some way as well?"

"Why, yes, that makes them your great-grandparents."

"Wow, I'm getting so many new relatives all in the same day!" Jonathan remarked. "Thanks for letting me know that. You can begin your story now."

"Well, Jonathan. My parents, and your great-grandparents, were the most remarkable people who I ever have known. My mother's name is

'Marietta,' but we called her 'Marie,' and my father's name is 'Michael,' but we called him 'Mickey.'"

"So, I guess they didn't mind people calling them by their short names. Please go on."

"Mickey and Marie grew up extremely poor. Their families both came from Southern Italy. My mom's mom, who is my grandmother and is your great-great-grandmother, was born in a small town called Benevento, which is Northeast of Naples."

"Have you ever been there?" Jonathan wanted to know.

"Yes, only once. But that time I was in Benevento was so incredible, and though I had never been there before, I felt right at home. It was a quaint, lovely town and the local people were so warm and friendly. Everyone I met there went out of their way to help a foreigner, as I was. It's hard to describe, Jonathan, but I was so connected to my surroundings and the people who lived there. I noticed walking through the beautiful town where my grandmother grew up that faith, family, and food so obviously were important to the people who lived there."

"I don't understand," Jonathan interjected. "I get how you noticed the food. But how can you notice faith and family?"

"An excellent question. Let me clarify. You can't actually see faith, but you can feel it, in your heart, your soul, and how you choose to live your life. Faith has always been such an important part of my family's history."

"That must be the reason why you loved the town so, but I still don't understand how you could have noticed faith there."

"I noticed it by the magnificent churches, the ever-present sign of the cross, the topics of conversation, and how often the people pray there. But most importantly, I noticed faith in Benevento by how the people who lived there held their heads up high, looked like they had not a care in the world, and were so at peace with themselves. People of faith, Jonathan, are moved by God's blessings, and as Jesus walked on water, they often feel like they're walking on air because they are touched by God's love for them, and that makes them so joyful and fulfilled."

Mary Ann paused to catch her breath and drink a glass of iced water that was on her hospital tray.

"And regarding your question about how I noticed family there, I observed it in the way older people were treated as being so wise, valued, and respected. I also saw how an extended family (which means people related to each other live together under the same roof) was viewed there as such a positive thing. It was welcomed, as opposed to just having to do it out of necessity, but not wanting it to be that way."

"Wow, Grandma, you sure do notice things. Thanks for explaining it to me."

"Any time, sweetheart."

After adjusting the pillow behind her for support, Mary Ann continued, "When my mom was a young girl, her father left her family."

"So, she too, grew up without a father, just like Julia and me. I don't understand how a father, who is supposed to love his kids, could just leave them."

"Nor can I, Jonathan," Mary Ann said, shaking her head in disapproval.

"Her father's absence made my mom realize she needed to drop out of school to help support her family financially. Her mother had little education and was desperately poor. The only job my mom could find required that she leave her family. Though only a girl herself, she moved from New York to Pennsylvania and took a job as a nanny to watch the children, and clean the house, of a wealthy couple. She didn't earn much, but anything was better than nothing. Whatever money she did make, she sent to her mom to help pay the bills. It was difficult for her, and she missed her family terribly. But you know, Jonathan, you do what you need to do, and you make the best of it. Despite her pain of separation from her family, she was thankful she could make a living to help them. She saw that as her role in life once her father left – she had a plan, found a way, and made it work. Not bad for a young girl with no money and little education, but a big heart and great determination."

"Your mom sounds like a really strong lady," Jonathan remarked.

"That she was, Jonathan, that she was, and thankfully so for her family's sake."

"Not only did Marie miss her family, but she also had the pain of leaving behind a man she madly was in love with, her Mickey, who, as I mentioned, was my dad."

"I'm happy that you had a dad who didn't leave you."

Upon hearing Jonathan's comment, Mary Ann smiled. "And he was the best father." She briefly reflected on wonderful experiences they shared together, and the "dates" they had when she was a young girl, enjoying their time together at the ice cream parlor or a double feature movie.

"Now, when Marie returned to New York after finishing her job in Pennsylvania, her and Mickey's relationship blossomed, and they finally got married to each other. They both wanted to have children so much as an expression of their great love for each other. The problem was, they found it very difficult to have a child, and my mom lost several children before they were born, and one who died when she was just days old. You can imagine the pain and sorrow they experienced. Yet, they never gave up hope and were faithful that their dream of becoming parents would come true one day. When I was born, it finally did, and I was their lone surviving child."

Mary Ann smiled again at Jonathan and then continued.

"I'm sure if you asked them, they would have loved to have four or more children as they both came from large families and had many brothers and sisters. That probably was their expectation too. Did that upset them or make them sad? Absolutely not. Rather, they were so thrilled the miracle of parenthood finally came their way, and they were rewarded for their continuous efforts to make it happen. That's such an important thing in life, you know, Jonathan. Celebrate what you do have, and don't despair or be saddened by what you don't have. Sure, you shouldn't give up hope of getting what you want and following your dreams. But at the same time, realize that if it's meant to be, it will, and if it's not meant to be, it won't."

"Say, for example, I was never born, and my parents' dream of parenthood had not happened for them. That certainly wasn't in their plan and was not the future they envisioned for themselves. But this, I know. Even if they ultimately were to have been childless, they still would have been joyous. They would have seen all the other blessings God gave them, even if that did not include parenthood."

"What other blessings did they have, Grandma?"

"My dad was an electrician, and his hard work helped to build skyscrapers in Manhattan. He had steady work, earned good pay, and, while not wealthy in money, earned enough of it to live comfortably. Also, as I've said, they both had wonderful mothers and many brothers and sisters, with whom they had great relationships, so they experienced the beauty of a strong and loving family, even if I wasn't in it. And, most importantly, they had each other and their shared solid faith. You know, Jonathan, one of my most treasured possessions is a statue of the Sacred Heart. It has little, or no, monetary value, but I wouldn't sell it for all the money on Earth. It was given to my mom as a gift by her church for her hard work cleaning it for many years. Even though she desperately was poor, she did that for no pay, but for her love of God. To me, that statue represents my mom's faith, which carried her through the best of times and the worst of times. And along with the joys and many blessings they both had, there were also difficult times."

Just then, a nurse walked into the room to administer medication. Upon seeing Jonathan's body leaning toward Mary Ann and his eyes being focused on her, the nurse turned to Jonathan and cheerfully asked him, "Having a good conversation?"

Jonathan replied, "The best. My Grandma is telling me about my great-grandparents. I find it very interesting, and I'm learning new things about life."

The nurse then asked Jonathan, "Hadn't you heard it before?"

"Oh, no. She just became my Grandma today, and this is my very first time meeting her."

The nurse, quite puzzled by Jonathan's response, simply said, "Well, have a good day and enjoy the rest of your conversation," as she exited the room.

"What difficult times did they have, Grandma?"

"Don't get me wrong; my parents had wonderful lives. But everyone has their good times and their bad times. As I mentioned, Marie grew up without a father. Luckily, her mother, Marie Antonio Mariano, gave such love and devotion to her children that the absence of a father did not bring down my mom, and her love of life and optimism never were diminished. Mickey and Marie had serious health issues, particularly as they got older.

My parents both got diabetes, had high blood pressure, and my dad developed painful bone cancer. But they didn't complain, and they suffered in silence. Ultimately, my mom lost both of her legs."

"Did she find them?" Jonathan asked.

Both Mary Ann and Julia smiled at the innocence of Jonathan's question. "No, Jonathan. Her diabetes got so bad she needed to have both of her legs removed by a surgeon, which is called a double amputation."

"How did she walk then?"

"She couldn't ever again. She was confined to her bed and a wheelchair for the rest of her life. She was in bed so much she developed terrible bedsores, which caused her excruciating pain. But you know what? She was as happy as could be. And if you asked her how she was feeling, even at the very end of her life, she would say 'great, no, greater than great.' Even though she had no legs, she still had her arms and hands, which she used to knit wonderful blankets, sweaters, and scarves to keep her family warm. So, you see, Jonathan, you use what you have, and you can remain happy even under the most difficult of circumstances."

Julia added, "they lived close to us, so I was able to see them often. They were like a second set of parents to me."

Mary Ann continued, "Indeed, we were blessed that they were such an important part of our lives. I find it so remarkable that every single night of their married lives when they went to bed, Marie and Mickey would kiss each other, tell the other they loved them, and hold hands 'till they fell asleep. Mind you, that was even on those nights when my parents might have had an argument or fight, which was rare. I'm not saying my parents were perfect. They, like any couple, had their differences. But that they could so freely put aside those differences each night and hold each other's hands no matter what shows why their relationship was so strong. Regardless of how upset Marie and Mickey might have been with the other before they went to sleep, when they did, it was as each other's best friend. When I look back on my life, I have never known two people who lived their lives with such joy, love, and gusto as my parents had. They clearly modeled what a great relationship looked, and felt, like."

"Wow, Grandma. I know I'm going to love them so much when I get the chance to meet them."

"I'm afraid to inform you, Jonathan, they both have passed on."

"Oh, I know that. Julia already told me. But I mean when I meet them in Heaven."

"Oh, I see, my dear. Absolutely!"

Mary Ann was so enjoying her time with Jonathan. She appreciated that he was listening intently to her story and trying to understand the life lessons she was sharing with him. She quickly witnessed his wonderful spirit Julia told her about, and she relished the opportunity to get to know him better.

Julia then shared one of her special remembrances. "The last time our family was with your great-grandma we all joined her around her bed, and she was in such a great spirit, despite her pain and suffering. So much so that we all started to sing Christmas songs together in September! Why we did, I'm not sure. But I know that your great-grandma's positive energy, happiness, and love of life helped make that our final time spent with her. It was a perfect send-off, as I believe that it was meant to be."

"Shortly after my mother died, I had this beautiful dream, Jonathan, I'd like to share with you now. It was years ago, but I remember it clearly, like it was yesterday. I hardly ever dream, at least not that I can remember, but this is the one dream I have never forgotten."

"I'd love to hear it, Grandma."

"At the time of my dream, my mom had passed, but my father was still alive. He moved out of their house, and it was empty, waiting to be sold. I go there for memory's sake and see that their front door is wide open. I don't intend to go inside. But since the door is open, I do go into the house."

"I notice on the kitchen table is a plate overflowing with Italian pastries, one of which is partially eaten, and I smile thinking of my mom and her love of food. I then walk down the narrow hallway to the bedroom, the same room where my parents held the other's hand each night at bedtime, where we sang Christmas songs unknowingly as a final goodbye to my mom, and where she passed away. The room is freshly painted and is very clean and bright. The paint is so white, and the sun is shining so brightly through the windows around the top of the room, that my eyes hurt. Rays of sunlight are coming into the room in all directions. At first, I feel a little strange because it is the first time I have been in that room since my mom was gone. But its warmth overwhelms me, and I feel very comforted."

"Suddenly, out of nowhere, I hear a voice coming from the living room, where I just passed to get to the bedroom, yet I know I am the only person in the house. I could be frightened, but I'm not. I follow the voice into the living room."

"When I enter that room, I cannot believe my eyes. There, on her favorite chair, is my mom, rocking away and knitting, as she always did, singing to Italian music playing on her record player. I am shocked because she has both of her legs, which, as I told you, were amputated before she passed away. She looks my way and gives me a wonderful smile. She then says, 'Hi, sweetheart.' At that moment, I feel so loved and totally at peace."

"Just then, my mom gets up from her chair, and the knitting she had on her lap disappears into thin air. She walks on her legs and gives me a long, tender hug and kiss, tells me she loves me, and, as if to apologize, says, 'I have to leave now.' While still in our embrace, she states in a very gentle, soothing, and reassuring voice that was almost a whisper, 'I want you to know I am doing fine and I love you so very much.' Pulling herself back slightly so that I can see her face, she radiates, as she did throughout her life, and gives me an incredible smile. I tell her I love her too. While I do not want her to go, I know there is nothing I can do to stop it from happening, and I see her walk out the front door and disappear."

"I then try to close the door, but I can't. I keep trying, and finally, it comes off its hinges. I guess the neighbors witnessed my struggles because, one by one, they ask me if I am alright, and they offer to help. I decline their offer of assistance, and I thank them. Then, I woke up."

"That sounds like more than a dream, Grandma. What do you think it means?"

"I think my mom was trying to comfort me and let me know she's in Heaven, represented by the brilliantly bright white light, and her walking into it at the end of my dream. And she's doing great, and everything is fine. In Heaven, there are no disabilities; that's why my mom had both of her legs. And in Heaven, you have things you enjoy, shown by the desserts, the Italian music, and my mom's knitting. Also, the fact I couldn't close the door at the end of my dream, I believe, means we cannot close the door on our past, the door to a deceased loved one is always open, and then, ultimately, the open door will lead us to Heaven when it is our time to rejoin them."

"What an amazing dream, Grandma."

"My parents were my best friends; we were so close. They were each an original, and they broke the mold when they were born."

Mary Ann turned to Jonathan and Julia and said, "I know you two have a lot to do. Jonathan, your questions brought me down memory lane, and I so enjoyed describing my wonderful parents to you."

"I'm glad I got to hear about them from you. They were so great. I guess that makes them my great great-grandparents."

"I always love to hear those stories, Mom. I feel their blessings in my life each day," Julia said as she reached for Jonathan's hand.

CHAPTER 19

Meeting God and Representing Ourselves Well

"**B**ut Grandma, I have another question I should ask you now. It is something I think of from time to time," Jonathan said to Mary Ann.

"What is that, sweetheart? You know, Jonathan, I just love it you're thinking of so many questions, and you take the time to ask them."

"Grandma, if you're not afraid of death, then I imagine you're not afraid of meeting with God either, right?"

"Absolutely, right. My passing on will bring me home to Him."

"What do you think that meeting will be like? I close my eyes, but I can't picture it."

Julia then cut in, "You know, Jonathan, one of my favorite Christian songs is *I Can Only Imagine* by MercyMe. It addresses the precise question you just asked Grandma. That is, what meeting your God, for the very first time, would be like for you. The song contemplates several different possibilities as a likely response to that incredible meeting. They are: to dance, be still in awe, stand in His presence, fall to your knees, sing *Hallelujah,* or not be able to speak at all. It's such a beautiful song, and I can't wait for you to hear it."

"Which of those do you think would be most likely for you, Grandma?"

"Another great question, my Jonathan. Well, of those choices in the song, I think for me it would be a combination of falling to my knees and

122

singing. Falling to my knees because given my spectacular joy, I wouldn't have the strength to stand. Singing because God has blessed each of us with a unique voice. It's one of His special gifts to us. Imagine what it would be like in a world without our voices. If no one could speak, sing, or make sounds, we'd have to write everything down to communicate with each other, or use hand, or body, gestures. How inconvenient that would be! And God has created each of us with our unique voice, which is different from anyone else's. Oh, two voices may sound the same to us, at times; but to Him, I'm sure He can hear each voice as its own, and He will know when He hears your voice it is from you and nobody else."

"Now, how better to use my voice before God, while on my knees, than to express my joy by singing? What song I would choose to sing, I have no idea; it's a very difficult choice. Two of my favorites are *Paper Moon* and *What a Wonderful World*, because they are so positive and uplifting. But, I imagine we would not be limited by the songs we know and love here on Earth, and have been created and produced by man, including arias, hymns, chants, chorales, odes, psalms, carols, and Christmas songs. When you are in church, Jonathan, look at the faces of the people who are there when they are singing together to God. Their faces are so peaceful, expressive, and alive. I just love to look at them, and to feel the energy and serenity they give me in our shared expression of love and gratitude for Him."

Mary Ann continued, "Now when it's our time to be with Him, we leave so much more than our bodies behind. Those who love us at the time of our death will remember our goodness and the special experiences we shared and enjoyed with them, and the lessons we have taught them during our life journey. Everything you do, everything you say, every thought you think, or you don't do, or you don't say, or you don't think, but that you should have, is a reflection and statement of who you are, and what makes you, you. So, you want to present yourself the best you can. If you can do that effectively, and lead a life that is good, virtuous, and pure, then when it is your time to pass, you leave behind such a remarkable legacy and gift to those still here, as my parents have done for me."

Mary Ann, a bit out of breath, took another short break before continuing.

"Of course, we all have our moments we'd rather forget and hope others will as well, whether it's in a drunken stupor, shouting out of control during an argument, losing our temper in a 'road rage' incident, or doing or saying anything that doesn't properly portray who we are. I believe our setting a high example for others, particularly parents setting a high standard for their child or children, is a special gift you leave them when your body gives out. If you can do that, then when they think of you and feel your presence, long after that time, they will have learned from you, honored your teachings, and celebrated your life, and those will provide them peace, happiness, and guidance for the rest of theirs."

"I think far too often, we see the trees, but not the forest. Meaning, we live our lives too much just aimlessly living it without fully focusing on or appreciating the effect we have on others, whether positive to emulate or negative to avoid. Doing good things and simple acts of kindness can brighten the world one person at a time and help those who may be in need or are less fortunate. Every one of us has our part to play. As my parents were to me, Jonathan, I know my Julia will be to you. And she will do her best to set a great example of how to have a well-lived life. Be open and guided by her lessons and learn from her wisdom. And always remember that love of God, love of family, and love of yourself (in being happy, as well as content within yourself), can carry you through anything."

Mary Ann took Jonathan's hand in hers and continued, "And one last thing before you leave. Life is what you make it, Jonathan. Focus on the positives God has put in your life and appreciate and feel blessed by them while they are still here. Life is constantly changing. Experiences, pets, acquaintances, friends, and even family members will all come and go, but the things that will remain with you for your entire life are your values, how you view and enjoy life, and God. I always am awestruck by the beauty of the oceans, the majesty of the mountains, the incredibleness of the universe, and the diversity and uniqueness of each life, from the microscopic cell to the great blue whale. Treasure them always and feel blessed by God's loving gifts. There's a kind of love that God only knows."

Mary Ann then gently kissed the back of Jonathan's hand and released it from her grasp.

"I'm so glad that we got to meet, Grandma. You are even more special than I could have imagined!"

"Thanks for your beautiful words, Mom," Julia said as she hugged her. "Now, get some rest. I hope we didn't tire you out too much. Love you, Mom," Julia called back as she took Jonathan's hand once again, and they headed to the door.

"Bye, dear. Bye, my Jonathan."

CHAPTER 20

Jonathan's Diagnosis

In making her decision to care full-time for Jonathan, Julia had numerous discussions with his medical team and participated in two lengthy meetings. Julia remembered her unease as she walked into a room of doctors to inform her more fully of Jonathan's unfortunate plight.

Attending the meetings was Jonathan's lead doctor, Dr. Sirowski, and three junior male doctors. Ms. Campbell, a hospital administrator who coordinated the meetings, also was in attendance. Julia believed Dr. Sirowski was in his mid-fifties. He wore gold wire-rimmed glasses and had a long expressionless face. His black hair was greying around his sideburns. He was distinguished-looking, and he carried himself with an air of authority.

Dr. Sirowski began, "Good morning, Ms. Richards. We have each received, and have read, a copy of your application and supporting letter detailing how you met Jonathan, the bond you have formed with him, and the reasons as to why you now seek to move him from St. Peter's to live with you and ultimately to adopt him. Let me start by saying your letter was sincere, and we have no questions about your admirable intentions. We want to make sure you fully understand Jonathan's diagnosis and the challenges likely to arise if the application is approved, and you choose to proceed with your plan."

"Thank you for meeting with me."

As Julia listened to Dr. Sirowski's welcome and opening remarks, she immediately noted he spoke with such certainty as if he never doubted any of his medical evaluations and prognoses. However difficult his words would be to hear, she knew the information he would provide would be essential for her to understand, even if she had less faith in it than he appeared to have and more faith in a higher authority. Julia wondered if he believed in God.

"Jonathan is an ideal patient as he listens well, and he does as he is instructed to do. He has a remarkable fighting spirit and a great determination, assets that will help him as his body weakens. Understand we would be doing you a disservice if we did not give you our frank assessment as to Jonathan's current condition and what you could expect going forward as his potential caretaker."

Julia braced herself as he continued.

"As you know, Jonathan is a very sick boy. We are disadvantaged because we cannot meet his parents and have access to their respective medical histories. But what little we do know, we suspect Jonathan's health issues likely stem from his mother's abuse of alcohol, cigarettes, and possibly drugs during her pregnancy. What remains unknown is whether either of Jonathan's parents had a history of genetic disorders in their families. Clinically, mental retardation is a less than average general intellectual functioning that includes some degree of impaired adaptation in learning, social adjustment, or maturation, or in Jonathan's case, all three of them at once, and is classified as 'developmental disability.' He recently had several months of relatively robust health with few medical complications. But you cannot expect his health to improve or to stay constant."

"What can I expect? How much time do you think he has left?" Julia asked, deeply fearful of the answer but needing to know and appreciate Jonathan's reality from his doctors' perspective. As she asked those questions, Julia could feel her throat tightening and her eyes moistening. In anticipation of hearing horrible news as to Jonathan's life expectancy, she developed a throbbing migraine.

"Jonathan is in the final stages of his life – his time left could be anywhere from a couple of months to half a year. The chances of his living a full year are less than ten percent. The cause of his death most probably will be from heart disease or cerebrovascular diseases, including stroke."

How do they determine precise percentages, anyway? Julia wondered. *And how reliable are they?* But she understood very clearly Dr. Sirowski believed Jonathan did not have long to live, however much time it proved to be. While she was saddened, she was no less determined. Given Jonathan's remaining time with her was very restricted according to his doctors' report, it was all the more important to her to provide Jonathan with the experiences and fulfillment she believed he so richly deserved.

Upon hearing the disheartening news, Julia could not fully conceal her emotions, and she shed a few tears, which appeared to be unnoticed by the doctors. Ms. Campbell quickly got up and placed a box of Kleenex in front of Julia and handed her one.

The remaining doctors each briefly introduced themselves and informed Julia of their specific involvement with Jonathan's care and health management. While they spoke less authoritatively than did Dr. Sirowski, their talk was dominated by technical, medical terms and presented without any hint of emotion. Only when Julia rose to leave the meeting did Ms. Campbell gave her a quick hug.

"If you need anything or have any questions, I am here to help you, so please reach out to me. I'll set up the next meeting and provide you with some available dates and times."

Julia was thankful for the hug and the offer of assistance.

At their second meeting several days later, Dr. Sirowski informed Julia, "The problem faced by any caretaker of a child in Jonathan's condition is his heart could give out at any time with little or no warning. Accordingly, he will continue to need 24/7 care and quick access to a hospital. We know this is something you do not want to hear, but it is our collective best judgment, given what we expect regarding Jonathan's increasingly fragile and deteriorating state, that he remains here at St. Peter's and be given hospice care in the coming months. The question you need to ask yourself and become comfortable with is whether you have the ability and resources to sufficiently care for Jonathan. Any decision must first and foremost consider what is in Jonathan's best interest, given his medical and emotional challenges."

Trying as best as she could to maintain her composure, Julia responded,

"I appreciate your recommendation. As I've stated in my letter, I have given this much thought, and I have fully planned for it. I wouldn't take it on unless I was convinced it is in Jonathan's best interest, and I can handle it. After all, while your focus rightly is on prolonging Jonathan's life, my focus is to enrich and enhance his remaining life."

"Understood, Ms. Richards," Dr. Sirowski replied. "If your application is approved and you proceed with it, we wish you and Jonathan well, and we will do all we can to support you both."

While the doctors' reports and recommendations were devastating news that cost Julia several sleepless nights, she was prepared for them. She arranged for a meeting with her boss, explained her plan, and obtained pre-approval for up to six months' absence from work. Additionally, the hospital staff stated they would work closely with her and provide any needed medical assistance. It also helped that Julia lived within a twenty minutes' drive to St. Peter's, and knew well the hospital and many of its personnel, given her Mother's numerous stays there.

Julia had a spare room in her apartment she used as a library. In preparation for Jonathan's arrival, she converted it to his new bedroom and tried to make it as comfortable as possible.

The steps Julia took to date for Jonathan were the easy part, she knew. She was less confident in her ability to play the mother and caretaker roles that would be required, particularly with Mary Ann's declining health and Julia's need to be there for her. But freed from work obligations and the need to finalize wedding plans, she believed she had a fighting chance to succeed.

Julia hoped before her last meeting with Ben that he would provide emotional support. Now she would need to go it alone and do the best possible under current circumstances. But growing up a child of a single parent who needed to work to support the family, Julia spent most of her life fending for herself, and when younger, always believed herself more capable than were her peers. While she had so looked forward to being married to Ben, Julia nevertheless was self-assured she did not need him, or anyone else, other than Jonathan's doctors, to take care of Jonathan. Moreover, that he was diagnosed to be in the final stages of his life gave her a new mission to make whatever time he had left to be as incredible and exciting and as normal as possible.

While the thought of Jonathan passing away under her watch was frightening to Julia, it was not as troubling as him living the rest of his life uncommunicative and miserable at St. Peter's. Before bringing Jonathan home, Julia decided she would need to find a proper balance of playing it safe for health reasons but not too severely restricting him. While she appreciated she had no control over prolonging Jonathan's life, which, after all, was God's will, she had total control over its quality. It was vital to her that Jonathan experience the wondrous world that was just outside of his window at St. Peter's to the fullest. And she very much looked forward to opening that window and exploring it with him.

At Dr. Sirowski's recommendation, Julia purchased a pendant Jonathan would wear around his neck so he would be able to summon for help on his own. It is similar to the device from a commercial she remembered from years ago that sold under the slogan, "Help me, I'm falling, and I can't get up!" Julia stressed to Jonathan that he was not to remove his pendant without first obtaining her permission.

She also purchased a cell phone for him, his first, with extra-large keys that were marketed to elderly consumers with bad eyesight. She programmed her and Mary Ann's cell numbers and the number of St. Peter's emergency department. Those were the only designated numbers he needed, and the shortlist was easy for him to remember: 1. for Julia, 2. for Mary Ann, and 3. for St. Peter's.

Lastly, Julia also purchased a metal bracelet for Jonathan that contained his medical condition and her cell number, despite his protests that bracelets were for girls.

Julia was well aware and wasn't under any false illusion that no pendant, cell phone, or bracelet could save Jonathan's life when God was ready for him. Nevertheless, she wanted to give him as much capacity for help if he ever were in a stressed health condition without her being present.

Unlike several of the children who lived at St. Peter's, Jonathan was able to walk and move independently without the aid of a wheelchair, crutches, braces, or other support. His mobility was a huge asset and would permit Julia to expand his universe more readily, although as she was about to discover, outside of St. Peter's, Jonathan tired quickly and would need intermittent periods of rest.

With Dr. Sirowski informing Julia that Jonathan's mother's substance abuse likely caused or, at least, aggravated Jonathan's illnesses, she made a mental note of her intention to write an article for *The Globe* upon her return to work addressing that subject. To prepare for it, she would interview women who gave birth to physically or mentally challenged children. Under cover of different names, she would tell their stories as an example of the lifetime of hardships that might easily have been avoided had they not allowed drugs, alcohol, and/or smoke to enter their bodies during their pregnancies. That a newborn should enter the world so disadvantaged from the start, like Jonathan, deeply disturbed Julia. She made it her priority to do what she could to arm a pregnant woman with the knowledge needed to make wise choices for her fetus's and baby's health and well-being.

CHAPTER 21

A New-Found Freedom

As she reached the visitors' parking lot at St. Peter's and stepped out of her car to bring Jonathan home for the first time, Julia was elated. When she approached the window where they first met, she stopped and searched for Jonathan. All the other children of St. Peter's, excited by his surprising news, surrounded him. After all, Jonathan was accomplishing a feat no child who entered the hospital ever had. To leave the hospital, especially after calling it home for more than a decade, was unprecedented. When the children parted, and Jonathan caught sight of Julia, he ran to the window, clapped his unusual clap, and pressed his right hand against the window with his fingers spread widely apart. And then, his tears of joy came. Upon witnessing his incredible happiness, Julia rushed to hug him.

Saying his goodbye to each of his fellow patients at St. Peter's and the nurses, staff, and Ms. Thornburg, was not easy for Jonathan. He was leaving behind the only "home" and "family" he could remember. Julia was proud of Jonathan as he correctly remembered each child's name in saying his parting words.

Ms. Thornburg gave him a present, which was a photograph of all the children she took just for him, set in a shiny 8" x 12" gold frame. "Don't forget us, and come back to visit soon," she said as she handed him her gift. The children all encircled him, and they shared a group hug. As he exited his hospital room, Jonathan gave a final wave goodbye and told Julia he would miss the people he had lived with, but not the room itself. At his request, they made one last stop to the chapel to say a quick prayer for those he was leaving behind.

As Julia pulled her vehicle out of St. Peter's parking lot and onto the side street abutting the hospital, Jonathan asked her if she would stop the car. As she did, he opened the door, stepped outside, raised both of his arms high in the air, and yelled out loud, "I'm free!"

It was Jonathan's first time in a car, and that he had not stood on St. Peter's property, that he could recall. The only places he could remember being at were his ward, the hospital cafeteria, the chapel, the hallways, and, just recently, his Grandmother's room. He also experienced St. Peter's playground and garden, and the grass surrounding the hospital parking lot; quite a limited universe for someone as full of life as Jonathan. He often thought how even a prisoner confined to a jail cell probably had seen and done more than him.

Until he met Julia, Jonathan thought very infrequently of the place just outside his hospital window. Before her, the only "outsiders" he encountered were visitors to the other children, mailmen, groundskeepers, and a person who plowed the snow out of the parking lot in the winter months. But Jonathan rarely had an opportunity to speak with them, and even if he did, they all had a purpose for being there that did not include him, so they didn't focus on a lonely boy. Moreover, he thought, they did not notice him or care to see him.

Before Julia entered his life, what Jonathan knew of the outside came from a 28" TV screen in his ward shared with all the other patients there. Since many of them were more vocal than he was, he often had no interest in watching what was playing on that small screen, and his "education" from it was quite limited. Jonathan often wondered how precise and encompassing the outside was portrayed on the TV screen pixels. The only accurate thing, he thought, were the news reports which the other children seldom watched. Even when he had the limited opportunity to watch them, Jonathan often was confused and couldn't understand their relevance to him. Additionally, the reports mostly were depressing and negative. He liked it the most when sometimes, at the very end, the newscasters would take a minute or two to present something positive, like a dog rescuing a kitten from a frozen pond. *Now watch*, Jonathan would say sarcastically to himself at seeing such a story on the TV, *to make the news the dog and kitten will both drown!*

One of the few shows Jonathan regularly watched was *Keeping Up With The Kardashians*, which won by majority rule of the other kids, especially the girls. He wasn't sure how they were all related to each other or what happened to Bruce, but he got to know them in a sort of personal way that led him to be interested in their lives, much like the rest of America, living vicariously through them. He also wondered what acting school they attended, as they were quite unlike the other serious actors and actresses he'd seen before. He would be upset when he missed a *Kardashian* show. Without a VCR or a smart TV, when he missed a show, he missed it for good. He wondered how the Kardashians could hold his attention and imagination over the years, but, somehow, they succeeded when others failed.

Meeting Julia changed all that for Jonathan. She spoke with him at length about her job, places she visited, events she attended, her church, and the many interesting people in her life. Julia whetted his appetite to learn as much as possible about the foreign ways of life outside of St. Peter's. Upon leaving the hospital, he felt almost like an alien from outer space, setting foot on his own planet for the very first time.

There was so much to experience. Jonathan had never been to a movie theater, a bowling alley, or played a sport. He had never seen the ocean firsthand, flew on a plane or been to a zoo. He also had never seen a skyscraper, experienced an elevator, or an escalator, eaten at a restaurant, been in a shopping mall, or rode a bicycle. So too, he had never been stuck in traffic, had to wait in a line, or had a cell phone battery die on him. The world outside appeared to him to be so big, bold, and beautiful, but also a bit overwhelming. Having Julia by his side to share it with him was a perfectly splendid way for him to take it all in.

The first stop was Jonathan's new home. The apartment was not large, but it was roomy enough for two. As Julia lived on the upper-most, nineteenth floor, Jonathan experienced his first elevator ride. Entering his bedroom for the first time, he jumped up and down on his bed. It was so much more comfortable and cozier than his stiff mattress at St. Peter's.

What impressed Jonathan the most was Julia's gigantic 65" curved smart HDTV. He wasn't sure he liked a curved TV until she turned it on. "Wow, that's an amazing picture. I never imagined a TV could look so real." She soon introduced him to the on-demand features of Netflix, Amazon Prime, and Hulu. On Hulu, he soon discovered that he could catch up on every *Kardashian* show he had ever missed with the press of a button. And no one to compete against him as to what to watch! His enthusiasm was tempered a bit when Julia explained what a "couch potato" was and that he should not become one. "There is so much you'd be missing if you ex-perienced life primarily through a TV screen, or even a movie screen," she warned him. "No, I want for you to enjoy the world first-hand, in the best color – God's color, that no HDTV (or whatever other names manufactur-ers could think of to sell more TVs these days) could match. It's unlikely you'll ever meet a Kardashian live, but the trade-off is so worth it. And I promise you will not be bored."

It took Julia all of ten minutes to unpack Jonathan's belongings and to settle him in. The first order of business was to introduce Jonathan to Belle, the cutest ball of fluff he had ever seen. Belle's tail wagged furiously when she was around him. In Belle, Jonathan found total and unconditional love, with no judgment of any kind. She was the ideal playmate for him, as Julia knew she would be. The two of them would play hide and seek, by Jonathan putting her in his room, closing the door, but with it being left ajar just enough for Belle to stick out her little paw to open it, by which time Jonathan found his hiding place. Julia hadn't informed Jonathan of Belle's acute sense of smell, which gave her a very unfair advantage in their game. After they finished playing, Jonathan and Belle would crawl into his bed to rest and Julia often would find them sound asleep, with Belle laying on top of him.

Julia also showed Jonathan the benefits their apartment building of-fered, including the indoor swimming pool, game room, and gym that, each in its way, fascinated Jonathan. Upon seeing the gym, Jonathan said in a serious tone, "now I can work out and get muscles like The Rock, Dwayne Johnson, and impress all the girls."

"I have a little secret for you," Julia told him, upon hearing his "muscle" statement. "The girls will be more impressed by your soul and goodness than they will be by your muscles. A smile and a wink can go a long way."

"There's so many choices, Julia, I don't know what to do first."

"I have a few ideas," she replied. "Let's go back upstairs, I'll cook your dinner, and then, if you'd like, for tonight, we can stay in and watch *The Kardashians* while munching on popcorn."

"A perfect night, and I get to spend it with my best friends. The only thing that would make it better is if Grandma could join us. Maybe we could surprise her someday, bring some popcorn, and watch TV with Grandma in her room. Her TV's not as awesome as yours is, but I'd rather have Grandma than a bigger picture."

Julia filled the ensuing weeks with nonstop fascination and excitement. Among the highlights, she took Jonathan to The Franklin Park Zoo and explored 72 acres in which they saw up close kangaroos, ostriches, giraffes, lions, tigers, bears, indoor butterflies (one of which landed on Jonathan's nose), and all kinds of other animals and birds. Jonathan enjoyed the zoo's playground, but he avoided the swings. His favorite place, however, was the petting farm at the contact corral.

They also visited the New England Aquarium. Jonathan loved the sea lions and meeting Myrtle the Green Sea Turtle through a glass window. The penguins, though, stole his heart. Julia laughed upon seeing Jonathan mimicking the way a cool penguin walked. Some creatures were downright scary, which caught Jonathan off-guard as he stepped backward when they approached him by the glass window of their tanks. Jonathan was particularly frightened by the giant octopus and the great white sharks. "Thank God for the window," he exclaimed. Before exiting, they stopped in the gift shop, which was conveniently placed to be unavoidable. Julia surprised him by buying him a stuffed toy sea lion pup, dolphin, and penguin. She gave them to him by putting them neatly on his bed when they arrived home so they would be waiting for him when he went to sleep. He named the sea lion pup, "Sammy," the dolphin, "Dolin," and the penguin, "Peter." The trio was a great comfort to Jonathan and a constant reminder of Julia's thoughtfulness and love. He fell asleep virtually every night thereafter, holding all of them in his arms.

The only downside to their aquarium adventure was the crowds every-where they went and Jonathan's need to wedge his way in to look at what the crowds constantly seemed to block from his view. This made Jonathan extremely tired. Julia quickly learned to slow down her pace to accommo-date Jonathan's needs. She found that while a slower pace resulted in them seeing and doing less, taking a more leisurely stroll enhanced the enjoy-ment of each of the sights and experiences they were able to take in.

Julia also taught Jonathan about Boston's history, including its role in the Revolutionary War, as well as Boston Common, which she informed him was the oldest city park in the United States, and a model for New York City's Central Park. She then surprised him with a visit to the Common on a bright sunny day. She made sure to include visits to the Soldiers and Sailors Monument, the Boston Massacre Memorial, the Parkman Bandstand, and Frog Pond.

The roaming musicians, jugglers, and magicians in the Common fas-cinated Jonathan, to the point where he'd follow them after a performance to their next spot to start all over again. Jonathan never tired of seeing the same act numerous times in a row. One magician named "Merlin," upon noticing Jonathan had seen his show repeatedly, made him a "magic" hat out of balloons he wore for the rest of the day until they started to deflate, and the hat could no longer remain on his head. Jonathan remarked he never heard the name "Merlin" before, and what a strange name it was. Julia explained it likely is his "stage" name and not his real mother-given name. Wrapping up their adventure in Boston was a Swan Boat ride in the Public Garden. Strolling there with Jonathan, Julia was reminded of her first date with Ben and the incredible time they shared that evening. She missed Ben terribly but tried her best to remain positive and thankful de-spite the pain of separation and disengagement.

A subsequent trip brought them to Faneuil Hall where they grabbed a bite to eat at one of its many eateries, and to the Museum of Science, where Jonathan saw his first IMAX film, to which he noted, "this makes my old TV at St. Peter's look pitiful!" His trip to the museum made him "very smart." Upon leaving it, he told Julia, "I learned so much today; I'm afraid it will all be gone from my head tomorrow." Finishing up their day was a

Super Duck Tour ride with other families. Jonathan was amazed when the vehicle entered Boston Harbor and floated away, spraying water all around them.

On Sunday morning, Julia introduced Jonathan to virtually everyone she knew at the Cathedral of Holy Cross in Boston's South End. Jonathan stood in amazement at the numerous large colorful stained-glass windows and the huge columns leading to the altar. Before attending, Julia read to him the church's online welcome and mission statement:

"We glorify God by being peacemakers, by being people of reconciliation and mercy. We all have opportunities to be peacemakers in a world where there are so many divisions, so many tensions, so many conflicting interests. As we journey together with Christians around the world, Jesus invites you and me to become a seeker and become the best version of ourselves. May God bless you!"

To which Jonathan asked, "How do I become the best version of myself?"

"To be your best," Julia began, "you would need to do good in God's eyes. To do good in God's eyes, you should be loving, caring, a peacemaker by avoiding arguments and fights, always trying to do positive things, by helping those who need help, being optimistic and hopeful, praying for things, not for yourself but instead for others, and being generous and kind. A good rule to ask yourself in any situation is 'what would God do, or want me to do?'"

After giving it further thought, Julia added, "My Mom has always encouraged me to be the best I can throughout my life. I remember when I was in school, and it was report card time, she didn't focus on my letter, or number, grades. Much more important to her than such metrics the school used to differentiate their students was whether I tried as hard as I could. She'd say, 'if you can look in the mirror and honestly say you tried as hard as possible, then that is all you, or anyone else, can ask, regardless of the ultimate grade. The grade quickly will become ancient history, but what will remain is your drive to succeed and do your best.' Her words of wisdom have never left me, and I continue to strive to meet her standard in everything I do to this day."

"Another thing that I've learned as I got older is it's crucial to your well-being to be an optimistic person."

"I'm not sure what that means," remarked Jonathan.

"I'll try to explain it. To be optimistic is to see the bright side of things – some people say, to see a glass half full, rather than half empty. Optimistic people genuinely are happy because they are hopeful; they believe good ultimately wins over evil. The opposite is a pessimistic person who always sees the glass half empty. In my life, my Mom is the best example of an optimistic person. She always taught me by her actions and comments that no matter how bad things get, no matter how beaten down you may be, always be thankful and hopeful. Despite her cancer, pain, and the awful chemo treatments she must endure, all that ugliness did not change who she is, her spirit, or her outlook on life. She still has a huge smile on her face, a twinkle in her eyes, and determination that never gives in and never gives up. If my Mom's optimism spread as her cancer has, the world would be such a better place."

After a slight pause, Julia continued. "Optimism isn't something you're born with; it's something you acquire. Optimistic people are more likely to be peacemakers and to be the best they can be. They draw people to them like magnets rather than push people away from them, as pessimistic people do."

"Julia, you are so smart. I want to be optimistic."

"You already are. Even though you have more reason to complain than others do, you don't. You take life's challenges, and you meet them head-on with a smile on your face. Your optimism drew me in, helped me to believe in you, and do what I can to support you."

"So, you wouldn't have done what you have for me if I were pessimistic?"

"I didn't say that, but it certainly would have been harder for me. I love being around optimistic people – they lift and nourish my soul."

"Just like your Mom."

"Just like my Mom. Yes."

"And my Grandma!"

CHAPTER 22

More Firsts

When they arrived home from church, Julia informed Jonathan she had a special surprise for him. Some more firsts in his life, she told him.

"What is it? I need to know," Jonathan pleaded.

"See that suitcase in the corner of your room? We're going to pack it and leave tomorrow for a trip on a plane."

"How do you know that?" Jonathan asked innocently.

"Because I arranged it. Trips don't pop up out of thin air. You plan where you want to travel, make the plane, and hotel, reservations, and organize events and activities for your trip."

"How did you know where to go and what to do?"

"I arranged everything based on how much I think you will enjoy them. And I believe you," Julia then corrected herself, "we will have a fun and memorable trip. And I've discussed it with your doctors, and they were fine with it."

"Is Ben coming?"

"No, he's not. It's you and I." As she answered Jonathan, she remembered her last three words were the title of her and Ben's intended wedding song. She continued to miss Ben terribly. But being Jonathan's caretaker, event planner, teacher, spiritual guide, and soon-to-be travel companion were a full-time job, and she loved every minute of her new roles.

"Oh my God, I'm so excited. Where are we going, Julia?"

"If I told you, then it wouldn't be a surprise, now would it?"

"Wow, Julia, you are good at planning things."

"Yes, it may be considered a virtue, but also a nuisance. I plan every-thing, and sometimes, I admit, to a fault. It can drive people crazy at times. And, in case you have not noticed, I can be controlling and very stubborn when something is important to me, and I need to be. Just giving you a warning, Jonathan, I'm not the perfect mom you may have been expecting. I have my faults, you know, just like everyone else!"

Julia was so happy to see Jonathan's eager and ecstatic face by her mention of their trip. It made her excited that she could bring Jonathan so many "firsts," including his first suitcase, first airplane ride, and first vaca-tion. The thought of giving Jonathan "first" experiences, particularly fun and exciting ones, was pleasing to Julia and Jonathan.

Later that day, Jonathan and Julia returned to St. Peter's to pay a quick visit with her Mom. In advance of her surprise for Jonathan, she informed Mary Ann that they would be away for several days.

"Hey, you two. You're looking great, Jonathan. I love that you always smile."

"Not always, but a lot when I see you!"

"Have you grown since I've seen you last?" Mary Ann joked with Jonathan.

"Not in height, but wisdom. Julia's smart about everything, including optimism."

"That's my girl. She's always been that way. And I love her for it."

"How are you feeling, Mom? You look good."

"I'm doing fantastic. I would run a race around the hospital if they would just let me out of this bed. But I couldn't bribe a nurse to help me."

She continued, "I finally got up my strength to have another chemo treatment, my last for a while. I'm glad it's over. Now, it's time to rest and recuperate. What else do I do? I haven't been able to keep my food down, so I think I've lost 15 pounds in the last week – my very own diet. I should write a book named *The Chemo Diet – How To Lose More Than Two Pounds a Day Guaranteed*. It's not for everyone, but as long as I'm losing my hair, I should also lose some weight, so I regain my girlish figure. So, Jonathan, I hear you are going on an exciting trip tomorrow.

I wish I could join you two. Do you think you have room for me in your suitcase?"

"No, my suitcase isn't that large. I still don't know where we're going. It's a big surprise."

"That's my Julia. She always keeps you guessing."

"Mom, is there anything I can get for you before we leave?"

"No, dear, I have everything I need right here. The nurses are so attentive and pleasant. They take good care of me. And there's a new young guy down the hall who visits me. His name is Neb, and he is also undergoing chemo for his cancer. So, we have a lot in common. We have conversations a couple of times a day. It is a little strange to discuss anything and everything with a stranger, but the more we know about each other, the less strange it feels. I enjoy his company. He tells me he doesn't believe in God. That's where our similarities end, although I'm trying my best to convince him otherwise. But so far, no luck."

After a slight pause, Mary Ann continued, "Now, you two go and have a wonderful time. I'm thrilled for you both. Even though I won't physically be with you, I'll be with you in spirit," she said while winking at them.

"Well, if you do think of anything, just let me know."

"And Jonathan, one thing that I meant to tell you. I understand Caren loved you very much. The thing to remember is now she is your guardian angel who is watching after you from above. If you believe that, she will never be far away from you or your heart."

Mary Ann then took Jonathan's hand in hers and looking at him, lovingly said, "Jonathan, I want you to know that you're everything I've ever dreamed about in a grandchild and more. You're perfect to me and you're Nana's boy. And any time the going gets rough, come to Nana. I can't wait to see you again!" She ended with giving him a tender kiss.

"Thanks. I won't forget that. I'll miss you so much!"

"Bye, Mom. Thanks for all your beautiful words. I love you tons!" Julia leaned over and hugged and kissed her Mother goodbye.

"Jonathan, please look after my precious daughter for me."

"I certainly will, Grandma," Jonathan said proudly.

"See you soon, my Jonathan," Mary Ann called to him.

Julia stopped to say a quick hello to Ms. Thornburg and let her see how well Jonathan was doing. She also wanted him to spend a few minutes with the children of St. Peter's. He purposely didn't mention his upcoming trip and smiled the whole time he was with them, so unlike the Jonathan who left the ward just a few weeks ago.

Julia then ran some necessary errands, including purchasing a new bathing suit for Jonathan, another first. She let him pick it out. It was all shades of yellow with a wild, crazy pattern. As he stepped out of the fitting room in his new attire, she remarked how cool he looked. "Now, the girls will notice me," he replied.

As Julia and Jonathan entered their apartment, she told him the *Kardashians* would have to wait until their return as they both needed to get an early night's sleep for their exciting adventure that awaited them tomorrow. The morning couldn't come soon enough for Jonathan. He slept without Sammy, Dolin, and Peter for the first time since they entered his life, as he packed them in his new suitcase before going to bed to make sure he didn't forget them in the morning.

Jonathan woke quickly to Julia's pleasant call, "Time to rise and shine." Julia helped him get dressed, which he did in record time. As they neared Logan airport, a plane flew over their car. Jonathan was surprised by how large and loud it was. He closed his eyes and covered his ears with both of his hands.

Having a plane fly overhead was one matter; being in one that was about to take off was quite another. Jonathan shut his eyes and professed to Julia how nervous he was as their plane picked up speed on the runway. *How does something so heavy, with all these people and bags, suddenly become lighter than air?* he asked himself. Julia smiled reassuringly to Jonathan as she saw his body begin to tremble. She put her head over his, held his hand, and whispered to him, "Don't worry, I've got you."

Jonathan summoned the courage to peer outside the small plane window to view the sights below. As they flew over cars entering Logan, he wondered if any boys or girls in those cars were closing their eyes and covering their ears, as he had done a short while before.

The flight lasted two hours and forty minutes, which seemed like an eternity to Jonathan. The plane couldn't land soon enough for him. To his delight, he did manage to catch up on several *Kardashians* shows on his very own tiny screen attached to the rear of the seat in front of him. That helped to calm him and make his time in the air pass more quickly. He was amazed at how everything looked so small on the ground and how miniature everything was in his section of the plane. In addition to the screens, he noticed the tiny size of the seats, the knobs and buttons overhead, the restrooms and faucets in them, the bottles of liquors and juices, and the packet of pretzels. Passing the seats in the first-class section of the plane when he boarded, Jonathan saw how much bigger everything appeared to be there, including, especially, the size of the passengers. He was thankful that one of those large passengers was not sitting next to him in the small section of the plane.

Upon entering the airport terminal, Jonathan saw a big sign that read, "Welcome to Orlando."

"What's in Orlando, Julia? Where is Orlando?"

"It's in Florida, and you'll see what's here very quickly."

On the cab ride to their hotel, Jonathan checked to ensure Sammy, Dolin, and Peter survived the flight. He was excited they were joining him on his vacation, and they would be there for him every night he was away.

When they checked into the Portofino Bay Hotel at Universal Studios, they were met by a man of Indian nationality at the reception desk, wearing a name tag "JJ Ailu Nahtano." Upon seeing that, Jonathan joked, "I guess people call you 'JJ' as a short name." The man smiled and then handed Jonathan a gift, which was a pail and shovel for the man-made beach, loaded with all kinds of mouthwatering candies and snacks. Jonathan walked over to a surprised "JJ" and gave him a quick hug to express his appreciation. He was being treated like a prince, and he loved every minute of it. Julia and Jonathan spent the remainder of the day exploring what their hotel had to offer them. Resting and relaxing by the pool, Jonathan was on the lookout for attractive girls so he could stand up from this chaise lounge and model his new bathing suit.

About a half-hour after they started relaxing by the pool and enjoying the Florida sun and their beautiful new surroundings, Jonathan noticed a girl whom Julia could tell had similar mental challenges as did Jonathan. The girl had short red hair, freckles and was in a tan bikini. As Julia saw Jonathan looking at her, whom he found to be very attractive, Julia suggested he introduce himself.

"I can't. I know how badly I'd feel if the girl didn't like me."

"Jonathan, she is nice-looking, and I think you should meet her. If you don't go to introduce yourself, you will never know how she feels about you. Wouldn't you always wonder what you missed if you didn't speak with her?"

"Yes, I would. But I don't think I could handle it if the girl decides not to talk with me. I don't want to shake and look frightened. Girls can pick up on that sort of thing, you know."

"Jonathan, your Grandma said something to me my whole life that I think is appropriate to share with you now. And that is, 'it's better to try and fail than not try at all.' And I can guarantee you one thing; if you approached her and she chose not to speak with you, it's her loss, not yours. She would never get to see you for the incredible person you are, and she would be missing out on an awesome experience."

"Okay, okay. I'll try it. First, let me think of what to say to get her attention." After a minute of thought, Jonathan, with additional encouragement from Julia, approached the girl.

"Hi, like my new bathing suit?" he asked her.

Not quite sure how to respond to that question, she simply said, "Hi, my name's Ali. It's my first time in Florida, and we're having so much fun here."

"Where you guys from? We're from Massachusetts."

"We live in Nebraska. While I like it there, it is nothing like Orlando."

"I know. Massachusetts is nothing like Orlando, either."

Trying his best to impress Ali, Jonathan continued, "Nebraska comes right before Orlando in the alphabet – N then O."

"You're right, and Massachusetts comes just before Nebraska – so it's Massachusetts, Nebraska, and Orlando – M, N, and O."

Jonathan was impressed she figured that out by herself and thought she must be smarter than he is. A little awkwardly, he continued, "I'm not sure where Nebraska is, but you should come to visit us in Massachusetts. I think you will like it there, and I will be there."

"What's your name?"

"It's Jonathan. Is your name really Ali, or is it short for another name?"

"My long name is 'Alison,' but everyone has always called me by my short name, and I like it better than Alison, so that's good."

"I never knew anyone having the name 'Ali' before. At least, not as a first name. It is an unusual and very nice name. Liking the pool?"

"Yes, I am. We have one in our backyard at home, so I do swim a lot when the weather is hot."

"We have an indoor pool where I live, but I have not been in it yet."

"Why not, don't you like to swim?"

"I think I would, but I have never tried it."

"Never, why not?"

"Because until just a little while ago, I lived my whole life in a hospital, and the hospital doesn't have a pool."

"Are you sick?"

"No, I'm feeling fine."

"No, I mean, why would you live in a hospital if you're not sick? I don't understand."

"Well, I have no parents and no family, and nowhere else to live until recently."

Still confused, the girl asked, "Isn't that pretty lady there your mom? If not, who is she?"

"Not yet, but I do hope someday soon she will be."

Giving up trying to understand their line of discussion, the girl continued with a simpler question. "So, what have you seen so far in Orlando?"

"Just this hotel and pool area."

"Don't you want to see more than this?"

"This has been great, and I don't know what else there is."

"Oh, there is so much more. My parents and I are leaving tomorrow morning. We've been here an entire week, and we have seen a lot that is truly incredible. But, since you have not seen it yet, I don't want to spoil it for you. You will experience it for yourself and see how magical it all is."

"I didn't know it's magical. Thanks for telling me. Now I really can't wait." Jonathan continued, obviously enjoying their conversation, "What's it like in Nebraska?"

"Well, it is very scenic, with wide-open plains, where buffalo used to roam wild. It gets its name from the Indians who lived there, and the word Nebraska meant to them 'flat water.'"

"How can water be flat?"

"I'm not sure; you would need to ask them. I do think you would like it there. I would love to show you my state someday, Jonathan, if you are ever out West."

"I would love to see it. And if you are ever in Massachusetts, please remember to visit me there. But don't ask me what Massachusetts means because I have no idea."

"Great. Hopefully, we can make that happen someday."

After a short pause, Ali continued. "My mom is motioning me that we need to leave. We still have to pack and get ready for our flight back to Omaha tomorrow."

"I thought you said you lived in Nebraska?"

"We do. Omaha is the largest city in Nebraska, and we live close to it. It's where the planes fly into when they come to Nebraska. Well, I must be going now. Nice to meet you."

Ali then approached Jonathan and kissed him on his cheek. "See ya in Nebraska someday!"

As Ali walked away from him, Jonathan touched the spot where she kissed him. He was so excited by Ali's kiss that he threw himself in the shallow part of the pool to cool off.

Julia saw how engaged Jonathan was in speaking with the girl, and she witnessed the kiss. She was delighted that he followed her advice, with an obviously positive result.

As Jonathan dried himself off from his sudden plunge into the pool, he told Julia speaking with girls was not as difficult as he thought it would be.

"You see, if you take chances or risks in life, you may just get what you want, and there's only one way to find out. I'm thrilled it worked out so well for you, even better than you expected. Next time, I hope you will have more self-confidence and not struggle with the thought of approaching a girl whom you find to be attractive."

"I don't know. We'll see. Only if I'm wearing this bathing suit because I'm sure it impressed her, and that's what got it started for me in the first place."

After finishing an enjoyable day at the pool, that evening while they were sitting out on their room deck overlooking the hotel grounds, Jonathan asked Julia how their hotel got its name. She explained Portofino is a charming and picturesque fishing village on the West coast of Italy, south of a larger town named Genoa. She informed him it's a famous tourist spot and showed him several online pictures of the village from her iPhone.

"I've never seen such a beautiful place," Jonathan remarked. "Can we go there on our next trip?" Jonathan wanted to know.

"I would love to take you to Portofino someday. But, until we can go, let's pretend we're there, okay? Like we celebrated your birthday on a day that really wasn't."

"Pretend?" Jonathan asked.

"You know, your mind is so powerful. Even though you may not have the time or the money to travel to all the places you would like to visit, never let that interfere with your imagination of what it would be like to be there. We can look up and study any place in the world on our computer or smartphone and then take those images and knowledge to create our special version of it in our minds. Now with virtual reality, you can see it in 360 degrees and feel like you're actually there! You can be as creative as your imagination lets you be."

Julia continued. "In your mind, unlike in reality, there is no limit to where you can go, what you can see, and how stunning and breathtaking it is. God has given everyone such a special instrument in the mind. We use it all the time without thinking about it. But when we use our imagination to focus on things, such as a visit to Portofino, Italy, and what that would look and feel like, we can create it in our minds, and the possibilities are endless. You know, you could go anywhere at any time, without having to make any arrangements, spending time packing and unpacking, beating traffic, being nervous flying in an airplane, or spending any money. Now, isn't that truly special?"

Julia then had an idea, turned to Jonathan, and eagerly said to him, "Forget the pictures of Portofino I just showed you. Erase them completely from your mind. I want you to take a few minutes and describe what your Portofino would look like and be to you if you were the architect and the builder of the city of your dreams. Let your imagination run free and describe it to me, Jonathan."

"I don't know. While I was at St. Peter's, I tried to imagine the outside world. My imagination was not too good because I couldn't picture a place like Orlando before."

"But, Jonathan," Julia interrupted him, "don't let that interfere with the picture you will paint in your mind for me of your Portofino. Unlike a snapshot or a photo, which just takes what's already there and converts it into pixels printed onto paper, you get to create a painting of it as the artist. Now, Jonathan, imagine what it would look like and describe it."

Jonathan spent several minutes deep in thought and concentration to determine what his Portofino would be to him.

"Well," he began slowly, "it would be a very fun and happy place. There would be Ferris wheels and other rides, and games, fireworks, and parades."

"Anything else?" she coaxed him.

"There would be candy shops and toy stores and people who smile, and laugh, a lot."

"And?"

"And big, beautiful churches and chapels, so people had wonderful places to pray, Christmas trees, Christmas lights and all things Christmas."

"And?"

"And donkeys, sheep, and other animals roaming around without cages, and they are happy too."

"And?"

"And no one kills the animals or each other, and there is no crime or sin."

"And?"

"And no fires, floods, hurricanes, tornadoes, earthquakes, or other disasters."

"And?"

"And no money, so everything is free, there would be no bills, and no one had to worry about whether they could pay for places to live, food, or other things."

"And?"

"No strangers, so everyone knows and understands each other. They would all be friends, and there would be no hatred or wars."

"And?"

"And no disease or illness, and no one there is like the children of St. Peter's and me with huge problems."

"And?"

"And no pollution, so the land and water are clean, and the night sky is so clear to see all the stars and planets, and you can feel closer to it because nothing is blocking your view of it."

"Wow, Jonathan! See, you just showed how incredible your imagination is. Isn't it great to imagine things? Take the time to stroll down your Portofino and feel what that would be like for you. Even though the real one is breathtaking, I'm certain the one you just painted in your mind is so much better still!"

"Well, even though God did not give me a brain like normal kids, at least he gave me an imagination. I never thought I had one until just now."

While Jonathan loved their hotel surroundings, especially armed with his wild imagination Julia helped to unleash, the best was yet to come.

Julia and Jonathan spent the following day at Disney World. Everything was so magnificent and magical, just as Ali told him it would be. They got their picture taken arm-in-arm in front of Cinderella's Castle. Jonathan blushed as Cinderella herself kissed him on the top of his head as they approached her. Jonathan mused he didn't even need to wear his new crazy bathing suit to get her attention. He noticed Julia left her high-heeled shoes at home, although she was still overdressed compared to the other women at the Park. *Good thing, with all the walking we're doing today,* Jonathan thought.

Julia stopped numerous times throughout the day, so Jonathan, and she, could rest. During one of their stops, they noticed an old man with long white wavy hair sketching a picture of Mickey Mouse standing in front of Disney World, his arms open wide and held high over his head, welcoming the guests to the Park. His picture put onto paper the sheer joy of Disney. Julia was impressed with how much pride he took in his artwork and his obvious enjoyment when guests would stop to admire his creations. Upon its completion, she purchased it for Jonathan.

Julia then asked the old man to draw a caricature of Jonathan and her standing in front of Cinderella's Castle. The man took an immediate fancy to Julia, and they shared, in a ten-minute discussion, their families, pasts, and views of life, which were very similar. The man's name was Angelo, and his family came by boat to America from Naples to enjoy the freedoms of this great land, he said. He spoke English with a slight Italian accent and smiled and laughed a lot. Jonathan noticed that when he talked with them, he used his arms and hands to emphasize what he was saying and was energetic in his discussions. *Angelo is one of the happiest people I've ever met. Who better to make drawings of a fun Disney trip than him?* Jonathan thought.

Angelo turned to Jonathan and asked him what he wanted to be shown wearing in the caricature. He chose his new bathing suit, describing its crazy yellow pattern as best he could. Julia chose Cinderella's gown. When it was completed and handed to them, the contrast between their two outfits in Angelo's masterpiece was so hysterical they could not contain their laughter. The old man was so amused and overjoyed by their reaction, he insisted they keep it without pay. It was his special gift to them and something always to remember him by, he said, as he hugged them, waved his goodbye, and wished them a wonderful day and trip ahead.

As the afternoon gave way to the night, Julia had a final surprise for Jonathan – the fireworks and the Festival of Fantasy Parade, which included all the main Disney characters, most importantly, Mickey and Minnie Mouse. Jonathan always wished to see a parade in person, but he could not have imagined what was passing before his eyes. He skipped, jumped, clapped his hands, and wore a smile the whole time of the parade. St. Peter's seemed to him so long ago and so far away from the likes of Disney World. He wondered if the robins outside of his window at St.

Peter's were smart enough to go to Disney World for the winter. *If only they knew about this place, they'd be here too*, he guessed, as he skipped along to the parade's happy music.

That day and night in Orlando were perfect for both Jonathan and Julia. For Julia, it brought back so many wonderful childhood memories when Mary Ann surprised her with a trip to Disney World. Now, she got to relive those memories and create new ones with Jonathan. Julia was sure all these many years later she still kept a princess necklace and matching earrings Mary Ann purchased for her at a Disney gift shop. She kept them to always remind herself of the incredible jubilation experienced on that trip. As her Mom struggled financially in those days, it was the only vacation they had taken together during Julia's youth, making it all the more special to her.

The next morning, the first words Jonathan spoke as he woke to Julia's sweet words "time to rise and shine," were "are we going back to Disney World today?"

"No. But today we're going somewhere just as fun. We're taking a short boat ride from our hotel to Universal Studios. And tomorrow we go to Sea World." Those names didn't mean anything to Jonathan, but he was sure that they'd be incredible. Anywhere with Julia as his guide would be fantastic, he knew.

Upon reaching Universal's entrance, Julia attempted to convince Jonathan it would be best to rent a wheelchair. Yesterday took its toll. He never walked so much in one day and, despite his excitement and eagerness to see everything Disney, he needed to rest more frequently than was usual for him. At first, he protested the wheelchair idea because he didn't want to be different from the other guests. But as he debated with Julia, Jonathan noticed numerous other guests already in the Park being pushed in wheel-chairs. *Maybe I wouldn't stand out, after all*, he thought. And she convinced him with a wheelchair they could see, and do, much more, and there would be no need for rest breaks, that is unless she herself needed them.

Standing at the entrance, a man wearing sunglasses and a sporty outfit stopped to speak with Julia.

"Hi, ma'am. Sorry to bother you. I was just wondering if you know where I can purchase express passes?"

"No, I'm sorry. But if you ask one of the people standing over there collecting tickets, I'm sure they can direct you."

"Have we met before?" asked the man as he neared Julia.

"I don't think we have. We were at Disney yesterday, so possibly there?"

"I'm from Los Angeles and a Dean of USC. Could we have met there?"

"No, that's unlikely."

"My name's Garrett, by the way. Happy to make your acquaintance."

"Hi. I'm Julia, and this is Jonathan." Jonathan then felt obligated to meekly wave to him.

"Anyone tell you what a beautiful smile you have? It has brightened my day, for sure."

"Thanks. I was just in the process of getting Jonathan a wheelchair. We haven't been to Universal before, and we have much ground to cover."

"I don't mean to hold you up. Do you want to meet later for lunch? It would be my treat."

"That's mighty kind of you, but I'm not sure of our schedule yet and what time, or where, we'll be eating. But thanks anyway and enjoy the Park."

"Sure. Take care, ma'am. Same to you."

Jonathan smiled as he witnessed the same encounters frequently yesterday at Disney World. Men of all shapes, sizes, and ages would pause to look at Julia. Many of them would go out of their way to speak with her, asking her for directions, saying she looked familiar, or inquiring as to the time, even though, oddly, they wore their own watch. He figured out they found her to be pretty, and she drew attention to herself simply by being herself. He wondered if Julia knew that as well. *Maybe it's that optimism thing*, Jonathan surmised. Noticing this pattern, Jonathan believed himself to be so very privileged this beautiful woman was there for him and only for him. *They can be jealous all they want*, he'd say to himself, and he'd smile with amusement and pride as each new man made an excuse to approach her.

After a full day of seeing the rest of the Park, Julia left the Wizarding World of Harry Potter for last, as she knew it would be the most special for Jonathan. Long before their Florida vacation, Jonathan spoke often of Harry Potter, having seen the first two movies of the series on the TV at St. Peter's. He let her know then that for Halloween he wanted to dress up as Harry. His familiarity with Harry, Ron, Hermione, Dumbledore, Draco, Malfoy, Voldemort, Neville Longbottom, and all things Hogwarts and wizardry, first gave Julia the idea taking Jonathan to this attraction would be his ultimate surprise of the trip. Strolling down the village of Hogsmeade made Jonathan almost believe he was in a Harry Potter movie. Upon tasting Butterbeer sold at the Park in a souvenir cup, Jonathan proclaimed it to be the best drink he ever tasted "in his whole life." He tried on a Harry Potter hat and cape in one of the shops and thrust Harry's wand high in the air, wishing it were Halloween in July. Julia snapped some candid photos of him to enlarge the best one and put it in the 8" by 12" Harry Potter picture frame she would surprise him with at a later date. It would look perfect on his nightstand, she was sure.

Julia was just about to snap a picture of Jonathan out of his wheelchair in front of the model train at Hogsmeade Station when her cell phone rang. It was barely audible, but looking at her iPhone, she recognized the call was coming from St. Peter's. Taking a deep breath, she answered the call.

"Hi, Julia." The man on the other end of the call waited for a response before continuing. "This is Doctor Ingram. I don't mean to frighten you, but your Mom has had a turn for the worse. The next 24 hours are critical. I don't know if she'll make it."

Fighting back her tears, Julia explained to Dr. Ingram she was in Florida with Jonathan on vacation. She wasn't sure what the earliest flight back to Boston was but told him they would be there as soon as possible. Julia asked Dr. Ingram to please keep her updated as she helped Jonathan back into his wheelchair. They raced through the Park to the nearest exit, flying by surprised bystanders, nearly knocking some of them over. Julia had a new mission – to be by her Mom's side and support her struggle to survive.

CHAPTER 23

A Most Important Speech

Julia was on overdrive. She quickly packed her and Jonathan's clothes and possessions, checked out of the hotel, returned the rental car, and boarded the first flight out to Logan. It wasn't until she strapped herself and Jonathan into their airplane seats that Julia reflected on the gravity of Dr. Ingram's voice and her Mother's unknown fate. Having Jonathan by her side and not wanting to alarm him more than he already was, she quickly controlled her emotions and tried her best to be as stoic as possible. Odd, Julia thought, that the last couple of hours were a complete blur. How did they get from having a fabulous and fun time in Hogsmeade to boarding the plane as quickly as they did? The details escaped her, but no matter, they were on their way to being where they needed to be. Jonathan was so frightened for Julia that he rushed as much as he could, skipping his typical rest, to get to the plane for takeoff. Once strapped in, he intentionally remained quiet, held her hand, and placed his head on her shoulder.

"Don't worry, Julia. God is with us, and I'm here for you," is all he whispered to her.

Julia did her best not to think the unthinkable and stay positive. She kept her cell phone on airplane mode and as soon as they landed at Logan and were taxiing to the gate, upon turning off that feature, she saw Dr. Ingram had called her. Julia immediately listened to his voice message.

"Hi, Julia. This is Dr. Ingram again. I promised you I'd keep you updated." Hearing the message, Julia wondered what time it was left, as her phone logged the call at the present time. "I'm so sorry. We did everything we could do to save your Mom. She passed away about thirty-five minutes ago. I wish I had the opportunity to give you this news in person. My sincere condolences."

Julia looked at Jonathan and gave him a huge hug, almost as a lost swimmer fighting to survive would hug a buoy upon finding one and holding on for dear life.

Still in their embrace, Julia told Jonathan, "She's gone."

"I know, just keep holding me."

"My dear Jonathan, God put you in my life just as I was to experience my biggest loss. You know, as a little girl, younger than you are, I'd sometimes have nightmares about losing my Mom, nightmares of this very moment. She was all I had at the time, and I would wake up in a sweat, wondering what would happen to me if I lost her. I remember constantly thinking to myself, how could I go on living without my Mom by my side."

Julia paused as she became misty-eyed and then bravely continued. "Now that time has arrived, and I know, despite our tremendous loss, we'll be fine. Grandma always would say, 'God wouldn't give us more than we can handle.' I trust all will be as it should be, and now we have our guardian angel in Heaven watching over us."

Thinking of her wedding that was no longer to be, Julia continued, "I know she tried her hardest to survive, and so looked forward to attending my wedding, walking me down the aisle, and celebrating with me. I know my Mom would have loved that day. And I appreciate how much she longed to share the rest of her life with me, you, and her future grandchildren, and tried her best to make that happen. But some things are not meant to be, despite our hopes, prayers, and dreams."

It was then Julia realized for the first time the need to rush to be by her Mom's side suddenly ended. Now instead of wedding plans, she needed to notify her Mom's few surviving relatives and many friends and arrange the funeral plans. How was it, Julia wondered, that Mary Ann's impending death was known for such a long time, yet when the news finally came, she nevertheless was so shocked by it? *I guess we never are prepared to lose a loved one, especially someone as amazing as Mom*, Julia told herself.

Reflecting on her Mom's life, Julia was struck by the unfairness of Mary Ann's illness and how it didn't differentiate who it was to attack. It hurt Julia that her Mother, who for more than a half-century was so loving and giving, had to endure the extreme pain and the many losses that came with her incurable disease. The double mastectomy robbed her of femininity, and hair loss affected her appearance. But the most significant loss of all was of life itself and the incremental difficulties and intrusions that led to an abrupt end. Julia's children to come would now be deprived of the opportunity to share their lives directly with their Grandmother. Mary Ann's absences from the future births, baptisms, communions, graduations, birthdays, weddings, holidays, and other special occasions, were a loss not only for Mary Ann and herself but also for the rest of their family and loved ones. Such circumstances gave Julia a heightened awareness that she would need to represent Mary Ann as best as possible and be a substitute teacher of her lessons and wisdom. She prayed for the ability to fill that role well for the benefit of Jonathan and future generations.

As soon as they arrived home, Julia wrote an obituary for her Mom, and *The Globe* displayed it prominently on each of the following three days. Next, she wrote a eulogy to deliver at the funeral. Julia had never given a eulogy before and was unsure if she could finish delivering it without getting overly emotional. But Julia brushed those fears aside and knew it had to be presented as such a well-deserved tribute. She felt an obligation to pay respect in her own words.

All the planning for a funeral and burial condensed into a few short days helped keep Julia's mind away from the sadness and despair that could have otherwise overwhelmed her. Instead, she focused on celebrating what Mary Ann has meant to her and so many others. The flower arrangements were predominantly red roses with white baby's breath. The final song to end the funeral service, *You'll Never Know*, had the perfect lyrics for how she felt.

Julia purchased Jonathan's first suit, patent leather shoes, dress shirt, and tie. He looked incredibly well put together, and, in an unfamiliar way, Julia drew energy by his presence. Maintaining a focus on Jonathan helped her through the most trying moment of her life. She was proud that

Jonathan felt blessed by having Mary Ann as his Grandma, even for such a short time, and how that experience changed his life and benefitted him.

Julia had the same numbness she experienced on the flight from Orlando to Boston a few days before, during the preparation for her Mother's funeral. With all the funeral arrangements being finalized, she devoted her energies to finishing the eulogy. Given her line of work, Julia wrote many articles and news stories of crucial topics of the day, yet none came close in importance to choosing the best words now to summarize her Mother's life and legacy.

While in a daze-like fog the days before, the morning of the funeral, Julia awoke with such clarity and a sense of purpose. Her mission that day was to celebrate Mary Ann's life and share her goodness. She barely heard the priest's words inviting her to the podium at the head of the altar, surrounded by tributes of red hearts and flowers. It was the same altar that would have been used for her wedding, had it happened. Taking a deep breath and canvassing the crowd, Julia began:

"If the measure of a great person is how deeply they touch and affect others' lives, then my Mother truly was a great person. Her warmth and kindness were obvious to anyone she met. My Mom was the closest thing to human sunshine I know of. The glow of her smile, the twinkle in her eyes, and the warmth of her heart gave us all great comfort and joy.

The essence of my Mother was an open-heartedness that greeted everyone who walked through our door with a big hug and a welcoming smile. She was a mother to anyone who came into our home.

Loving, caring, giving, gentle, warm, uplifting, brave, elegant, and beautiful – both inside and out – she epitomized those words.

My Mom was so much more than my Mother; she was my teacher and friend as well. She taught me so many things about life:

to be caring and loving,
to be respectful of others,

to be myself,
to look on the bright side of things,
to love life and to be happy,
to enjoy and celebrate the warmth, comfort, and fun of a close family, and
to have an undying love for one another.

For whatever reason, she also was chosen to teach me about death – about dying with dignity and grace, and all the while never, never feeling sorry for herself. Not once did I hear her ask, 'why me?' or complain about her situation. More than that, she was a calming influence in dealing with her illness and her impending passing.

While her body was weakening, her spirit was as alive and healthy as ever. She always made home such a warm, welcoming place to be. And no time of the year was a better time than at Christmas when God, family, and giving came into sharpest focus. Each year she would decorate the house and the Christmas tree, bake a tableful of breads and cookies, place mistletoe in the foyer, and the nativity in the living room. And the family would gather together, we would exchange gifts, and she would cook and serve a wonderful meal, Christmas music would fill the air, friends would then arrive, and we would finish the day playing games and having a great time.

And no time of the year was more important to me than on Christmas eve when my Mom and I would come to this church for midnight mass. We would sit right over there [Julia pointed] and thank God for all He has given us. And the 'all He has given us' had nothing to do with possessions or money, but instead everything to do with our family and the many, many memorable moments we shared.

One of the things I heard her often say was, 'everything happens for a reason.' It gave me strength and comfort. Mom also gave me great faith in God's will. I may not understand why someone with such beauty would be taken from our lives so early, but I know it happened for a reason.

Mom's life truly was a gift from God. And gifts of love don't end; they get passed on. Her grandmother gave it to her mother, her mother gave it to her, and she gave it to me. And I, in turn, will pass it on to those who follow me.

While my Mom's life ended early, I can only be extremely grateful for the miracle that was my Mother. I'll take a few minutes of magnificent over a lifetime of mediocrity. And I had many years of magnificent. Without Mom, life will never again seem so simple and uncomplicated, but she has shown me the way, and her great example will forever guide me.

I'd like to share with you a poem which is very special to me. I read it many years ago in a newspaper, cut it out, and have kept it ever since. It reads:

'This day comes with sad regret,
it brings a day we will never forget.
The blow was hard, the shock severe,
we never thought your death so near.
It's lonely here without you,
we miss you more each day.
Life is not the same to us
since you've been called away.
The joys we shared together
are the memories we hold dear.
And the happiness you gave us
keeps you forever near.
To your resting place we visit
and place the flowers with care.
But no one knows the heartache
when we turn and leave you there.
Please God, forgive our silent tears,

our secret wish that you were here.
Others have sorrows, this we know,
but you were ours, and we loved you so.'

I'd like to close with some words of wisdom my Mom gave me recently upon the passing of a special young girl named Caren. She said, 'this is not a time for tears and sorrow, rather this is a time for smiles, thanks, and wonderful memories.'

I also want to recognize a special person in attendance today. His name is Jonathan, and he adopted my Mom as his Grandmother shortly before her passing. Jonathan brought her such joy, love, and happiness, and he fulfilled her dream of being a grandmother. I'm comforted by the fact that she finally had that opportunity and experienced the affection of a grandchild just before her body left us. She taught him so much in so little time; it's truly remarkable. And they formed an eternal bond that has blessed him and will continue to bless him.

When you think of my Mom, I hope you feel deeply touched and smile as I do and will continue to do.

Mom, I am so proud of you and honored and privileged to have been a part of your life and family.

Thank you from the bottom of my heart for all you have given me and taught me.

May you rest in peace with the Lord, your parents, and grandparents, and those others of our family who have gone before you, and may you continue to watch over and guide us.

I love you so much, sweetheart!!!"

Julia was weak in her knees and almost faint from the energy it took to present the eulogy. She delivered her message as Mary Ann would have wanted. Her chosen words were a celebration of a life well-lived and a tribute to an amazing woman.

As Julia sat down next to Jonathan, he put his hand in hers, and he said,

"You just put into words the Grandma I knew. Thanks for including me in your speech."

While Julia was presenting her eulogy, she noticed Ben entered the church and sat in the last pew. She was both surprised to see him and comforted by his presence. It was the first time they saw each other since the night they parted ways.

At the end of the funeral mass, Ben made a point of greeting Julia and paying his respects and condolences.

"Julia, I want you to know how sorry I am. I saw the obituary a couple of days ago, and I knew I had to be here. Your Mom was an extraordinary lady. I loved her very much, and I know how much we all will miss her."

"Thanks, Ben," Julia said softly. "It means a lot to me."

"So, you must be Jonathan," Ben remarked upon seeing a young man standing next to Julia. "I've heard so much about you."

"Oh, I'm sorry. Ben, this is Jonathan and Jonathan, this is Ben." Julia had not mentioned to Jonathan the wedding was called off because she didn't want him to associate them living together with that occurrence. She prayed that Jonathan would not mention the wedding that was no longer to be, not here and now. Luckily, Jonathan simply said, "I've heard a lot about you, too. All good."

"Well, I do hope to see you again soon, Jonathan. Bye, Julia. You take care of yourself."

Julia went to greet the others who came to pay their respects, including Ms. Thornburg, numerous of her co-workers, and some distant relatives whom Julia hadn't heard from, or seen, in many years. They asked her why Mary Ann's casket wasn't open, as they expressed their desire to see her one last time. Julia replied that her Mother always wanted a closed casket, believing it easiest on everyone that way. *If you wanted to see her one last time, wouldn't it have been better to have seen her when she was alive instead of after she passed,* Julia thought but dared not say. Mary Ann often stressed there was no need to go to cemeteries to pay respects to lost love ones. "Pay your respects and bring me flowers when I'm alive so I can enjoy them, not when I'm gone," she'd frequently tell Julia.

As Julia stepped outside the church, she was approached by a gaunt, young man. He wore a suit that looked to be two sizes too big for him.

"Hi, Julia. I know we haven't previously met. I'm Neb. I am a patient at St. Peter's, and my room is on the same floor as Mary Ann's was."

"Yes, I know. My Mom told me how much she enjoyed meeting with you."

"I knew I had to be here when I entered her room to have one of our chats, and her bed was empty and freshly made. I learned of her passing, and I'm heartbroken. 'Grant me a release,' I demanded of my doctors so I could leave the hospital and be here today. I insisted on it, and I wouldn't have missed paying my respects. Your mom did not need to tell me how much she loved you. I could see it in her eyes and face whenever she spoke about you, which was often. I so admire a parent's unconditional love that I never had but wished that I did. She became like a parent to me and was truly concerned about my well-being."

Neb then took a nervous sigh as his eyes began to tear.

"I am terminally ill with cancer, as well. Even though I was a total stranger to her, your Mom gave me the hope and determination to fight on as best I can. She tried to convert me to Christianity and abandon my agnostic beliefs. That hasn't happened yet, but she did give me tremendous inspiration and encouragement. I'll miss her each day I have left. I'm very thankful I got the opportunity to know her as well as I have. She is a special person in my life, and I will never forget her."

Julia told Neb how much his kind words and attending the funeral meant to her. She hugged him and wished him well. "May God bless you, Neb."

In addition to the eulogy, Julia had a unique way of paying respects to Mary Ann. Throughout her adult life, Julia collected a listing of songs with lyrics that were perfect to describe what her Mom meant to her. As the years passed, her list of songs continued to grow. Typing all the lyrics to those songs and explaining their meaning in the context of her Mother's love and life, and making playlists of them to share with others, Julia created her own special tribute. The songs included: *A Dream With Your Name On It* (Jennifer Holiday), *Butterfly Kisses* (Bob Carlisle), *Dreams*

To Dream (Linda Ronstadt), *You're The Best Thing That's Ever Happened To Me* (Gladys Knight), *When I See You Smile* (Bad English), *All That Matters* (Cliff Richard), *The Love I Found In You* (Jim Brickman), *What A Wonderful World* (Eva Cassidy), *You Are So Beautiful* (Joe Cocker), *May I Have This Dance?* (Scott Kippayne), *Wind Beneath Your Wings* (Sheena Easton), *Hero* (Enrique Iglesias), *Without You* (Jim Brickman and Tara McLean), *If We Hold On Together* (Diana Ross), *My Sweet Lady* (Cliff De Young), *Time to Say Goodbye* (Sara Brightman and Andrea Bocelli), *Remember Me* (Diana Ross), *To Where You Are* (Josh Grobin), *I Don't Know How To Say Goodbye* (Linda Eder), *You're Still You* (Josh Grobin), *When The World Was Mine* (Ronan Keating), *This Is Your Song* (Ronan Keating), *This Is Your Time* (Michael W. Smith), *Memories* (Elvis Presley), *Wanting Memories* (Sweet Honey In The Rock), *She Was There* (David Sills), *There You'll Be* (Faith Hill), *God Loves You* (Jaci Velasquez), *Goon Too Soon* (Michael Jackson), *Love Never Dies* (Patti LaBelle), *Unforgettable* (Nat King Cole and Natalie Cole) and *You'll Never Know* (Barbra Streisand).

Whenever Julia wanted her Mom just a little closer, she could always play those songs and be reminded of the incredible power of music to express her love and feelings for Mary Ann. And when she happened to hear one of them on the radio in her car, in a store, or elsewhere, she felt her Mother's presence and a huge smile naturally appeared on her face. "I love you too," she would say out loud.

CHAPTER 24

Momisms and Forgiveness

When they returned home after the funeral, Jonathan asked Julia why that was the first time he met Ben, and she and Ben spent no time together. "I hope it's not because of me. That would kill me to hurt you!"

"Thanks, Jonathan, but don't think such thoughts. Remember, only positive thinking while you live here."

"Yeah, I remember. Ben does not look at all like I was expecting. He is much better looking than I thought he would be. That's positive, right?"

"You know, Jonathan, thinking about it further, I don't mean to cut off your negative thoughts. I want you to discuss anything with me, positive or negative, and I welcome it. I do hope you share with me what you are feeling. So, let's change our promise. Our new promise should be always to be honest with each other. Is that okay with you?"

"That works for me."

"This is my first time acting as a mom, so I have to learn as I go. Thanks for your patience."

In the days that followed, Julia was left with the task of cleaning out her Mom's house, which was to be sold. In doing so, she found pictures of her father she had never seen before kept in a box in the attic.

Julia always respected her Mom for how she spoke of her father, even though the man abandoned his family and left Mary Ann poor and destitute, and a jobless, single parent. Not once did her Mom say a bad word about him, as Julia was a child of that man and shared his blood and genes.

Julia believed that he was someone who deserved only contempt for what he did to his family, yet by the simple fact of being Julia's father, Mary Ann accorded him her full respect.

Looking at her father's pictures, Julia tried to imagine the time when her parents were in love with each other and were looking forward to starting their new family. She often dreamed of what it would have been like if she had a father who was there for her. Julia wondered what became of him and if he had a good life. She also questioned whether he ever thought of her and, if so, what those thoughts were. When Julia was a child, the hurt she felt from his absence caused her essentially to erase him from her mind, just the way he seemed to erase her from his. But with the distance of time and the hurt subsided, she permitted herself to contemplate the man she never quite knew.

Julia also discovered numerous love letters written by her grandparents when Marie temporarily lived in Pennsylvania, and Mickey resided in New York, all neatly wrapped together in a rubber band. While she knew them well, she was excited to read the words they chose so many years ago to express their love for each other during a period when circumstances dictated their separation. Had that disunion not happened, Julia appreciated this window on their lives, in their own words, would not have existed. It would allow her to bring their past alive simply by some ink on pieces of paper they had the foresight to save, and Mary Ann had the wisdom to store and preserve so Julia could hold them in her hands today.

With her Mom now gone, and Jonathan no longer able to learn life lessons directly from Mary Ann, Julia often spoke of her in his presence. "She taught me so much by her many sayings, which I called 'Momisms.' One of the things she would frequently say is 'Do onto others as you would have them do onto you.' This is referred to as 'the Golden Rule' of the Bible. It means you should treat people the way you want them to treat you. If you want to be treated with respect, you need to be respectful of others. It allows us to understand and see things through their eyes. We wouldn't be mean or hurtful to a person if we could picture ourselves being that person and 'walk in their shoes.' It is similar to another of her sayings, 'What goes around comes around,' which means if you freely give goodness to others, you are more likely to receive it back, or it could be the opposite. Very often we're unaware of it, but we all give off an energy which says a lot about who we are."

"I know what you mean, Julia. I first time I met Grandma she gave me a couple of winks. They so touched me. I didn't know her at all, yet I felt like I totally knew her."

"I'm glad you experienced that. I was so fortunate to be blessed by my Mom's winks my whole life. No matter how miserable my day was going, no matter if I was sick or down, one of her winks was all I needed to brighten my day and make me better. It was her signature gesture that so represented her great spirit and who she was. And despite losing her health, as you know, she never lost her wink."

After a slight pause, Julia continued, "Another thing I will never forget, as I grew older and started to drive, whenever I would leave my Mom she would, without fail, be waiting at the door to see me off and wave her goodbye just before we parted. She did that as well when I was young, and I would leave the house to walk to school. It showed me how important I was to her. It's never easy for a loving parent when their child leaves them, but, of course, it's necessary. It is the little things, such as a wave, that may seem so insignificant at the time but gain importance with their absence in our lives, which we will never forget. As I drove away from her house for the last time, I looked back, almost expecting to see my Mom at her door but knowing that could not be. Nevertheless, I smiled as I thought of her wave and her great love for me."

Given Jonathan's reaction to Caren's death and his sense of guilt he still carried with him, Julia believed Jonathan could benefit greatly by learning how to forgive himself. She shared with him an unforgettable mass she attended many years ago. Halfway through the priest's sermon on forgiveness, the priest asked everyone in church that morning for a simple favor.

"He said, 'Ready? Every one of you will make a fist with your right hand. Squeeze your fist as tightly as you possibly can for twenty seconds. Keep trying to squeeze your fist tighter and tighter, even if it hurts. I will count to twenty. When I say the word twenty, fully release your fist.' The priest then finished his count down, 'twenty, now release.' He explained, 'sometimes in life, we encounter things that make us upset with others, even those we love the most. We let our anger take hold of us and say, or do, things we did not intend to say, or do, to hurt the other person. When we released our fists, that is a physical representation of forgiving the person with whom we are angry. Forgiveness benefits not only that person but, perhaps most importantly, yourself. If you can forgive someone who has wronged you or forgive yourself in certain circumstances, you'll feel much better and relieved. If you exercise that power often and freely, you will benefit tremendously from it. Let the other person know how they hurt you but then also let them know you fully forgive them. If you model forgiveness to others, as God wants you to do, they will more likely be forgiving toward you. The simple act of forgiveness can break the cycle of negative feelings and lead to healing and repair. Try it, and practice it, often throughout your life,' he said."

"It was a straightforward message, Jonathan, but one of the most powerful ones I have learned in my life. My Mom would often say, 'Find peace and happiness within yourself, and others will find them in you as well.' One of the ways you find peace and happiness is in forgiveness."

Julia then tried to relate this lesson specifically to Jonathan.

"Caren's death is upsetting. Part of the reason is that you didn't tell her how you truly felt about her before she died. If you had the chance for a do-over, you would certainly let her know that now. But don't blame yourself – forgive yourself. None of us is perfect. We all make mistakes in life. I have made many, many mistakes, but I try to learn something from each of them. If we can learn from our mistakes, that's how we become closer to being the best that we can be."

Julia hoped and trusted her Mother's teachings would help Jonathan. In that way, she thought, her Mom would continue to do great things even though she no longer physically was present.

"Okay, Jonathan, here goes. Put up your right hand, make a fist, I'm going to count to twenty, and squeeze your fist really, really tightly." Then Julia modeled the fist lesson to help release his sense of guilt.

CHAPTER 25

The Mysterious Boxes

Julia kept a few of Mary Ann's former possessions in a special place in her closet. It was comforting for Julia each morning as she selected clothes to wear for that day to glance over and feel blessed by Mary Ann simply gazing at her former possessions.

One morning when Julia was in her closet, a clear plastic bag fell from the nearby shelf. Julia knew the bag well. One of the nurses had given it to her after her Mom had passed. It was filled with Mary Ann's clothes, jewelry, pocketbook, car keys, and other personal items. As she went to place the fallen objects back in the bag, she saw a box that was still there, previously hidden by the fallen material.

Julia promptly removed the box to get a better view. It was square, brilliantly gold, with the letters "MA," in a rose gold etched on top, which she figured was short for "Mary Ann." She had never seen it before which Julia thought was odd because she knew well all her Mom's belongings. As Julia moved to the bedroom to get a better look, the box suddenly sparkled from the sunshine streaming through the window. The sides were etched with a solid line, similar in coloring to the lettering's rose gold on top of the box. Julia shook it but heard nothing. It had little weight, and she wondered if it was empty.

Julia spent the next five minutes trying to open the box. After her last attempt failed, she returned it to the closet, sure it wouldn't be too long before her next try. Although Julia became busy with chores that morning, her thoughts continually returned to the box. When she had the opportunity in the early afternoon, Julia called the hospital and was informed that nurse Ruth packed the bag shortly after her Mom had passed. As it was Ruth's day off, Julia couldn't speak with her until tomorrow.

Upon arriving home later that day, Julia headed straight to the box, as if guided to it. This time, however, she got a screwdriver and a small hammer from the junk drawer. She carefully aligned the screwdriver to the edge of the line surrounding the box and lightly tapped it with the hammer. After each unsuccessful try, Julia slightly increased the force of her strike until there was a slight separation of the two sides delineated by the rose gold line. She repeated the process on the other side of the box. Finally, the two sides fully separated, and the top popped off. *Wow, that was not made easy*, Julia thought.

Somewhat disappointed, Julia removed a smaller box that looked identical to the larger outer box that had encased it. However, six small dials with the numbers 0 through 9 on each dial presented a lock on top. Upon further examination, Julia discovered a type-written one line message taped to the bottom of the second box. It read, "MA's favorite number x3." That clue was an easy one for Julia, as she knew her Mom's favorite number was "35," which was the number of the house where Mary Ann lived for most of her life. Upon dialing "353535", the top separated off the second box. Julia felt her heart race removing its contents. On the top was an old photograph of her Mom in the middle, and on either side of Mary Ann were herself and Tommy as young kids. All three of them were hugging each other and looked particularly happy. Underneath the photograph was a letter, folded several times to fit in the box. Julia's hands trembled as she unfolded it. She immediately knew it was from her father, as it began, "Dear Precious." Julia forgot his nickname for her until she saw the handwritten letter all these many years later. It reads:

"Dear Precious,
Let me start by apologizing that I disappeared without notice and without having the chance personally to say goodbye. I'm sorry I hurt my family, but I left so that I could best protect you. I needed

to work undercover for the US Government, and there was a risk involved to which I could not subject you or your Mom. To mitigate that risk, please understand I needed to disappear.

Over the years, I kept tabs on you and your Mother from a distance. I became aware that she was terminally ill and knew her declining health effectively eliminated the risk of my reappearing at the end of her life. Her illness gave me the perfect opportunity to be with her one last time. But I needed to do it in such a way to best protect you, by my avoiding contact and slipping the outer box into her clothes that I know you will be given by St. Peter's.

As I am writing this, I am sitting on your Mom's hospital bed. Your Mom and I had a good cry, and she told me words I longed for her to say – that she never gave up on me and continued to love me throughout the years. I told her how much I loved her too, and believe my brief visit brought long overdue closure and peace. She informed me as to what an amazing lady you have become and about Jonathan. I am extremely happy because I understand you are. Her last words, almost in a whisper, were 'I tried.' And it was apparent to me how hard she tried – to overcome her illness, be there for you, meet her future grandchildren someday, and share directly in their lives. She certainly gave it her all. Your Mom has weakened, slipped into unconsciousness, and I know the remaining time is limited. I will be leaving soon, but I couldn't disappear again without taking this opportunity to sincerely apologize, tell you why I had left, and inform you of your Mom's final moments.

Please burn this letter and dispose of it.

All my best. I'll never stop loving you!!!

Love Forever,

Dad"

Upon finishing the letter, Julia smiled broadly. Her dad's few chosen words instantly erased all the hurt and anger she harbored against him for decades. No longer would she bear the heavy burden of thinking she was an abandoned child of a father without feelings or love for her or her Mom.

Julia was thrilled that her Mother's life ended on such a positive note. "No one deserved it more, Mom," she said as she lit a match to the letter and watched her father's written words disappear in flames and smoke. While Julia would have loved to share this exciting news with Jonathan, she determined it was best for her father's safety, and theirs, to tell no one, and his letter be lost to history but never forgotten. Inhaling the smokey smell of the burnt letter, she thought what picture of her Dad would look best in a frame to place on her fireplace mantel, next to her Mom's picture already there.

CHAPTER 26

The Committee's Decision

Julia knew that without her Mom, life would never be the same again. And she was aware that her reaction to Mary Ann's death would be modeling behavior for Jonathan. She stressed it was essential to get back to a usual routine and feel blessed because, most importantly, that's how his Grandma would want it. "It's perfectly natural to greatly miss loved ones when they are no longer physically with us, but feeling depressed, lonely, and miserable are not the recipe for a prompt recovery," she informed him.

Julia had not yet been permitted to adopt Jonathan. But she realized that wasn't necessary for her to act as a mother should to him. Julia felt even closer to her Mom by functioning as a mother for the first time. Well aware of Mary Ann's many sacrifices for her over the years, Julia now got to experience her sacrifices for Jonathan, which helped her appreciate Mary Ann even more.

Jonathan and Julia did everything together, to the point where she became familiar with the Kardashians. But she didn't want him glued to a TV as his primary source of entertainment and enrichment.

Julia was ever-present to encourage Jonathan to do his best as he experienced new challenges, including riding a bicycle she purchased for him, swimming in their apartment building's pool, and bowling. She recorded his many adventures and played them back for him on their curved TV. "You're a star," Julia would remark, as Jonathan saw himself on the big screen.

The most challenging activity for Jonathan was roller skating. He quickly became frustrated when he attempted to stand on his own but couldn't. Every time he thought he was able to skate, he'd fall. One day he vowed to quit. "That's it. I'm never doing this again. I'm not going to make a fool of myself in front of all these people," he declared. It took much coaching, coaxing, and Julia's choice of the right words to provide him with the courage and determination to try it again the following week. It didn't go well. He fell in a loud thump despite Julia's trying to hold him up. Three kids behind him could not get out of his way, causing each of them to topple over him and each other. At first, they gave Jonathan dirty looks, but when they mixed in taunting, derogatory language, and curse words, they crossed the line. Julia spoke with the kids to get them to settle down. But when they nevertheless persisted, she proceeded directly to management to complain about their inappropriate behavior, and they were expelled from skating for the remainder of the day. The following week they were back and apparently got the message as they ignored Jonathan completely, going out of their way to avoid skating anywhere close to him. Julia told Jonathan, for his part, it was best to avoid negative people and ignore their ignorance. "They likely have been skating years before you were, and they undoubtedly had their share of falls when they began, which they conveniently have forgotten about and, in any event, wouldn't admit in front of their friends," she told him.

While Jonathan was generally familiar with contemporary songs that played almost nonstop from the overhead speakers throughout St. Peter's, it was intended as background noise and typically went unnoticed. Occasionally when he was at the hospital, Jonathan would recognize a song playing through the speakers and hum along. But the music he was exposed to was limited. Julia shared some of her favorite Christian songs, instrumental, classic rock, country, and classical music. Jonathan expressed his love of piano, which was his, as well as Julia's, favorite instrument. She also enjoyed theatre and introduced him to songs from *Les Miserables, Do I Hear A Waltz?, Wicked, Jekyll & Hyde, Pippin,* and many others.

Julia read numerous books to Jonathan, including *Moby Dick, The Adventures of Huckleberry Finn, The Adventures of Tom Sawyer, Treasure*

Island, Charlie and the Chocolate Factory, The Catcher in the Rye, and several of the *Hardy Boys* mysteries, which fascinated him, and, of course, the *Harry Potter* series. In their reading time, Julia did all the reading, Jonathan, all the listening, which suited Jonathan just fine. But she insisted he begin to learn how to read. In going through her Mom's belongings, Julia found a *Dick and Jane* book that had been hers. She patiently taught him to read it.

When she read with Jonathan, Julia often thought of Tommy and his love of books and felt his presence with them. She could picture Tommy's facial expressions at each new adventure and smiled at Jonathan's reaction and anticipation at the turning of each page. When Julia closed a book they finished together, Jonathan would often comment, "I love it so much I wished it didn't end."

Julia reserved Sundays for Bible study. Despite taking a class at her church years ago, she was far from a Bible expert. Julia did have several favorite passages, including Proverbs 3 and Philippians 4, which she read and discussed with Jonathan.

"Trust in the Lord with all your heart; do not depend on your own understanding.

Seek his will in all you do, and he will show you which path to take. . . ."

Proverbs 3, lines 5 and 6.

"Don't worry about anything; instead pray about everything. Tell God what you need and thank him for all he has done. Then you will experience God's peace, which exceeds anything we can understand. His peace will guard your hearts and minds as you live in Jesus Christ.

And now dear brothers and sisters, one final thing. Fix your thoughts on what is true, and honorable, and right, and pure, and lovely, and admirable, think about things that are excellent and worthy of praise. Keep putting into practice all you learned and saw me doing. Then the God of peace will be with you."

Philippians 4, lines 6 – 9.

As Julia and Jonathan settled into an established routine, they grew closer. She quickly learned he had a great sense of humor and loved to laugh. Julia bought him a book of jokes he begged her to read.

Opening the book, Julia began, "What time is it when an elephant sits on your fence?"

"What time?" Jonathan asked in reply.

"Time to get a new fence."

Upon hearing the punchline, Jonathan dropped to the floor having a giggling fit. That happened often as Julia continued to read the book. Julia loved those times, for they showed Jonathan's lighter side and joyousness.

Some of Jonathan's favorite times were spent with Belle. He loved playing with her. In addition to hide and seek, he taught Belle to play fetch and wait patiently for treats. He introduced her to Sammy, Dolin, and Peter, who he was very protective of, and made sure Belle did not attempt to munch on them. When he left the apartment, he remembered to close the door to his bedroom, fearful he might return to find his three amigos became unrecognizable stuffing scattered all over in Belle's attempt to play with them. *Belle has no idea how important they are to me*, he thought. When Jonathan was at home, Belle was his constant companion, and she quickly became more important in his life than any Kardashian.

When they were in public places, Jonathan often took Julia's hand in his. At first, he did so for his protection to avoid getting lost in the vastness of his new world. But as the weeks passed, he held hands with her due to their strong connection and because he was so proud to be by her side.

After their initial thirty-day trial period ended, Julia and Jonathan returned to St. Peter's for their meetings with the Hospital Oversight Management Committee. The purpose of those meetings was so "the powers that be" could assess whether Julia's plan was beneficial to Jonathan and should be permitted to continue to allow for Jonathan's adoption. They attended three meetings, which could also be described as interviews or, at times, interrogations. Two of them were each an hour-long with Julia and Jonathan appearing separately; the third lasted a half-hour, with both of them participating together.

When Julia entered the room for her separate meeting, she could feel her hands become sweaty, given its importance to the Committee's ulti-mate decision. A bright light overhead felt like a spotlight to Julia, focused squarely on her. As the nine Committee members settled into their chairs and began their inquiry, her muscles tightened.

"So, Julia, we understand you would visit Jonathan at St. Peter's fairly regularly when you first met him. Is that correct?"

"Yes, and I very much looked forward to those meetings."

"We understand your Mom also was a patient at St. Peter's. Is that right?"

"Yes, her room was a couple of halls away from Jonathan's."

"Did you ever visit with Jonathan without visiting with your Mother as well? In other words, did you ever come to visit only Jonathan, rather than just stopping by his room after you finished with her visits?"

Julia paused for a few seconds to think of an appropriate response. "Honestly, no. I always visited both of them when I came to the hospital, which was pretty much daily."

"So, to repeat, you never came to visit only with Jonathan?"

"It would have been difficult for me to do that, given my Mom was in the final stages of her life and how close our relationship was."

"Okay, let's move on. You are not married, correct?"

"Yes, that's correct."

"Do you have any relatives who live within a twenty-mile radius of where you live who could assist you with Jonathan?"

"No. I have no siblings, aunts or uncles, or other relatives, unfortu-nately. But I am contemplating hiring a nurse or nurse's aide. And I've taken six months' leave of absence from my job so I will be with Jonathan all the time."

"Yes, for those six months. What happens after that time is finished?"

"I will do whatever is necessary, including requesting additional time from work."

"And, if your boss doesn't grant that request? What then?"

"I will hire someone to be available for Jonathan 24/7, after my rigor-ously interviewing them."

"Do you have any concern your absence from work, and your potential request for additional time off to care for Jonathan, might jeopardize your employment?"

Wow, thought Julia. *I wasn't fully prepared for this hostile questioning.*

"No, none. I will do whatever it takes. If that means losing my job, I am ready for it."

"How long do you think you could support yourself, and Jonathan, without being employed?"

"I have considerable savings and investments and have carefully reviewed my financial situation. I could easily go without pay for a year or more."

"Are you willing to provide the Committee with your most recent bank account and financial statements?"

"Certainly. That is not a problem."

"Does your estimate of a year without a paycheck include the expense of hiring a full-time nurse or nurse's aide?"

"Yes, it does. I have taken all of my known potential expenses into consideration."

"Now, let's turn to a rather unfortunate incident. We were informed on a recent visit with Jonathan you took him outside without hospital staff present, correct?"

Julia straightened herself on her chair as she knew where this line of questioning was leading. "Yes, I asked permission from Ms. Thornburg, and I received it. Jonathan requested to go, and I thought it would be good for him to get fresh air. You know, he is a very inquisitive young man, and I hated to see him every day without much ability to explore outside."

"Isn't it true you helped him get onto the big swing, pushed him, he fell off and landed on his face, and cut his check?"

"Yes, it's true. But you should understand I was with Jonathan the whole time, and I never had him out of my sight. Also, I encouraged him not to go too high and hold on tightly. I want to be honest and transparent with you. I so much want Jonathan to explore and have fun in the process and not be a wallflower who is petrified of taking any risks. I understand that risks are necessary to live and learn, and he would benefit from them, even if they sometimes hurt. I was so deeply sorry that Jonathan experienced pain on that occasion. Luckily, it turned out to be a superficial wound. And I have confidence it won't happen again."

After their questioning, the Committee members permitted Julia a five-minute "closing argument" to support her stated purpose of adopting Jonathan. She told them of Jonathan's pain from losing Caren and how she helped him process death and put it in its proper place of the broader picture of God and His plan. She explained while he had no friends at St. Peter's following Caren's death, he now had Sammy, Dolin, and Peter, as well as Belle, and for a very short while, he had a Grandmother who loved him so. Julia informed them instead of a TV as this primary source of entertainment and education, he now was exploring, experiencing, and excelling in the real world for the first time. And instead of his looking at pictures in the magazines by the login desk at the children's ward, she now was helping him read and comprehend the Bible and taught him how to pray to God. Julia described Jonathan's joy in the chapel and his excitement at each new adventure and how he expressed it by clapping, jumping, and skipping. She let them know of his holding her hand in public places, placing his head on her shoulders, his mid-waist hugs, and of their special hand gesture of saying hello and goodbye to each other. Julia also impressed the Committee by explaining her sacrifices for Jonathan, including limiting her time with Mary Ann so they could go on a vacation, and giving up her wedding to a man she deeply loved and considered her best friend, so that she could properly care for Jonathan. Lastly, Julia explained her belief that their first meeting was not an accident or happenstance but was designed by God's will and grace, and how that motivated her to do what was right. Julia gave a "closing argument" in a short five minutes that would have made a seasoned trial attorney envious of, supported by the conviction of her mission that was so fundamentally important to her, rather than the receipt of a paycheck.

When the Committee gave Jonathan the same opportunity to give his "closing argument" in his separate meeting, he did not need five minutes, only five seconds. Here was this small boy standing before a large, long table with nine unsmiling men of power sitting behind it, all staring at him at the same time and waiting for him to speak. He looked at each of them directly, refusing to look down or away, and he told them his reason why they should permit Julia's adoption of him simply as "Because I love her, and she loves me, and Julia gave me God, Grandma, and optimism."

In their joint meeting with the Committee, Julia and Jonathan needed no words to demonstrate their close relationship. It was evident by the way she held the door open for him, patted his shoulders to calm his nerves, and continually smiled and winked at him as he rocked back and forth. Julia told him before their meetings began that regardless of the Committee's decision, she would be there for him, and no decision by any Committee could deter her in fulfilling God's will.

Upon arriving home, Julia asked Jonathan to join her in the family room. "You know, Jonathan, I am immensely proud of how well you did today. I don't think you could have done better." After a slight pause, she continued. "Remember you asked me, the very first time we were in the chapel, whether I loved you?"

Jonathan shook his head, "yes."

"Well, at the time, I couldn't answer your question fully because I didn't know you well enough. But now I do, and I want to answer your question again. I love you for your happiness and the happiness you give to others. I love you for our smiles and hugs. I love you for your jokes, light-heartedness, and laughter. I love you for your optimism and your positivity. I love you for your thoughtfulness and your kindness. I love you for your new-found faith and how you so freely express it. I love you for being you. So, my Jonathan, I want you to know I do love you, and it would be my honor to be your mom."

As Julia spoke, Jonathan started to sob, which increased with each additional explanation by her as to why she loved him. Having been told for the first time in his life that he was loved meant everything to Jonathan and that Julia spoke those words made them perfect.

Within five days of their meetings, Julia received an envelope from the Committee in the mail. Hoping for the best, she called Jonathan over so they could open it together. When she read the Committee's approval to Jonathan, he picked up Belle and spun around with her in his arms several times, while shouting "Thank you, God." He then gave Julia a tremendous hug that lasted far longer than did his "closing argument."

Julia was now free to adopt Jonathan. With that fantastic news, Jonathan secluded himself in this room for an hour and emerged with an envelope he gave to Julia. It contained his very own hand-created Mother's Day card he proudly presented to her, even though that holiday was many months away. "I know it's not Mother's Day yet, but I couldn't wait for it to come," Jonathan told her. "Having you as my mother, every day should be Mother's Day!"

With the Committee's green light, Jonathan officially would have a mom. There was no doubt in Jonathan's mind he had the best one on the planet.

Julia took Jonathan to a fancy restaurant to celebrate their great news. He wore his only suit and tie, and she wore an elegant dress and high heels, and she arranged her hair in a neat, tight bun.

CHAPTER 27

Weakening

As the warmer weather receded to the Northeast's bitter cold, Jonathan's stamina and energy waned. In late October, Julia gave Jonathan his very own Harry Potter Halloween costume she purchased for him at Universal Studios and had it mailed to her apartment to surprise him. Despite Jonathan's enthusiasm to become Harry and get rewarded with candy for doing so, he could not trick or treat at more than five homes before his energy weakened too much for him to continue. Julia was thankful he had the experience, even if just briefly.

For Thanksgiving, Julia intended to surprise Jonathan by taking him on a trip to New York City to see the Macy's Thanksgiving Day Parade, in person, just as his great-grandparents had done for his Grandmother. This, she knew, would be quite different from the parade at Disney World, and she looked forward to seeing him awestruck when the Santa Claus float arrived before his very eyes, heralding the start of the Christmas season. But given that Jonathan tired much more frequently now, Julia determined it was best to watch it on their curved TV at home, without the maddening crowds. Instead, they munched on kettle corn and enjoyed the warmth of the fire burning in their fireplace as they watched all the festivities. As expected, Jonathan's favorite float was the very last one – the Santa float, with both Mr. and Mrs. Claus, surrounded by reindeer and elves, waving to the crowd, and looking so welcoming and jolly. When Jonathan saw it, he became excited for the coming of Christmas and started to think what he possibly could buy that Julia would love as a gift from her new son.

By the end of November, Jonathan was no longer able to do any physical activities. His days primarily were confined to reading, music, and Bible study. His more sedentary lifestyle caused his muscles to weaken. When Jonathan did leave the apartment, Julia pushed him in a wheelchair, obtained from St. Peter's.

"I feel like an old man in this thing," Jonathan would protest when Julia struggled to lift the heavy chair from her car's trunk and open it for him.

"It's the best way for us to travel. I wish someone would push me around all day," she kidded him.

Jonathan adapted to the wheelchair quickly, given his experience at Universal Studios. He appreciated Caren's aversion to using it, as he disliked having to rely on Julia and his loss of independence and self-sufficiency. He was able to wheel himself in his chair, but for only short distances. Around the apartment, he opted to use crutches, which took some practicing. Jonathan laughed when Belle would bark upon seeing him on his crutches as she didn't know what to make of him.

When Julia pushed him in his wheelchair, Jonathan requested that she avoid rolling him over any nonuniform cracks in the sidewalk or pavement, believing it would bring them bad luck if she did. It was a superstition she tried to honor whenever possible, reminding her of when she was a little girl and would take extra-long steps on the sidewalk around her house to avoid stepping on the cracks in them. Once, when he came upon a sidewalk that contained a curse word written on it, Jonathan had Julia go to the nearest store to buy him chalk to write over it as best he could. He explained he didn't want the little children to see "that" word, and the chance of that happening bothered him.

Visits outside their apartment were now, for the most part, limited to the hospital and church. That Julia needed to run errands from time to time caused an issue to arise between them as to whether she should hire a nurse to watch Jonathan during her short absences from the apartment. He protested vehemently.

"I don't need anyone with me when you're gone. I'm capable of taking care of myself."

"I know. But the doctors told me you need to be around someone who could help you if you experienced problems."

"You're treating me like a young kid. I don't like it."

"Jonathan, I'm only trying to do what's best for you. I understand you feel capable. That's good. But we must also think of your health issues."

"I can't be like Belle, with a leash around my neck. You've got to respect that!"

"I do. But I also respect the doctors' advice as to how best to care for you. You were not with me at the time, and you did not hear them."

"As you know, doctors aren't always right. They don't know everything about me and what I can do on my own."

"Understand, I'm taking this position because I love you, and I want what's best for you."

"Fine, but that doesn't mean you can control everything about me. I need to have a voice too. It's my life, after all, not yours!"

"Let's take a break and pick up our discussion later tonight. In the meantime, think about possible solutions."

Later that evening, Jonathan and Julia persisted in their arguments, failing to convince the other. Jonathan was learning the art of persuasion by reminding Julia he had his alarm pendant, and her errands were close enough she could be home quickly if necessary. He also argued he could call the emergency room at St. Peter's. Ultimately, they reached an agreement that if her time away from him were to be longer than an hour, she would contact St. Peter's to send a nurse for Jonathan. He settled for that compromise and was grateful Julia heard and considered his arguments in reaching an acceptable resolution. She conditioned the agreement on St. Peter's approving of it. Both Julia and Jonathan were grateful when Dr. Sirowski's assistant informed them the hospital would not stand in the way of their mutually acceptable pact.

When Boston was covered with its first snowfall one early December morning, Julia wheeled Jonathan to the rear of their apartment building and had a gentle snowball fight. At Jonathan's request, she built him a snowman complete with button eyes, a carrot nose, and black licorice curved upwards at the ends for his mouth. "Our snowman needs to smile," Jonathan told Julia. He wished to call him "Samson," the Biblical figure, whose great strength led him to destroy a temple, killing thousands of Philistines, which freed the Israelites from the Philistine rule.

"Well, we'll need to give him long hair, then, Jonathan. Samson is famous for drawing his strength from his hair. If it were cut, he would have lost his strength."

Julia disappeared into their apartment building, and shortly thereafter, she emerged with a small mop, a saw, and a knitted cap. She asked Jonathan to help her to saw the wooden mop handle, put the mop on Samson's head and cover the small stump of the former mop handle with the knitted cap. Samson, the snowman, now looked more like Samson, the Biblical figure, if one had only a tremendous imagination. Julia and Jonathan laughed at the sight of their creation made from snow and spare parts.

"I know that I'm getting weaker, but now Samson will help me! From now on, no more haircuts for me. I'll have long hair like Samson, and I'll draw my strength from him," Jonathan proclaimed.

However, knowing Samson the snowman could be gone with one upcoming mild day or buried in some future snowstorm, never to be seen again, Julia added, "Yes, and from God as well."

Getting to Know Ben

One morning in mid-December, Jonathan found Julia's iPhone on the kitchen table. She accidentally left it unlocked and ready to go. Having a cell phone, Jonathan was familiar with switching screens and pulling up the phone's contacts list. Jonathan quickly found the name "Ben Anderson." He was not aware of Ben's last name, but since that was the only "Ben" he saw on the list, he believed he had the right contact information. He was glad Ben's name was an easy one for him to spell. He wrote down the cell phone number with his intention to call Ben soon.

A couple of days later, when Julia was running errands, Jonathan called Ben. He was nervous because he spoke with Ben only once, briefly following his Grandmother's funeral. Jonathan hoped Ben would remember him.

After an initial introduction, Jonathan continued, "I know you and Julia have not seen each other lately. I'm sorry if my move in with her is the reason. I hate to think you may be upset. When I ask her, she doesn't want to discuss it. I think she is not telling me the whole story."

"Why, thanks, Jonathan. I appreciate your concern. Yes, we have not spent much time together of late, as you know. You could say we both have a common trait – being stubborn!"

"I feel terrible, and I would like to make it better."

"Don't worry about it. It's not your fault. Julia and I are adults, and we solely are responsible for what happened between us."

"Ben, I have a special favor to ask you, and that is the reason for my call."

"What is it?"

"I would like you to come over when Julia isn't here and help me with girl issues I'm having. I need to ask you some questions in person about it."

"Did you ask Julia?"

"Not yet, but I want a guy's view. I met a girl who I very much like, and I need to speak to her again. Can you help me?"

"Sure, under one condition. You need to let Julia know I'll be meeting with you."

"No problem. Julia has an appointment with my doctors starting at 6:00 tomorrow night, so that would be a good time for you to come over."

The following evening, Ben met with Jonathan. As soon as Jonathan saw Ben, he rushed over and gave him a waist-high hug, which caught Ben off-guard.

"The last time I saw you was at my Grandma's funeral for only a few seconds. That was the saddest day of my life. I'm still not over it. I feel so sorry for Julia that she has lost her Mom."

"Yes, she was incredibly special to me as well. I had a great relationship with her, and I miss her too."

After a slight pause, Ben then asked Jonathan, "So, tell me, who is this girl you met?"

"Her name is Ali. Julia took me on a trip to Orlando, and I met her at our hotel's pool. Julia told me to speak with her, and finally, I did. She even kissed me goodbye."

"I wasn't aware of your trip. When did you go?"

"It was several months ago. Ali lives in Nebraska, and I've been thinking of her ever since."

"So, you didn't try to reach her before now?"

"No. We've been too busy. Julia is a great mom, and she has filled my days with activities and fun. She does her best to let me forget about my problems and to enjoy things."

"So, how can I help you with Ali?"

"I haven't spoken to her since we returned home from our vacation.

When I was in Orlando, I invited Ali to visit me here in Massachusetts, and she invited me to see her in Nebraska. I want to remind her of me. But the problem is I don't know how to reach her."

"Do you know how to use Facebook?"

"No. What is Facebook?"

"Well, it's an online site. On Facebook, you can type in a name, and with a little information, the chances are you can find that person if they created a profile. I can help you with a search if you want."

"Thanks, Ben."

Ben opened his iPhone to start the search. Since Jonathan didn't know Ali's last name or other useful information, the task was rendered difficult. Jonathan felt embarrassed that he forgot to ask Ali more questions about herself. He then remembered she hadn't asked him for any information about himself. *Maybe that's the reason she didn't reach out to me*, he thought.

After his several online attempts failed, Ben said, "Sorry we couldn't find her. But I'm glad you met someone whom you liked, and you both made a strong connection. That can happen again, you know."

"I'm not good with girls yet. I don't understand them at all and the way they think."

"The trick is to find common ground. Discover things you both like to do or share an interest or passion. Try to be understanding of your differences. Learn from your arguments and mistakes. Always strive to make things better and apologize when you do something wrong."

"Is that what you've done with Julia?"

Ben reflected on their last argument.

"Looking back, I have to admit I could have done a better job. I said some things that hurt her, and I never apologized for them."

"Well, as you said, we could learn from our mistakes, right, Ben?"

Without waiting for a response, Jonathan continued.

"I need to tell you I'm sorry. I was very jealous of you when Julia first told me about you and how much she was looking forward to your wedding day and becoming your wife. Since I love Julia, your relationship with her bothered me. I didn't want to share her with anyone, including you. I guess I didn't understand then that Julia could love both of us at the same time and her love for you had nothing to do with her love for me. I'm glad I figured that out on my own."

"You're a smart young man, Jonathan. I'm not sure I would have realized that at your age."

"You are very lucky. You have so much going for you, Ben, that I will never have. If you don't mind, I need to sit down for a while. My legs are not as strong as they used to be."

"Sure. You know, I started from a humble beginning. I did not have an ideal childhood. I was on the heavy side when I was in junior high and high school, and other kids picked on me. I was bullied at a time when it was viewed as cool. Because of my weight problem and not standing up for myself, none of the girls wanted anything to do with me. I didn't make friends easily."

"Wow, you've come a long way. There's hope for the rest of us then. Right, Ben?"

"There's always hope, and I'm glad you got to experience what some confidence can do for you. I first gained confidence when I went to college and moved away from home. In college, I played sports and started meeting so many new people. I had my first date and first kiss. You can say I was a late bloomer! Law school was a great experience when I studied hard and did well. I lost a lot of weight, and I began to work out regularly. I started believing in myself when nobody else did. Slowly, I felt better about what I could achieve in my life. It didn't come naturally for me, and I worked hard at it."

"Wow, I can't believe that I had my first kiss at a younger age than you. What interests do you and Julia share?"

"Very many. But perhaps most importantly, how much we both look forward to becoming parents and raising kids. I knew without question, and I still do, that fatherhood is my ultimate goal. Maybe because of the difficulties I experienced in my younger days, I look forward to raising my children someday and unlocking their full potential. I know it will be my greatest accomplishment in life when it happens."

"Given how good-looking you both are, I imagine if you had kids with

Julia, your kids would look amazing. And I can tell you better than anyone; Julia is a great mother. She has taught me so much these past few months. I can't imagine my life without her. For the first time, she made me feel good. And that's so different from the hole I dug for myself after my friend, Caren, died."

"I'm sorry to hear that, Jonathan. What do you mean by 'the hole' you 'dug' for yourself?"

"Losing Caren was so hard on me. Have you ever lost anyone you loved, Ben?"

"Yes, unfortunately, several times."

"After Caren died, I had little interest in anything. I didn't want to wake up, eat, or see people other than Julia. My life just kind of stopped. And I didn't know how to move on. At the time, I pictured myself falling into a deeper and deeper hole I could not get out of. And the deeper I fell, the worse it was. I had no idea how to stop falling. My body was squished up, my arms wrapped around my knees. I felt that I was jumping in a pool like a cannonball, except there was no water and nothing surrounding me other than darkness. I kept on going in a downward motion without end. It was very frightening."

"I'm so sorry you experienced that pain," Ben said as he put his hand on Jonathan's shoulder.

"I wasn't acting like myself for weeks. I didn't want to speak with or see anyone or take the covers off from over my head. I just wanted to be left alone, but that made me even sadder. I believed that nobody understood what I was going through. It was the most terrible thing. I felt guilty because I didn't treat Caren as good as I should have. The only thing that stopped my fall was Julia by bringing me here. She saved me. I don't know what I would have done without her."

"A lot of lessons can be learned from your experience."

Jonathan glanced at Ben's face and saw his concerned look. He then continued.

"I thank God for Julia in my life. She's been so kind to me. She even taught me how to pray at the beautiful chapel at St. Peter's. That's my favorite place in the whole world. I owe her so much. I want to do something nice for her, but I don't know how."

"Well, Christmas is coming. Think of something to purchase for her."

"I can't get Julia anything. I have no money and asking her for money to buy her own present is so uncool."

"Here, use this," Ben said as he reached for his wallet and gave Jonathan two fifty-dollar bills.

"Thanks for helping me. Now, I can't wait for Christmas! You know, the first time I met Julia, she wore very sparkly earrings. I want to get her something like that. Sparkly things are made for her." Jonathan was careful to put Ben's money in his pants pocket and not to lose it.

After a brief pause, Jonathan continued, "What's the most important thing that you've learned in your life, Ben?"

"Good question. I'd say never to give up. I've been down several times before but always have found a way to pick myself up, clean myself off, and press forward. And if you really want something, do not take 'no' for an answer. Find a way to make it happen. Be persistent and do your best to achieve your goals."

"What's your number one goal, Ben?"

"Settling down with the right person and starting my family. I'm not getting any younger."

"Can you wait a minute? I have something to give you. I'll be right back."

Jonathan then went into his bedroom, opened the drawer of his night-stand, took out an envelope, and handed it to Ben.

"Here, this is for Julia. Please give it to her for me when the time is right."

"I don't understand."

"Oh, it's not for Christmas. I won't be here forever, and I want to thank her after I'm gone. Please don't tell her about it. Promise?"

"I promise."

"I know I can trust you to do that for me. It's my special gift to my mom, more important than any present I can think of buying for her. And it is our special secret."

"I'll give it to her, Jonathan. You are very thoughtful. But don't think such thoughts. Instead, continue to enjoy your time with Julia. I'm glad you have her."

"So am I, believe me!"

"I have a football in my car. How about I get it, and we have a catch outside?"

"Yeah. Some more firsts. I have never thrown a football before. Now I can be more like Tom Brady! I have seen him on TV many times. He's terrific, you know."

CHAPTER 29

The Shared Miracle of Christmas

A couple of weeks before Christmas, Jonathan pleaded with Julia to take him to the nearby shopping mall. "What do you need at the mall?" she wanted to know.

"I need to get your presents."

At the mall, Jonathan insisted Julia leave him alone to buy her gifts so they would be a surprise. As he was in his wheelchair and had his cell phone and alarm pendant, Julia hesitantly agreed. "Call me if you need anything, and I'll be right over to you," she told him as they parted ways.

Jonathan bought two presents and the most joyous-looking wrapping paper he could find.

Back home, Jonathan was faced with the arduous task of wrapping his gifts for Julia. He never wrapped before and didn't want Julia to do it herself or show him. Instead, he found and watched several YouTube videos instructing how to accomplish it. Armed with this knowledge and believing himself capable, Jonathan spent the next couple of hours trying his best to wrap for the first time. When he'd completed one box and was not happy with the result, he'd rip the paper off it and start all over again, wanting it to be perfect for his new mom. After this happened several times, Jonathan became worried that the large roll of paper he bought was not going to be enough. After his last attempt and given the shortage of remaining paper to try again, Jonathan finally was willing to accept the results of his labor. Looking at the packages, with bumps and being far from neat, or anything that resembled the boxes in the YouTube videos he used as his guide, Jonathan said to himself, *a little messy, but I think mom will be pleased.* Now, with Julia's freshly wrapped gifts secretly hidden under his bed, he couldn't wait for Christmas to arrive. Jonathan tried to picture her face when she opened them.

Julia was not a person who took her holidays lightly. She had a large, designated storage area in the basement of their apartment building that was overflowing with her many decorations. Two weeks before Christmas, when Jonathan awoke from his slumber and stepped outside his bedroom, he couldn't believe his eyes. His mom transformed their apartment into a holiday wonderland. Furniture was moved, pictures were swapped, an unadorned artificial tree was in the living room window for all to see, and the smell of the season (thanks to air fresheners) was in the air. Julia also had a light that created merry red and green patterns all over the ceiling. Jonathan thought it miraculous as to how Julia brought Christmas to their home in such a tangible and cheerful way.

"It's soooo beautiful!!!," he gushed, still rubbing his eyes in amazement.

He went straight over to the carefully placed nativity set and touched the head of baby Jesus, who was warmly wrapped in the manager, being lovingly watched over by a kneeling, praying Mary and a standing Joseph, cane in hand.

"My Jesus," Jonathan said. "Now I know we will be blessed for Christmas."

"It's not complete yet. We have one more thing to purchase before we're ready for the holiday." Later that day, Julia and Jonathan went to a local vendor who sold real trees. They both agreed on the same large pine, took its height and width measurements to confirm it would fit in their apartment, and happily brought home the perfect tree.

With the apartment being fully decorated, there was only one place left for the newest addition – in Jonathan's room, next to Julia's "Christmas Chapel I" painting by Thomas Kinkade. Jonathan was thankful to have the tree close to him, and fall asleep each night, and wake up each morning to the strong scent of real pine that was not produced by man and stuffed in a little container, but instead was created by almighty God.

Later that evening, Julia lit the woodpile waiting in the fireplace to provide its warmth, unpacked the tree ornaments, played classic Christmas songs, and made a sparkling fruit punch. Julia and Jonathan decorated their two trees together, as they both sang along to the holiday music filling the air. When the trees were completed, they flipped on the switches to illuminate the strung bulbs, to Jonathan's delight. The artificial one had large multicolored bulbs that paired by Bluetooth with Julia's iPhone, and with the turn of a dial on her phone, Jonathan could, to his amazement, instantly change the color of each bulb and create different patterns that mesmerized him for hours. The real tree in Jonathan's room had bright white miniature bulbs that alternated coded patterns that Jonathan watched so often he memorized them.

After Julia removed the empty containers that had held her ornaments back to the basement, she entered Jonathan's room and found him fast asleep under his tree, with Sammy, Dolin, and Peter held tightly in his arms. Belle was sleeping on top of them all. Jonathan looked so peaceful and content, the many small white bulbs casting their lights over him, which so pleased Julia she snapped his picture.

Though Julia knew she could not replicate, in quite the same way, the many special memories her Mother created for her, she tried her best to make this season an unforgettable experience for Jonathan. She carried on her Mom's traditions, including reading to Jonathan one of her favorite books, *The Christmas Miracle of Jonathan Toomey* by Susan Wojciechowski. Jonathan was thrilled that his name was in the title. Before Julia could start reading, Jonathan asked her to tell him what it was about.

"It's absolutely one of my favorite books, such a great, uplifting story of a young boy and his mother who become friendly with a grumpy and joyless woodcarver, whom they ask to make for them a nativity set for the holiday. The woodcarver takes a liking to the boy (and his mother), and that relationship transforms his life. It's perfect for Christmas reading," she told Jonathan.

By the time Julia finished reading the book, she and then Jonathan cried at its miraculous ending. Jonathan learned he shared the same name not with the young boy in the story but with the woodcarver himself, who was transformed from being lonely and miserable to jubilant and uplifted.

"I didn't realize books can make you cry from happiness," Jonathan remarked.

Next, Julia experienced another of her Mom's traditions with Jonathan. She placed a DVD into the player, and, munching Italian pastries, they began watching *Ghost of Christmas Past*. Julia explained the show was about a runaway girl who, with the help of a caretaker of an old, unused theater, returns home for the holiday to be with her family.

Before the DVD started to play, Julia said, "The magical part of the video is the incredible music. It's like attending several concerts all rolled into one that combine to create a heartwarming story." During the movie, Jonathan rose and danced to the songs playing, as they both laughed.

The following evenings were filled with other video treats for Jonathan, including *Frosty the Snowman* (which reminded him of their Samson), *Rudolph The Red-Nosed Reindeer*, *The Polar Express*, and *Miracle on 34th Street*, both the original and a remake. Each video was so magical to a young boy who never previously experienced movies like these.

As Christmas neared, Jonathan's excitement built. Julia was quick to remind Jonathan of the holiday's true meaning, which had nothing to do with decorations, trees, Santa, traditions, or gift-giving. "Christmas, most importantly, is about baby Jesus's birth in a manger in Bethlehem. That's what we're celebrating, and makes it so special and unlike anything else," she impressed on him. When Jonathan asked her if they could visit the manger someday, she told him it would be so incredible if they could but it was long gone from the face of the Earth.

"You see, Jonathan, some of the most cherished things you cannot go to visit, touch, or even see, but it's the concept of them, and their meaning to us, that truly are important."

As Christmas Eve came, Julia had two more of her Mom's traditions to share with Jonathan. First, she placed two trays on their kitchen table that had hand-painted on them the words "Cookies for Santa." They then baked cookies together and arranged them on the trays as a snack for Santa and placed carrots next to the trays for his reindeer. Julia would wake early on Christmas morning, check to make sure Jonathan was still asleep, take bites of several cookies, and put them back on the trays, intentionally leaving crumbs behind. Then she would snap a couple of the carrots and place them on the table next to the trays of half-eaten cookies. And with that, she would create irrefutable evidence that every young boy and girl wished for – a visit to their home by the jolly big-bellied man dressed in red, assisted by his able flying mode of transportation.

"I hope he doesn't get stuck in our chimney, Julia; what would we do if he did?"

"Don't worry, Santa has lots and lots of experience with chimneys, and he'll find a way to get all of the presents delivered on time, including yours."

That evening Julia shared her Mother's final tradition – going to midnight mass. She appreciated a late trip to church would be difficult for Jonathan, so she left the choice to him. He chose to go and, indeed, wouldn't have it any other way. They both dressed in their best clothes, and arm-in-arm they entered the church. Jonathan convinced Julia to leave his wheelchair in her car, advising her God would give him the strength to make it on his own, with her support. She could not argue with God's awesome power and a young boy's determination to have a perfect Christmas Eve mass.

Jonathan soaked up every word the priest presented to the congregation and joined, as best he could, every prayer jointly spoken, and every song collectively sung. As his Grandmother suggested to him, he intently watched the others' faces while they sang their praises, and, as she told him, he could feel their shared jubilation and peace, which so enhanced the experience for him.

However, most remarkable to Jonathan was toward the end of the mass, when the priest informed the parishioners that a special guest would be joining them. On cue, all the lights were dimmed, and in the back of the church, Santa walked in. As he slowly and deliberately made his way past the smiling adults and the astounded children, he reached the altar, and with a lone spotlight focused on him, knelt to pray. Jonathan guessed he asked

God to help him in his yearly task of delivering millions of presents world-wide. Upon finishing his prayers, Santa waved a Merry Christmas greeting to all who were lucky enough to attend that special occasion. Jonathan was so overjoyed he got the chance to wave back to him, his bright blue eyes all aglow.

After the mass ended and Julia and Jonathan shared their greetings with others at the church, he fell sound asleep on the car ride back home. Somehow, she found the strength to get him into his wheelchair and bed.

"Merry Christmas, my dear son," Julia whispered to Jonathan, while he was sleeping, as she tucked him in with Sammy, Dolin, and Peter, the soft white lights of the real tree illuminating their four faces, and she kissed his forehead.

Jonathan arose with a start at 5 a.m., having had less than four hours of sleep. He jumped out of bed, grabbed the two gifts hidden for weeks, and placed them gently under the tree of many bright colors in the living room. On his way back to his bedroom, he noticed with glee the physical evidence Santa indeed arrived on time. Jonathan then saw, for the first time, the three presents neatly wrapped under the tree in his bedroom. *How did I not see them when I just past that tree a minute ago*? he wondered. As soon as Jonathan's head hit his pillow, he fell into a deep sleep, content that the day ahead would be extraordinary.

Jonathan woke several hours later to the sound of festive Christmas music playing, a roaring fire in the fireplace, the sweet smell of real pine, and a waiting kiss from his mother. His first thought was that he couldn't wait for Julia to open her gifts.

Over the fireplace was hung a large stocking that bore his name in brilliant, shiny gold letters. It was filled with all kinds of goodies, each individually wrapped, that Jonathan hurriedly opened. Next, Jonathan went into his bedroom to open his presents, waiting for him under the pine tree.

"Merry Christmas, my Jonathan. I hope you like them."

Jonathan's first present from Santa was his picture at Hogsmeade in a Harry Potter frame. The second gift from Santa was a Harry Potter wand that lit up and played music from the Harry Potter films. His first present from his new mom was another creation by Angelo from Disney World that Julia shipped to her apartment as a surprise for him. It contained all the Disney characters he knew, arranged in a circle, smiling, and looking so very happy. *Just like a wreath*, he thought. Julia then directed Jonathan to an envelope lying at the back of the real tree he didn't see before. Opening it, Jonathan recognized Julia's handwriting. She helped him to read it, her voice full of emotion as she did.

"My Dear Jonathan,
I am so excited to spend Christmas together. You are such a treasure in my life, and I love you more than you know. I am very proud of the many accomplishments you have made over the past six months. I am sure God is smiling down on you, along with your Grandmother, and they are proud of you as well.

Keep up your fighting spirit, your quest to learn and grow, and your determination to be the best you can be. Don't let anyone or anything ever bring you down, as you deserve to soar.

Merry Christmas, my sweetheart!
Love always,
Mom

P.S. – I have one more present for you that I'll wheel into your room when we finish reading this letter."

Wiping away his tears, and after giving Julia a hug Jonathan-style, he thanked her "for the kindest words ever spoken to me." He then said, "Let me guess, my final present is a new wheelchair, right?"

Julia arranged to have Jonathan's final gift kept overnight in the large storage room down the hall from their apartment. "Hold the door open, sweetheart, and I will bring it to you."

Julia wheeled into their apartment and Jonathan's bedroom a player piano, one with its own set of hundreds of songs to be played with a press of a button, and the accompanying bench. As they sat together on the bench, Jonathan banged the keys to create his own improvised sounds. He was awestruck when she hit a button, and the words "Christmas Songs" appeared on the small digital screen like magic. She selected "White Christmas," and that very song started to play on the piano keys. It was a heavenly moment for two people who shared a passion for music, particularly from a piano. They both started to sing along to the music as best as they could, and when Jonathan forgot the words, he hummed along, as did Julia. After thanking his mom many times, he excitedly prompted her to open the two presents waiting for her in the living room.

As she gazed down at the bright, joyous wrapping paper, she asked him, "Did you wrap these yourself? How perfect. They're so beautiful; I almost hate to open them."

"But you've got to. How will you know what's inside if you don't?"

"You're so right, my Jonathan," Julia agreed, as she carefully started to unwrap her presents.

Julia's first present was a pair of sparkling, dangling imitation diamond earrings.

"I wish they were real," he explained to her as she gently took them out of their box to try them on. "But I didn't have enough money for real ones."

"They are so real and special to me. I will always treasure them!"

Julia then opened her last present from Jonathan. It was a gold, fine-chained necklace adorned with a cross that bore the image of Jesus and also sparkled brilliantly when the light hit it.

Julia gave Jonathan a hug and kiss, Julia-style. Returning to their new piano, they sampled the other Christmas songs that it could play, and they jovially sang along as Julia wore her sparkling new jewelry.

Later that afternoon, Jonathan asked his mom to visit with a friend, Samson, the snowman. Upon seeing him again, Samson was just how they left him, except his mop hair was tilted to one side. Jonathan walked over, fixed Samson's hair, kissed him on his snowy head, and left him one of the carrots initially intended for the reindeer. "The source of my great strength and magical powers is still standing," he remarked happily.

"This is by far my best Christmas ever! Thanks, mom."

CHAPTER 30

Extreme Sorrow and Tremendous Pride

Shortly after Christmas, Jonathan eagerly shared a secret with Julia.

"You know, mom, I have a final surprise for the holiday season," Jonathan began.

"What, my sweetheart?"

"Remember when we went to the chapel in St. Peter's? It was the day you first told me about Ben, and you were going to marry him."

"Yes," Julia replied, a bit hesitantly.

"When you left me alone there, I told God I didn't want to meet Ben or have anything to do with him since I thought that he wouldn't like me, and I wouldn't like him either." Jonathan paused to catch his breath as he began to share his surprise with Julia.

"Well, I was so wrong. I found Ben's cell number, and I called him. We had a nice talk, and I asked him to meet with me. I remembered what he looked like from Grandma's funeral. We finally got together shortly before Christmas while you were meeting with my doctors. He was the one who gave me the money to buy your Christmas presents. I like Ben now, and we became friends. I do hope to see him again."

"Well, Jonathan. That is a surprise. Thanks for sharing it with me. It's a real sign of maturity to take matters into your own hands and to take action as you have. But, even with all the King's horses and all the King's men, you can't put Humpty Dumpty together again. Only Ben and I can do that. Now, let's focus on celebrating the New Year ahead."

Spending New Year's Eve warm and cozy at home, Jonathan and Julia had a little party to celebrate, as winter continued its New England onslaught. As Jonathan climbed into his bed, he asked Julia, "Guess what I thought?"

"What? Did you make a New Year's resolution?"

"No. I haven't decided on one yet. But what I did think is I'm so lucky I have my illnesses because they brought you to me. If I weren't sick, I wouldn't have been at St. Peter's, and if I weren't at St. Peter's, then we wouldn't have met. Imagine that! I thank God for the time when I first met you every night when I say my prayers."

"Thanks for sharing that with me, my Jonathan. Believe me, me too! Happy New Year, my sweet son."

Julia took Jonathan back to St. Peter's for further evaluation, as he appeared to get weaker and her concern for him grew. Jonathan's doctors informed her there was nothing they could do to strengthen his weakened heart. Julia was thankful he was not in pain, only weak.

By the first week of January, Jonathan was confined to his wheelchair and bed full-time, as he no longer was strong enough to stand on his own. Unable to use his legs, he thought of his great-grandma, Marie. He had a better understanding of how difficult the loss of her legs at the end of her life must have been.

Jonathan realized he was not doing well, as it was apparent by the attention and commotion his visits to the hospital now caused, and his constant shortness of breath, difficulty in speaking, and inability to stand. On the way home in the car from their latest visit to St. Peter's, Jonathan asked his mom what the doctors told her. She felt obligated to let him know the seriousness of his condition without alarming him.

"Your heart is in a weakened state; that's why they want to continue to monitor you and run tests. I know you don't like testing, nobody does, and I'm sorry about that. But you're getting the care you need, and we're lucky St. Peter's is so close to us and is an excellent hospital."

"Did they tell you anything else about me?"

"Yes, you need plenty of rest and need to stay in your wheelchair and bed. You shouldn't overexert yourself."

"Anything else?" Jonathan persisted.

"They will need to monitor you more often, at least twice a week."

Jonathan had to rest before asking his final question.

"Did they tell you when they think I'm going to die?"

Julia knew that to answer Jonathan, she'd have to compromise on her promise always to be honest with each other, given her need to protect him from the truth. Julia took a deep breath and bravely continued, without showing the emotion she hid from him so well.

"Only God knows that, Jonathan. Doctors can think they know God's plan for you, but they don't."

Julia saw no need to tell Jonathan that his final diagnosis was "days to weeks" of his remaining life. Dr. Sirowski informed her personally, "It's highly unlikely he'll live to see February and his next birthday." When she investigated Jonathan's past with Ms. Thornburg's help, Julia learned his birthday was on February 14th.

Following every one of the discouraging visits to St. Peter's in the new year, Julia tried hard not to show Jonathan the gut-wrenching pain she experienced. Jonathan already outlived his expected passing according to Dr. Sirowski's original prognosis, but Julia too could sense the end was near. While they were direct, Jonathan's doctors were preparing her for what soon was to come. They recommended Jonathan be readmitted to St. Peter's, where he would get hospice care and "would be well taken care of." But Julia would have none of it. "It's home where he belongs," she told them, "and it's home where he'll stay until . . . ." Julia could not finish her sentence.

As Jonathan's skin turn yellow and ashen, his movements feeble, and his previously healthy appetite greatly diminished, Julia felt helpless. Her mission now was to make him as comfortable as possible and brighten his spirit. She appreciated, though, his spirit did not need her assistance. Despite his deteriorating physical condition, he remained the happy, inquisitive, high-spirited, and loving young man he was to the end. His heart was giving up, but his spirit never did. During his last few days, Julia would sit with him by the side of his bed and simply hold his hand in hers for hours, as they said little, but nothing needed to be said.

Surrounded by the browning pine tree Jonathan pleaded with Julia remain in his bedroom well after Christmas, their new piano, Belle, Sammy, Dolin, Peter, and Julia, Jonathan held up his right hand with his fingers widely spread, shaking and weak, trying with all his energy to keep his hand held high. Julia then smiled an endearing smile of an incredibly proud mother, held out her right hand, and spread her fingers to meet his and overlap them the best she could. He managed to open his bright blue eyes for the last time and give her one last smile and a squeeze of her hand, and then his heart stopped. Jonathan passed away at 9:35 a.m. on January 19th.

"My beautiful son." Julia leaned over and kissed Jonathan's lips and held him tightly in her arms upon sitting on his bed. She tried not to cry, but the more she tried to hold back her tears, the more they flowed as Julia started rocking back and forth with Jonathan still in her arms. All alone with her son, and with nobody with them for her to be strong for, Julia released all her emotions like never before. She experienced a chill and was cold and shaking despite there being no breeze in the apartment. Julia grabbed a nearby blanket and covered Jonathan's body and herself in it as she continued to hold him tightly and felt the warmth of his body next to hers in their own secluded bubble. Julia didn't want to let go and cried again upon letting his body slip from her grasp. Jonathan was the first person in her life she witnessed dying. As he passed, she felt his presence in the room and his spirit all around her. It provided her a comforting feeling and gave her the strength to make the necessary arrangements.

After Jonathan's body was removed, Julia took down the Christmas ornaments from Jonathan's tree, packed them away, and brought the tree to the rear of the building for trash pickup. She then noticed Samson was no longer standing, having been melted by the warm weather in the last few days. All that remained were a piece of licorice, a half-eaten carrot, three buttons, a knitted cap, and the top of a mop. She picked them all up and returned them to her apartment.

Julia then finalized the funeral arrangements that had been well-planned in advance. *The Globe* prominently displayed Jonathan's obituary for three consecutive days to announce her remarkable child had left us.

It was strange to Julia that while she lived by herself in her apartment for years before Jonathan had joined her there and never once felt lonely, she experienced an extreme loneliness and emptiness now that Jonathan suddenly was gone from her life. She kept Sammy, Dolin, and Peter sitting on his bed as if they were waiting for his return that was not to come.

Julia took it upon herself to give her son a eulogy, as she did for Mary Ann. It was vitally important to honor his memory to the best of her ability. Her emptiness lasted for three days, and then her "Mother" kicked in, and she thought how lucky she was to have met Jonathan, gotten to know him, care for him, teach him, share and explore with him, love him, and be his best friend and mother. It was the greatest honor of her life, and she prayed and thanked God for that opportunity.

It then dawned on Julia, for the first time, that rather than her simply being Jonathan's teacher, Jonathan was her teacher as well. He taught her so many things – how to love unconditionally as a parent, be nonjudgmental, be nurturing, be a mom, and be the best person she could be. Despite all the disabilities and obstacles he had to overcome, challenges that remained foreign and unknown to his more "normal" peers, and because of them, he triumphed throughout his young life and at the end of it.

Being the reporter she was, Julia decided to write an article about the life she shared with a young man who she cared for and she cared deeply for. Julia told a heartfelt story of this incredible person who suddenly and unexpectedly entered her world and had such innocence, faith, and optimism. *The Globe* readily published it in the "Living" section of the paper for all to see.

Julia believed it was her obligation to call Jill and inform her personally of her only child's passing. *She needs to know, and I should be the one who tells her, however difficult that call will be*, she thought. Julia searched online for Jill's cell number but had no luck finding it. *I need to reach her somehow.* Then, she remembered her lunch with Ron at "good 'ole Jim's." She hadn't used her blue purse since that trip, and Julia was sure the napkin containing Ron's cell number would still be there, just as she left it. Upon finding it, she called Ron.

"Hi, Ron. This is Julia, from Massachusetts. Remember me?"

"Sure, how could I forget you! You ready for me to show you Mexia yet?" Ron joked. "It's so nice to hear that Georgian-Northern accent again. What can I do for you, ma'am?"

"I need to speak with Jill, but I can't find her cell number. Would you happen to have it?"

"No, I never call her, but I do run into her from time to time. You know, come to think of it, Jill and I share a mutual acquaintance, and I'm sure she has it. Let me call her, and I'll get right back to you."

Fifteen minutes later, Julia received a call from Ron.

"Well, now you can't say I haven't done anything for you," Ron said, as he shared the ten digits that Julia was relieved to receive.

Upon hearing Ron's last three words, Julia was reminded of one of her favorite songs having the same title from the artist Brendan James. She knew that being a parent, she would have done anything for Jonathan and that he would have done anything for her. She was proud of the unqualified and unconditional love that they shared.

"Remember, Julia, upon our partin', you told me you hoped I followed my big dreams?" Ron continued. "Well, I quit the ranch and now live in Houston. I'm taking business classes at a local college. It's a first step. Not sure where it will lead but know I wouldn't have had the chance if I stayed at the ranch. Thank you for your words of encouragement. They helped me realize I needed to take action and rather quickly, as I ain't getting any younger."

"How wonderful. I'm so happy for you, Ron. Thanks for letting me know. Good luck and may all your dreams come true!" As she ended her call with Ron, Julia reminisced about the brief time they shared, and the promise and potential Ron had. *I do hope he has a wonderful life,* she thought.

Julia wasted no time making the difficult call to Jill. She knew Jill wouldn't recognize her cell number. *She'll be afraid it's a bill collector of some kind, and she won't answer, I'm sure. But I do owe it to her to try and for her to hear the news directly from me.* Julia's call went right to voice mail, and she left the gut-wrenching news and told Jill how sorry she was.

By the time Jonathan's funeral came three days later, Julia was ready to deliver the second eulogy of her life. As with Mary Ann, Jonathan had a closed casket. Jonathan was buried in his only suit, the one he wore to his Grandmother's funeral, and at their celebration dinner upon learning Julia could adopt him. The funeral home allowed her to place some item or items in Jonathan's casket. She chose Sammy, Dolin, and Peter to join him, along with his Harry Potter wand, his Bible, and her original hand-written Christmas letter to him, of which she kept a copy. She left the picture of him at Hogsmeade on his nightstand.

As Julia entered her car to head to the church for her son's funeral, she turned on the radio. The station it was set to started playing the very song she chose, from the many songs offered to her, to be the final song of Jonathan's service, *You Raise Me Up* by Josh Grobin. *What a coincidence,* she thought incredulously. *What are the odds of that happening?* But as she drove to the church and experienced the sun's warmth through her windshield, she no longer believed it to be a coincidence, as she smiled her broad smile and felt extreme serenity and peace.

Once at the church, Julia was amazed at the number of familiar, and the many unfamiliar, people waiting for her arrival. The article she wrote for *The Globe* was widely read, and the story touched many people who did not know Jonathan but wanted to experience firsthand the beauty that was her son. Upon reaching the top of the church stairs, she received a reassuring hug from Ms. Thornburg and the other nurses of St. Peter's.

Julia then noticed two other familiar faces in the crowd, those of Sam and Jill. Sam read Julia's article, forwarded it to Jill digitally, and generously offered to pay for her flight to Boston and her hotel bill to attend her son's funeral. Sam, her eyes bright and shining, came up to Julia and spread her condolences and her goodness that instantly touched Julia's soul, and she was so thankful for Sam's comforting presence.

"I know how difficult this day is for you, but I also realize that everything will be fine with God's love for us," Sam said to Julia.

Following their embrace, Sam left Julia alone as Jill approached so Jonathan's two moms could speak to each other privately.

Jill began, "I was hoping I'd see you again. I read your article. I'm so thankful you filled the role I could not play for Jonathan. You're a special woman, Julia. I'm so happy that Jonathan had you in his life. I still feel much regret, particularly today. But I'm glad to know Jonathan's life ended on such a high note, which would not have been possible without you. I'm sorry for how I treated you back in Texas. I was jealous of you; I must admit. But now, especially after reading your article, I can feel nothing but gratitude toward you."

Julia hugged Jill and thanked her for giving birth to Jonathan, being his original mom, making the difficult and courageous decision of doing what she believed to be best for him, and her kind words. Julia appreciated that if it had not been for that decision more than a decade ago, she would not have had the opportunity to become a part of Jonathan's life, as she did. "If I can ever be helpful to you, in any way, it would be my pleasure," Julia said, ending their heartfelt conversation smiling.

As Julia turned to enter the church, she felt someone tugging at her arm. Turning around, she saw Ben.

"That was an amazing article you wrote. I was so touched and moved by every word. Knowing you, I'm sure you have a eulogy prepared, and I'm looking forward to hearing it, as is everyone else. I'm certain your love of Jonathan will be in every word of it." Then, changing his tone, he asked her a pointed question. "Can I see you afterward? I need to speak with you." Julia thanked Ben for his remarks, and she shook her head affirmatively, still feeling a bit surreal in this environment, on this occasion.

As Julia entered the church, she reached for holy water and made the sign of the cross. The church was overflowing with people, standing room only. For a boy who had no friend but for her, and no connections, this was an extraordinary display of love and compassion, she marveled. As Julia entered, someone in the crowd, upon recognizing Julia's picture from the article, started clapping as if to thank her for the many sacrifices she made for Jonathan. That single clap grew infectious, as everyone in the church, including the priest, stood up and applauded until Julia, astonished and a bit embarrassed by the sudden display of affection, took her seat. She never before received such a warm welcome or so much love from so many people all at the same time. She knew it wouldn't have been possible without having had Jonathan in her life. She looked at the large multicolored stained-glass windows on all sides of her, glanced up toward Heaven, and believed herself remarkably blessed.

When her turn to give her eulogy arrived, she approached the pulpit and crossed her legs, squeezing them tightly together. She heard doing so causes the blood to flow more freely to the brain, so you are less likely to faint even when standing. She never addressed so many people before, was not accustomed to public speaking, and for an instant, grew alarmed and nervous as she felt a tingling sensation in each of her fingers. Then she saw a mental image of her Mother's smiling face, and she was good to go. Julia cleared her throat, took a deep breath, waited a few seconds to canvas the large crowd of people, all eyes on her, and then she began:

"I couldn't let this moment pass without saying a few words about our beloved Jonathan.

When I think of Jonathan, I think of all great things, of sunshine, beauty, love, and warmth.

Jonathan has touched all our lives and made our world a better place. A few weeks before he passed, I wrote Jonathan a note so that my words were tangible for him, and he could look at them whenever he wanted. He kept my note in his nightstand drawer next to his bed. I'd like to read it to you now.

'My dear Jonathan, I love being your mom. You have so much going for you. You have a big heart, are kind, understanding, caring, loving, appreciative, and the list goes on and on. Know you have many great qualities that make me so proud of you!

I think in life, we focus so much on our problems that often we don't see the strengths we possess, and others see in us.

As I've mentioned to you, I promise you I will do everything I can to show you how much I love you, help you when you may need help, and do anything I can to make your life better.

I want great things for you because you so deserve it!!!'

Jonathan's life ended much too early. That is so tragic and leaves us with an unimaginable loss. However, I am comforted by the fact he touched all of us with his life so beautifully, so genuinely, and so deeply. When God gives us a miracle such as Jonathan, it's extremely difficult to lose that. But I say Jonathan does not end here today – he remains a wonderful part of all of us – by having enriched our lives, making us laugh, and sharing himself with all of us so generously. Yes, Jonathan's vibrant flame was extinguished too early.

But I've learned through an amazing woman, my Mom, to appreciate what I did have, my dear and gentle son, and not focus on what I don't have now by his absence. I know I will always miss not being able to be with him physically, have a conversation with him, read him stories and see his reaction to them, witness his smile and hear his laughter, and hold his hand and feel his hugs around my waist.

But with his passing, we move from the physical to the spiritual. As with my Mom, who recently passed, I know he will always be with me, at a different, but no less important, realm. Just as he could always reach for my written words to him in his nightstand draw, I know I can always feel his presence without being able to see him. Jonathan himself taught me this. You see, the very first time we met, he told me he was able to feel my presence with his eyes completely shut and hidden in his sweater because he was so drawn to me. Jonathan explained he could feel, and feel blessed by, my goodness (as he described it), even though I was not visible to him. Now the tables are turned, and I know, without a doubt, my Jonathan's spirit is so alive and so vibrant, he will never leave me, even though his body has. And I feel an overwhelming sense of serenity in that.

Lastly, I take great comfort in knowing, with all my heart and soul, that Jonathan now is at peace in a better place, a place called Heaven, with his Father, and his beautiful Grandmother, where he suffers from no disabilities, and finally is just like everyone else with him there. Indeed, I trust he is with his Grandmother now, smiling at all of us, and he is being, and will continue to be, well taken care of.

I want to thank all of you for being here today; you've come from near and far. It means so much to me, and I will never forget it.

Jonathan, sweetheart, we all love you with all our hearts. Be well. I so look forward to the day when we meet again, and I can hug and kiss you. I love you tons, and I always will. Thank God for Jonathan!

Thank you."

As Julia went to sit back down in her pew, she almost collapsed into it, her strength weakened by her emotions and the words she needed to deliver.

When the funeral service ended, Julia searched for Sam and Jill, and upon meeting up with them, she expressed her gratitude for their being there. So many people leaving the church stopped to speak with Julia, she needed to rush to the cemetery so as not to miss her son's burial. She knew it would be so difficult for her to bear.

CHAPTER 31

A New Beginning

Unlike the crowds at the church, few people followed the hearse to the cemetery, which made the gathering there much more intimate. As Julia said her final goodbye to Jonathan, she knelt by his casket, said a loving prayer for him, and delicately placed a single brilliantly yellow rose on top. As she expected, it was a very emotional experience to watch Jonathan's small casket being lowered into the freshly dug ground.

After the short prayers for the burial, Ms. Thornburg, Sam, Jill, and those few others who attended, each, in turn, said their goodbye to Julia. She was weary and drained. With the priest having left as well, she had a few minutes alone with her son at his final resting place, as her numbness and disbelief overwhelmed her.

Kneeling by Jonathan's gravesite, Julia gently said in a voice that was almost a whisper, "I miss you already, sweetheart. Please know how much I loved sharing my life with you and being your mom. If I had to do it all over again, I wouldn't have done anything differently. I know if God grants me the opportunity to be a mom again, my future children will benefit from the lessons I have learned with you and that you have taught me. We were meant to be together, and even your passing will not fully separate us. I know that your Grandmother is already taking good care of you, as she did for me my entire life. You will forever be my son, and I couldn't be prouder of you and all of your many accomplishments in such a short period. Be well, my dear Jonathan. I so look forward to being with you again!"

After looking up at Heaven and feeling the midday sun's warmth, Julia turned to start her slow walk back to her car. As she headed in that direction, she could make out the figure of a person walking toward her from the nearby hill overlooking the cemetery. Julia waited as his figure grew, and she recognized Ben's face. In all the activities following the church service, she hadn't focused on her promise to meet Ben afterward, and it wasn't clear to her when that would be. Julia suspected Ben waited until everyone else left so they could speak alone. But for their very brief conversation just before she entered the church that morning, she hadn't seen or spoken to him since her Mom's funeral. As he got closer to her, she could see his eyes were red, and he had been crying.

As Ben approached Julia, he looked directly at her and spoke in a soothing voice. "I want you to know how sorry I am for not believing in your mission with Jonathan. I didn't quite understand it when we last spoke. But reading your article and hearing your eulogy, I do now." Ben continued, "You did a remarkably unselfish act. You gave up your plan to marry me to care for a young, dying, and challenged boy who desperately needed you. You generously gave of yourself to him without asking for, or expecting, anything in return. You adopted him and became his mother, so the last six months of his life could open a world to him that, but for you, he would not have known. Again, I pray you accept my deepest apology for not trusting your instincts and faith and seeing and understanding, at the time, your mission for Jonathan."

Julia could tell from the sincerity in Ben's voice, the look on his face, and his chosen words, he now understood her and believed she had made the right decision.

She smiled and then spoke to the man who she once intended to marry. "Thanks for your understanding, Ben. I want you to know despite our not communicating for months, I very much appreciate your attending my Mom's funeral and now Jonathan's. It's been a tough period for me, losing in rapid succession two people who have such incredible influences on my life. While losing them is so difficult, I am blessed they were here for me, as I was for them. I didn't want to lose you in the process, but it appeared I had no other choice, and I did what I needed to do. I know you understand that now, but I needed to say it, so you know I never intended to hurt you in any way."

When Julia finished speaking, a cloud overhead moved on, and the bright sun reappeared. The light from the sun reflected brilliantly off her shiny gold necklace with a cross that contained the image of Jesus upon it that Ben then noticed for the first time. Almost instantaneously, he remarked, "So, that's the necklace Jonathan gave you for Christmas? He told me he wanted to get you something sparkly."

Julia nodded her head "yes" and smiled back at him.

"I have something to share with you. Meeting Jonathan at your Mom's funeral and seeing how the two of you interacted with each other, I was quite impressed. Jonathan called me shortly before Christmas and requested we get together. At our meeting, he asked for, and I provided him advice about girls, and we went outside to throw a football to each other. I got to experience firsthand Jonathan's great spirit. He told me all about the special connection he had with you, what a fantastic mom you were to him, and how grateful he was to have you in his life. That brief meeting helped me better understand and appreciate your story, even before I read your article in *The Globe* or heard your eulogy this morning."

Julia then shared, "I know. Jonathan told me about your meeting. He must have taken some lessons from Maggie, as I am sure he was trying, in his way, to play matchmaker."

Julia told Ben she was happy he got to know Jonathan and better understand their rather unique, or "weird," relationship. She told him it meant a lot to her. Remembering then that it was Ben who gave Jonathan the money to purchase her Christmas presents, she said, "Thanks for what you did. It says a lot about the man who you are."

Ben then helped Julia, still weakened and shaken, to her car and made sure she would be fine to drive by herself. He offered to take her home, but Julia, being the independent person she was, politely declined his offer.

"Well, take good care of yourself. See you, Julia."

As she arrived in her apartment, Julia entered Jonathan's empty room and sat on his freshly made, vacant bed. She picked up and gently kissed his picture on his nightstand. Opening the nightstand draw, she found her note to him and his cell phone. Lifting the phone illuminated its wallpaper, which was a "selfie" of him standing in front of Disney's Festival of Fantasy Parade with a huge smile on his face. She thought of his elation during that parade and how he expressed it so freely by skipping, jumping, and clapping. The angle of the picture made it look as if Jonathan himself was a part of the parade. Thinking of Jonathan being in the parade, instead of merely observing it from afar, made her happy.

Leaving Jonathan's room, Julia sat on her comfy, easy chair as Belle jumped up on her lap to join her. She could sense that Belle was grieving too and experienced a similar loss without Jonathan's physical presence. She reflected on his too-short life and his innocent transparency at expressing how he was feeling. Julia thought how much better things would be if his more "normal" peers and adults had Jonathan's disposition and zest for learning and life. Julia realized how his disabilities and difficulties made him a better person by appreciating, to a heightened degree than others, what little he did have since he took nothing for granted and was thankful for everything. She felt comfort that Jonathan finally had no disabilities and no disadvantages. Julia smiled, thinking how overjoyed Caren was now that her "Jonnie" was with her again and, eventually, of Caren walking down the aisle in a pastel floral print on cloud white wedding gown to join him in a suave tuxedo waiting for her at the altar. Julia fell into a deep sleep as she thought of the beauty and spirit of her son.

The next morning, on Sunday, Julia was awakened by an early call from Ben.

"With all that went on yesterday, I forgot to give you something. It's a note of some sort Jonathan put in an envelope, and he wrote your name on it. The day we met, he gave it to me and asked that I give it to you at the appropriate time. I didn't think of it until I got home yesterday. Anyway, even if I had remembered, I think it better you received it after the funeral."

"Thanks. Being from Jonathan, I know it will be special. Where do you want to meet?"

"Well, Jonathan told me his favorite place is the chapel at St. Peter's. I've never been there before, but I intended to see it, given how important it was to him. Since he left you a special note, I should give it to you in a special place."

"The chapel it is then."

They agreed to meet at noon that day.

Julia intentionally arrived early at the hospital, so she had time to first visit with Ms. Thornburg, the other nurses, and the children of St. Peter's to thank them again personally for their support. She also figured she could assist with putting the children more at ease and seeing, by her example, life continues despite an excruciating loss. She hugged each one of them individually before leaving.

As Julia made her way to the chapel, she stopped by the visitors' window to Jonathan's ward. She closed her eyes and imagined Jonathan on the other side of it, sharing his special greeting with her. She gently placed her right hand, with her fingers wide apart, on the window, holding it there for a short while, as if to draw energy and strength from it.

As Julia entered the chapel, an elderly woman wearing a red scarf was just leaving it. The woman made eye contact with her, smiled, and wished her a blessed day, and Julia did the same in response.

Julia reflected on the peaceful and special times she experienced there with Jonathan and that it was his idea that she teach him to pray there. She then noticed Ben sitting in the first pew, waiting for her arrival. He rose as she approached him, digging into his pocket to reveal Jonathan's envelope. "This is a special delivery for an extraordinary person," he said, handing it to her.

As Julia opened it, her hands shaking, she noticed it was not a note or letter, but rather a drawing. In the center was a large red heart containing the words "I Love You Always. Thanks For Everything Mom." A smaller red heart was on each side of the large heart. On the white background was the sun, with yellow lines drawn in the direction of all three hearts representing the sunshine. Julia smiled as she showed it to Ben, and she started to cry at the innocence of her Jonathan.

"You know, Jonathan was right," Ben began. "This chapel is one of the most serene places I have ever been to. I've visited Notre Dame, St. Paul's, and many other exquisite grand cathedrals of Europe and the rest of the world. Yet, despite their elegance and master craftsmanship, I did not feel as warmly received and at peace as I do here."

Ben then turned to Julia and raised his hand to her cheeks, wiping away her tears.

"Julia, I have to ask you something. I've thought about it a lot, and I always came to the same conclusion. I wasn't happy these past six months. It was difficult for me to stay my distance from you, even though I knew in my heart it was best for you and Jonathan that I do so. I want you back in my life."

Ben then dropped on one knee in front of the altar, looked lovingly at Julia, and pulled a small box out of his coat pocket. He then asked her:

"Will you marry me *again*?"

Ben showed her the same ring that worked its charm the first time he asked Julia that very question without the word "*again*" at the end.

Julia smiled the smile only she could, and instead of answering him, she coyly asked, "You mean to give you a second chance?"

As Ben, still kneeling, shook his head "yes," Julia made a tight fist with her right hand hidden deep inside her jacket. She then quickly counted to twenty, possibly missing some of the numbers, and upon reaching the number twenty, she released her fist. She then dropped to her knees to join Ben on the ground, threw her arms around the man she still very much loved, and then replied with the words he longed for her to say.

"Yes, absolutely!" she gushed.

Julia and Ben embraced each other tightly for several minutes. They then rolled onto their backs, looking up at the chapel's vaulted ceiling and its depiction of Heaven.

As they stood up, straightened out, and brushed themselves off, Ben reached into his inner-most pocket, and out emerged, in his hand, a single white rose.

"I'm sorry, I had this waiting in my pocket to give you, if you, *once again*, accepted my proposal for your hand in matrimony. We got so carried away, I forgot it was even there until we just stood up and I could feel the end of the stem jab my thigh." Turning to Julia, a broad smile on his face still wet from his tears of joy, he asked her, "Julia, will you accept this rose?"

Before she responded to his question, she asked him, "I can't believe it was there. How did it not get crushed just now?"

Then she answered her question before giving him a chance to respond. "No need to answer. Some things we are not meant to know, and we leave those to faith," she said with a twinkle in her eyes, still wet from her tears of joy.

Pausing slightly for maximum effect, she responded with a forced overly-Southern accent, "My dear sir, I would be most honored to accept your rose. You have just made all of my dreams come true."

Dropping her Southern accent, she continued, "Just think, 'Julia Anderson.' I've spoken that name to myself many times before, you know, but now, somehow, with all we've been through, it sounds better to me than it ever did before!"

As they left the chapel, they strolled arm-in-arm, back to their cars, heading into their new lives together. As Ben escorted Julia to her vehicle and held her car door open for her, he whispered:

"Thanks for my second chance. I promise to do my best to be a great husband and never doubt you. I won't blow it again; you can rest assured! And I want you to know I see you, so very clearly now. And I have a new appreciation of all your beauty, and I love you more than ever because of it!"

Julia responded lovingly, "Isn't it amazing, Ben, that just before Jonathan was to suffer his greatest loss, God put me in his life, and just before I was to suffer mine, He put Jonathan in mine. Now, He has done it again, and after losing my Jonathan, He has given you back to me. I am so thankful, and I'm certain we will have a remarkable life together!"

Ben then embraced her with his big bear hug, kissed her passionately, and called back to her as he headed to his car, "Meet you at home, sweetheart."

As they drove away from St. Peter's in the direction of Julia's apartment, Julia looked up at the shining sun, winked, and said out loud, "Mom, you are so right; everything does happen for a reason! I love you tons too, Mom!"

Acknowledgments

I would like to thank especially my Mom for continuing to inspire and amaze me during all these many years, for the power of your faith, and for being the best you could be. You brighten the world and make it such a beautiful place. I would also like to thank my Dad, Edmund, for your lifelong sacrifices for our family and the many happy, loving years you gave to Mom and the rest of us.

A special thanks also to my Grandparents, Marie and Mickey Picarella, for creating, nurturing, and uplifting your precious daughter and for giving so much of yourselves to everyone else. You forever will be my role model as to how a couple should love and support each other.

This acknowledgment would not be complete without a special thank you to my five sons, Michael, Brendan, Grant, Garrett, and Dean. Beginning in my teen years, I would watch with envy as fathers would play with their children on playgrounds, put them on their shoulders walking the beach, hold them in their arms when they achieved a new milestone, play sports with, and nurture and support, them. As long as I can remember, whenever anyone asked me what I wanted to be when I grew up, my response was "a father." There is nothing quite like it. Being a parent is an incredible honor, and my most important and lasting achievements will be my raising and sharing life with each of you. To put it simply, you are so amazing in your own unique way, making me so proud. Also, I want to thank you for imagining and describing, at my prompting without telling you the context of this novel, what your "Portofino" would be like, which I used in Chapter

22. I also want to acknowledge your mom, Alecia, for going through the journey with me and caring so deeply for our family's welfare.

Next up are my siblings, Ed, Mary Ann, and Bob, and their respective spouses and children. We have been through and shared so much over the years, and we will always have our special bond despite our geographic separation. I know you are as proud of your children, Nicholas, Steven, Dani, Mariel, and Kaci, as I am of mine. And a special thank you to (i) Mary Ann, for helping me to edit this novel, providing insightful comments, and making my fictionalized Mom more closely resemble our real Mom and (ii) Bob for assisting with the cover design, graphics choices, and my webpage.

I also want to thank my editor, Mark Chimsky. Your patience and perseverance and believing I could take this novel to fruition are deeply appreciated. I am glad you signed on for this project, and I very much enjoyed navigating the creative process with you.

Lastly, but not least, thank you to all the Jonathans and Julias out there. For everyone who has a physical or mental disability (like Jonathan) or otherwise may be marginalized by our society, it's time we collectively recognize your specialness and uniqueness and honor and support you. And for all those who do directly support you (like Julia), thanks for your tireless efforts to better the lives and lift the spirits of those who are different. The world is such a better place when we are empathetic, caring, and loving toward each other.

Mom and Dad

Mom and her parents, Marie and Mickey Picarella

ME

Please share your thoughts, comments, questions, etc., regarding
Second Chances, or your own story, on my webpage:
www.MichaelEmrich.net. I would love to hear from you.
Thanks again for taking the time to read *Second Chances*.
I very much appreciate it!

www.ingramcontent.com/pod-product-compliance
Lightning Source LLC
Chambersburg PA
CBHW070001180726
48002CB00019B/1849